The Glassblower of Murano

Marina Fiorato

St. Martin's Griffin New York

This is a work of fiction. All of the characters, organizations, and events portrayed in this novel are either products of the author's imagination or are used fictitiously.

www.stmartins.com

Library of Congress Cataloging-in-Publication Data

Fiorato, Marina.
The glassblower of Murano / Marina Fiorato. — 1st U.S. ed.
p. cm.
ISBN-13: 978-0-312-38698-6
ISBN-10: 0-312-38698-2
1. Glassworkers—Italy—Fiction. 2. Glass blowing and working—Fiction. 3. Trade secrets—Fiction. 4. Venice (Italy)—Fiction. I. Title.
PR6106.I67G63 2009
823'.92—dc22

2009002564

First published in Great Britain by Beautiful Books Limited

First U.S. Edition: June 2009

10 9 8 7 6 5 4 3 2 1

For Conrad, Ruby and, most of all, Sacha;
you are all in this book somewhere.

CHAPTER 1

The Book

As Corradino Manin looked on the lights of San Marco for the last time, Venice from the lagoon seemed to him a golden constellation in the dark blue velvet dusk. How many of those windowpanes, that adorned his city like costly gems, had he made with his own hands? Now they were stars lit to guide him at the end of the journey of his life. Guide him home at last.

As the boat drew into San Zaccaria he thought not – for once – of how he would interpret the vista in glass with a *pulegoso* of leaf gold and hot lapis, but instead that he would never see this beloved sight again. He stood in the prow of the boat, a brine-flecked figurehead, and looked left to Santa Maria della Salute, straining to see the white-domed bulk looming in its newness from the dark. The foundations of the great church had been laid in 1631, the year of Corradino's birth, to thank the Virgin for delivering the city from the Plague. His childhood and adulthood had kept pace with the growing edifice. Now it was complete, in 1681, the year of his death. He had never seen its full splendour in daylight, and now never would. He heard a *traghetto* man mournfully calling for passenger trade as he traversed the Canal Grande. His black boat recalled a funeral gondola. Corradino shivered.

He considered whether he should remove his white *bauta* mask as soon as his feet touched the shore; a poetic moment – a grand gesture on his return to the *Serenissima.*

No, there is one more thing I must do before they find me.

He closed his black cloak over his shoulders against the darkling mists and made his way across the Piazzetta under cover of his tricorn and *bauta.* The traditional *tabarro* costume, black from head to foot save the white mask, should make him anonymous enough to buy the time he needed. The *bauta* itself, a spectral slab of a mask shaped like a gravedigger's shovel, had the short nose and long chin which would eerily alter his voice if he should speak. Little wonder, he thought, that the mask borrowed its name from the '*baubau*', the 'bad beast' which parents invoked to terrify their errant children.

From habit borne of superstition Corradino moved swiftly through the two columns of San Marco and the San Teodoro that rose, white and symmetrical, into the dark. The Saint and the chimera that topped their pediments were lost in the blackness. It was bad luck to linger there, as criminals were executed between the pillars – hung from above or buried alive below. Corradino made the sign of the cross, caught himself, and smiled. What more bad luck could befall him? And yet his step still quickened.

There is one misfortune that could yet undo me: to be prevented from completing my final task.

As he entered the Piazza San Marco he noted that all that was familiar and beloved had taken on an evil and threatening cast. In the bright moon the shadow of the Campanile was a dark knife slashing across the square. Roosting pigeons flew like malevolent phantoms in his face. Regiments of dark arches had the square surrounded – who lurked in their shadows? The great doors of the Basilica were open; Corradino saw the gleam of candles from the golden belly of the church. He was briefly cheered – an island of brightness in this threatening landscape.

Perhaps it is not too late to enter this house of God, throw myself on the mercy of the priests and seek sanctuary?

But those who sought him also paid for this jewelled shrine that housed the bones of Venice's shrivelled Saint, and tiled the walls with the priceless glittering mosaics that now sent the candlelight out into the night. There could be no sanctuary within for Corradino. No mercy.

Past the Basilica then and under the arch of the Torre

dell'Orologio he hurried, allowing himself one more glance at the face of the huge clock, where tonight it seemed the fantastical beasts of the zodiac revolved in a more solemn measure. A dance of death. Thereafter Corradino tortured himself no more with final glances, but fixed his eyes on the paving underfoot. Even this gave him no respite, for all he could think of was the beautiful *tessere* glasswork he used to make; fusing hot nuggets of irregular glass together, all shapes and hues, before blowing the whole into a wondrous vessel delicate and colourful as a butterfly's wing.

I know I will never touch the glass again.

As he entered the Merceria dell'Orologio the market traders were packing away their pitches for the night. Corradino passed a glass-seller, with his wares ranked jewel-like on his stall. In his mind's eye the goblets and trinkets began to glow rosily and their shapes began to shift – he could almost feel the heat of the furnace again, and smell the sulphur and silica. Since childhood such sights and smells had always reassured him. Now the memory seemed a premonition of hellfires. For was hell not where traitors were placed? The Florentine, Dante, was clear on the subject. Would Corradino – like Brutus and Cassius and Judas – be devoured by Lucifer, the Devil's tears mingling with his blood as he was ripped asunder? Or perhaps, like the traitors that had betrayed their families, he would be encased for all eternity in '. . . *un lago che per gelo avea di vetro e non d'acqua sembiante* . . . a lake that, frozen fast, had lost the look of water and seemed glass.' Corradino recalled the words of the poet and almost smiled. Yes, a fitting punishment – glass had been his life, why not his death also?

Not if I do this last thing. Not if I am granted absolution.

With a new urgency he doubled back as he had planned and took the narrow bridges and winding alleys or *calles* that led back to the Riva degli Schiavoni. Here and there shrines were set into the corners of the houses – well-tended flames burned and illumined the face of the Virgin.

I dare not look in her eyes, not yet.

At last the lights of the Orphanage at the Ospedale della Pietà drew near and as he saw the candlelight warmth he heard too the music of the viols.

Perhaps it is she that plays – I wish it were so – but I will never know.

He passed the grille without a glance inside and banged on the door. As the maid approached with a candle he did not wait for her inquisition before hissing: 'Padre Tommaso – *subito*!' He knew the maid – a surly, taciturn wench who delighted in being obstructive, but tonight his voice carried such urgency that even she turned at once and soon the priest came.

'*Signore*?'

Corradino opened his cloak and found the leather gourd of French gold. Into the bag he tucked the vellum notebook, so she would know how it had been and one day, perhaps, forgive him. He took a swift glance around the dim alley – no, no-one could have drawn close enough to see him.

They must not know she has the book.

In a voice too low for any but the priest to hear he said: '*Padre*, I give you this money for the care of the orphans of the Pietà.' The mask changed Corradino's voice as he had intended. The priest made as if to take the bag with the usual formula of thanks, but Corradino held it back until the father was forced to meet his eyes. Father Tommaso alone must know him for who he was. 'For the orphans,' said Corradino again, with emphasis.

Recognition reached the priest at last. He turned over the hand that held the bag and looked closely at the fingertips – smooth with no prints. He began to speak but the eyes in the mask flashed a warning. Changing his mind the father said, 'I will make sure they receive it,' and then, as if he knew; 'may God bless you.' A warm hand and a cold one clasped for an instant and the door was closed.

Corradino continued on, he knew not where, until he was well away from the Orphanage.

Then, finally, he removed his mask.

Shall I walk on till they find me? How will it be done?

At once, he knew where he should go. The night darkened as he passed through the streets, the canals whispering goodbye as they splashed the *calli*, and now at last Corradino could hear footsteps behind keeping pace. At last he reached the Calle della Morte – the street of death – and stopped. The footsteps stopped too. Corradino faced the water and, without turning, said 'Will Leonora be safe?'

The pause seemed interminable – splash, splash – then a voice as dry as dust replied.

'Yes. You have the word of The Ten.'

Corradino breathed relief and waited for the final act.

As the knife entered his back he felt the pain a moment after the recognition had already made him smile. The subtlety, the clarity with which the blade insinuated itself between his ribs could only mean one thing. He started to laugh. Here was the poetry, the irony he had searched for on the dock. What an idiot, romanticizing himself, supposing himself a hero in the drama and pathos of his final sacrifice. All the time it was *they* who had planned the final act with such a sense of theatre, of what was fitting, an amusing *Carnevale* exit. A Venetian exit. They had used a glass dagger – Murano glass.

Most likely one of my own making.

He laughed harder with the last of his breath. He felt the assassin's final twist of the blade to snap handle from haft, felt his skin close behind the blade to leave no more than an innocent graze at the point of entry. Corradino pitched forward into the water and just before he broke the surface he met his own eyes in his reflection for the first and last time in his life. He saw a fool laughing at his own death. As he submerged in the freezing depths, the water closed behind his body to leave no more than an innocent graze at the point of entry.

CHAPTER 2

Belmont

Nora Manin woke at 4am exactly. She was not surprised, but blinked sleepily as the digital numbers of her bedside clock blinked back. She had woken at this time every night since Stephen left.

Sometimes she read, sometimes she made a drink and watched TV, numbing her mind with the inane programming for insomniacs. But tonight was different – tonight she knew there was no point even trying to get back to sleep. Because tomorrow – today – she was leaving for Venice and a new life, as the old one was over.

The digital clock and the bed were all that remained in the room that didn't wait in a box or a bag. Nora's life had been neatly packed and was destined for storage or . . . or what? She rose with a groan and padded to the bathroom. Clicked on the fluorescent strip that blinked into life over the basin mirror. She splashed her face and then studied it in the glass, looking for resolve in her reflection, finding only fear. Nora pressed both hands to the place on her front between her ribs and stomach where her sadness seemed to reside. Stephen would no doubt have some medical term for it – something long and Latin. 'It wearies me,' she said aloud to her reflection.

It did. She was tired of being sad. Tired of being bright and breezy to those friends that knew Stephen's defection had left her shattered. Tired of the mundane workload of dividing what they had bought together. She remembered the excitement with which they had found and bought this house, in the first days of marriage, when Stephen had got his post at the Royal Free Hospital. She thought that Hampstead seemed impossibly grand for a teacher of glass and ceramics. 'Not when they marry surgeons,' her mother had dryly said. The house even had a name – Belmont. Nora was not accustomed to houses so grand that they deserved their own names. This one sat, appropriately, on the beautiful hill that led to Hampstead village. A model of pleasing Georgian architecture, square, white and symmetrical. They had loved the place instantly, made an offer and had, for a time, been happy. Nora supposed she should be glad. At least the money from Belmont had provided her with security. Security – she smiled wryly at the word.

I have never felt less secure. I am vulnerable now. It is cold outside of a marriage.

For the thousandth time she began to take an inventory of her reflection, looking for clues as to why Stephen had left. 'Item – two eyes, wide and indifferent green. Item – hair; blonde, long, straw-coloured. Item – skin; olive. Item – two lips; chapped with the perpetual chewing of self doubt.' She stopped. For one thing she was no Shakespearean widow, despite the fact that she felt bereaved. And for another, it gave her no comfort to know that she was younger and blonder and, yes, prettier than Stephen's mistress. He had fallen for a forty-year-old brunette hospital administrator who wore severe suits. Carol. Her antithesis. She knew that Carol wouldn't sleep in an ancient Brooklyn Dodgers t-shirt and a scruffy plait.

'He used to call me his Primavera,' Nora told her reflection. She remembered when she and Stephen had seen the Botticelli painting in Florence on their honeymoon. They were both taken by the figure of Spring in her flowing white gown sprigged with flowers, smiling her slight, hermetic smile, beautiful and full of promise. With her burnished blonde ropes of hair and her leaf-green hooded eyes she bore a startling resemblance to Nora. Stephen had stood her by the painting and taken down her hair while she blushed and squirmed. She remembered the Italians calling '*bellissima*', while the Japanese took photographs. Stephen had kissed her and put a hand on her stomach. 'You'll look even more like her when . . .'

It had been the first year they had been trying for a baby. They were full of optimism. They were both in their early thirties, both healthy – she was a runner and Stephen a gym fanatic – and their only vice was quantities of red wine, which they virtuously reduced. But a year went by and eventually they visited a colleague of Stephen's at the Royal Free, a round and cheerful aristocrat with a bow tie. Interminable tests later, nothing was found. 'Unspecific infertility'.

'You may as well try blue smarties, they'll work as well as anything,' said the colleague, flippantly. Nora had cried. She had not fulfilled the fruitful promise of the *Primavera*.

I wanted *something to be found – something that could be fixed*.

They put themselves through a number of invasive, intrusive and unsuccessful procedures. Procedures denoted by acronyms that had nothing to do with love or nature, or the miracles that Nora associated with conception. HSG, FSH, IVF. They became obsessed. They took their eyes off their marriage, and when they looked back, it was gone. By the time Nora entered her third cycle of IVF both knew, but neither admitted, that there was not enough love left between them to spare for a third party.

It was around this time that a well-meaning friend had begun to drop hints that she had seen Stephen in a Hampstead bar with a woman. Jane had been very nonchalant about the information – she had not been damning, as if to say; 'I'm just telling you this in case you don't know. It may be innocent. I will say nothing which you cannot ignore with impunity, if you choose to. Nothing from which you cannot draw back. Nothing is lost. Only be aware.'

But Nora was consumed by the insecurity of her infertility and challenged Stephen. She expected denial, or admission of guilt and pleas for forgiveness. She got neither. The situation backfired on her horribly. Stephen admitted full culpability and, in his misplaced conceit of honourable behavior, offered to move out and then did. Six months later she learned from him that Carol was pregnant. And that was when Nora decided to move to Venice.

I am the cliché after all. Stephen is not. He left a young blonde woman for an older brunette. A jeans-wearing artist for a bean-counter in a suit. I on the other hand, instantly enter a mid-life crisis and decide on a whim to leave for the city of my ancestors and start again, like some bad TV drama.

She turned away from the mirror and looked at her packing, wondering for the millionth time if she was doing the right thing.

But I can't stay here. I can't be always running into Stephen, or her, or the child.

It had happened, with astonishing bad luck, on a fairly

regular basis, despite Nora's attempts to scrupulously avoid the environs of the hospital. Once she met them on the Heath, of all places – all that square mileage and she had met them while running. It occurred to her to keep going, and had she not been attempting civility with Stephen over the division of Belmont, she would have. Stephen and Carol were hand in hand, wearing similar leisure clothes, looking happy and rested. Carol's pregnancy was clearly evident. Nora was bathed in sweat and confusion. After a stilted exchange about the weather and the house contracts, Nora ran on and cried all the way home, tears streaming into her ears. Yet Stephen had been more than generous – he had all but given her the house. He has acted well throughout, thought Nora.

He is no pantomime villain. I can't demonize him, I can't even hate him. Damn him.

The house sale had given her freedom. She could now embark on her adventure, or her mistake. She had told no-one what she planned, not even her mother Elinor. Especially not her mother. Her mother had no love for Venice.

Elinor Manin was an academic who specialized in Renaissance Art. In the seventies she had gone on a tutor exchange from King's College London with her opposite number in Ca' Foscari at the University of Venice. While there she had rejected the advances of the earnest baby professors from Oxford and Cambridge and fallen instead for Bruno Manin, simply because he looked like he had stepped from a painting.

Elinor had seen him every day on the Linea 52 *vaporetto* which took her from the Lido where she lived to the university. He worked on the boat – opening and closing the gate, tying and untying the boat at each *fermata* stop. Bruno twisted the heavy ropes between his long fingers and leapt from the boat to shore and back again with a curious catlike grace and skill. She studied his face, his aquiline nose, his trim beard, his curling black hair, and tried to identify the painting he had come from. Was it a Titian or a Tiepolo? A Bellini? Which Bellini? As Elinor looked from his profile to the impossibly beautiful *palazzi* of the Canal Grande, she was suddenly on fire with enthusiasm for this culture where the houses and the people kept their genetic essence so pure for millennia that they looked the same now as in the Renaissance. This fire that she felt, this continuity and rightness, did not leave her when Bruno noticed her glances and asked her for a drink. It did not leave her when he took her back to his shared house in Dorsoduro and bedded her. It did not even leave her when she found that she was pregnant.

They married in haste and decided to call the baby Corrado if it was a boy and Leonora if it was a girl, after Bruno's parents. As they lay in bed with the waters of the canal casting an undulating crystal mesh onto the ceiling,

Bruno told her of his ancestor, the famous *maestro* of glass-blowers, Corrado Manin, known as Corradino. Bruno told Elinor that Corradino was the best glass-maker in the world, and gave her a glass heart made by the *maestro's* own hand. It was all incredibly romantic. They were happy. Elinor made the heart reflect the light on to the ceiling, while Bruno lay with his hand on her belly. Here inside her, thought Elinor, was that fire, that continuity, that eternal flame of the Venetian genome. But the feeling faded as the modern world broke into theirs. Elinor's parents, not surprisingly, felt none of the respect for Bruno's profession that the Venetians feel for their boatmen. Nor were they impressed by his refusal to leave Venice and move to London.

For Elinor too, this was a shock. Her reverie ended abruptly, she was back in London in the seventies with a small daughter, and a promise from Bruno to write and visit. Baby Leonora spent her first months with her grandparents or at the University crèche. When Bruno did not write Elinor was hurt but not surprised. Her pride stopped her from getting in touch with him. She made a gesture of retaliation by anglicizing her daughter's name to Nora. She began to appreciate feminist ideas and spent a great deal of time at single mother's groups rubbishing Bruno and men in general. At the Christmas of Nora's first year, Elinor received a Christmas card from an Italian friend from Ca' Foscari. *Dottore* Padovani had been a colleague in her department, a middle-aged man of intelligence and biting humour, not one given to patronage or sympathy. But Elinor detected a note of sympathy in his Christmas greetings. She rang as soon as the Christmas vacation was over to demand why he thought that just because a woman was a single parent she deserved to be pitied. He told her gently that Bruno had died of a heart attack not long after she had left – he assumed that she had heard. Bruno had died at work, and Elinor pictured him as she had first seen him, but now clutching his chest and pitching forward into the canal, the city claiming its own. The fire was out. For Elinor her love affair with Venice was over. She continued in her studies but moved her sphere of interest south to Florence, and in the Botticellis and Giottos felt safe that she would not keep seeing Bruno's face.

Nora grew up amongst women. Her mother and grandmother, the women of Elinor's discussion groups; they were her family. She grew up to be taught to develop her own mind and her creativity. She was perpetually warned of the ways of men. Nora was sent to an all-girl school in Islington and showed an aptitude for arts. She was encouraged in her sculpture by Elinor who had dreams of her daughter following in the footsteps of Michelangelo. But Elinor had reckoned without the workings of fate and the call of Nora's ancestors.

For whilst studying sculpture and ceramics at Wimbledon School of Art Nora met a visiting tutor who had her own glass foundry in Snowdonia. Gaenor Davis was in her sixties and made glass *objets* to sell in London, and she encouraged Nora's interest in glass, and the blower's art. Nora's fascination for the medium grew with the amber-rose bubbles of glass that she blew and her expertise developed during a summer month spent at Gaenor's foundry. With the fanciful, pretentious nature of the naïve student she saw her own self in the glass. This strange material was at once liquid and solid, and had moods and a finite nature, a narrow window in which she would allow herself to be malleable before her nature cooled and her designs were set, until the heat freed her again. Elinor, watching her daughter's specialism become apparent, began to have the uneasy feeling that that continuity, that enduring genome that she had identified in Venice, would not be so easily dismissed and was rising to the surface in her daughter.

But Nora had distractions – she was discovering men. Having been largely ignorant of the male sex for the whole of her childhood and adolescence, she found that she adored them. None of her mother's bitterness had passed to her – she surrounded herself with male friends and cheerfully slept with most of them. After three years of sex and sculpture Nora embarked on a Masters degree in ceramics and glass at Central St Martin's and there began to tire of artistic men. They seemed to her without direction, without conviction, without responsibility. She was ripe for a man like Stephen Carey, and when they met in a Charing Cross bar, her attraction was immediate.

He came from not the arts but the sciences – he was

doctor. He wore a suit. He had a high-powered, well paid job at Charing Cross Hospital. He was handsome, but in a clean-shaven way – no stubble, no ironic seventies t-shirts, no skater clothes. Their courtship was accelerated by similar feeling on Stephen's side – here was a beautiful, free-thinking, artistic girl dressed in a slightly funky fashion, charming him with a world he knew nothing of.

When Nora brought Stephen home to Islington Elinor sighed inwardly. She liked Stephen – with his old-world manners and Cambridge education – but could see what was happening. In her womens' group her friends agreed. Nora was seeking out her father, but what could Elinor do?

Elinor gave her daughter the glass heart that Bruno had given her. She told Nora what she knew of her father's family, of the famous Corradino Manin, in an attempt to give her daughter a sense of paternal identity. But at that time Nora was no more than momentarily interested – her heart was full of Stephen. Nora finished her Masters and was offered a teaching post, Stephen got a surgical residency at the Royal Free, and there was nothing left to do but get married. They did so in a solid conventional fashion in Norfolk, with Stephen's wealthy family running the day. Elinor sat through the ceremony in her new hat and sighed again.

The couple went to Florence for their honeymoon at Elinor's suggestion. Nora was enchanted by Italy, Stephen less so.

Perhaps I should have sensed something wasn't right, even then.

She now remembered that Stephen detested the traffic and tourism of Florence. He resented her speaking to the locals in her hard-learnt but fluent Italian. It was as if he resented her heritage – felt threatened. In the Uffizi he himself braided her hair again after his brief, uncharacteristic moment of romance in front of the Botticelli. He said that her blondeness attracted too much unwanted attention in the street. Yet even with her hair bound she collected admiring glances from the immaculately dressed young men who hunted in designer-suited packs of five or ten, raising their sunglasses and whistling.

It was Stephen, too, who had resisted her suggestion to call herself Leonora again – too fancy, he said, too Mills and Boon. She had kept the name Manin for her work, as she exhibited her glassware in a small way in some London Galleries. Her chequebook and cashcards, however, said Carey.

Nora wondered if Stephen had only accepted Nora Manin because it sounded as if it could be English. Few people identified Manin as an Italian name, with no giveaway vowel at the end.

Is it because Stephen resented my 'Italian-ness' that I am anxious to embrace it so wholeheartedly, now he is gone?

Nora turned from the luggage and searched in her makeup bag for her talisman. Among the mascara wands and bright palettes of colour she found what she was looking for. She held the glass heart in her hand, marvelling at its iridescence. It seemed to capture the light of the bathroom's fluorescent tube and hold it within itself. She threaded a blue hair ribbon through the hole in its crease and tied it round her neck. Over the last horrible months it had become her rosary, her touchstone for all the hopes of the future. She would hold it tight as she cried at those 4am wakings and tell herself if she could only get to Venice, everything would be alright.

The second part of her plan she did not want to think about yet – she had told no-one, and could barely even say it to herself as it sounded such a ridiculous, fanciful notion. 'I am going to Venice to work as a glassblower. It is my birthright.' She spoke to her reflection, aloud, clearly and defiantly. She heard the words, unnaturally loud in the quiet of the small hours, and cringed. But in determination, she clasped the heart tighter and looked again at her reflection. She thought she looked a little more courageous and felt cheered.

CHAPTER 3

Corradino's Heart

There were letters cut into the stone.

The words on the plaque which adorned the Orphanage of the Pietà were thrown into sharp relief by the midday sun. Corradino's fingers scored the grooves of the inscription. He knew well what it said;

'*Fulmine il Signor Iddio maledetione e scomuniche* . . . May the Lord God strike with curses and excommunications all those who send or permit their sons and daughters – whether legitimate or natural – to be sent to this hospital of the Pietà, having the means and ability to bring them up.'

Did you read these words, Nunzio dei Vescovi, you old bastard? Seven years ago to this day, when you abandoned your only grandchild here? Did you feel the guilt pressing on your heart?

Did you look over your shoulder in fear of the Lord God and the Pope as you slunk home to your palazzo *and your coffers of gold?*

Corradino looked down at the worn step and pictured the newborn girl swaddled there, still slick with birthblood. Birthblood and deathblood, for her mother had died on her childbed. Corradino clenched his fists till the nails bit.

I do not want to think of Angelina.

He turned instead to find peace in the view across the lagoon. He liked to study the water and gauge its mood – today in sunshine the waves resembled his *ghiaccio* work – blown blue glass, several different hues, melted together and plunged in ice to give a finely crackled surface. Corradino had refined the art of *ghiaccio* by floating sulfate of silver on the surface of the iced water. This way the hot glass would accept the metal as it cracked and seal it within when it cooled, giving the impression of sunlit water. The sight of the *laguna* looking exactly thus gave him confidence.

I am a master. No-one can make the glass sing like I do. I am the best glassblower in the world. I hear the water reply; yes, but that is why the French want you *and no-one else.*

He looked across the lagoon to San Giorgio Maggiore, and watched the spice boats pass the unfinished church of Santa Maria della Salute. The rich reds and yellows of the spices and the dark hues of the merchants' skins were framed by the clean white stones of the vast structure. These were all sights that he relished. Gondolas sliced the water and courtesans rode bare-breasted and wanton in their *Carnevale* finery. Corradino admired not their flesh but the silk of their gowns. The colour and form of the falling material as it caught the sun. The rainbow of hues like the inside of an oyster. He watched for a while, enjoying one of his rare moments of freedom from the foundry, from the *fornace*, from Murano. He admired the axe shaped prow of the gondola, with the six branches to denote the six *sestiere* or regions of the city. The city he loved. The city he was leaving tomorrow. He said the names over to himself, rolling the words on his tongue like a poem or a prayer.

Cannaregio, Dorsoduro, Castello, Santa Croce, San Polo and San Marco.

In time the wash of the gondola reached him, slapping gently against the mossy marble of the dock, and brought him to himself. He must not tarry too long.

I have a present for her.

Corradino ducked down the *calle* at the side of the church of Santa Maria della Pietà which adjoined the Orphanage. He peered through the ornamental grille that allowed passersby to see through to the cool darkness within. He could see a group of the orphan girls with their viols and violoncellos, with their sheet music. Seated at the edge he could see her blonde head bobbing as she talked to her friends. He saw, too, the head of Father Tommaso at the front, tonsured by nature, instructing a group that stood ready to sing. Now was his moment.

With his indifferent voice echoing in the *calle*, Corradino began to sing a well known tune used by meat traders or pastry sellers to attract buyers to their wares. The words, however, were changed, so that only one person would know him for who he was, and she, alone, would come to him:

'Leonora *mia*, bo bo bo,

Leonora *mia*, bo bo bo.'

Soon she was there at the grille, her little fingers curled through the ornamental panel to touch his. '*Buon giorno* Leonora.'

'*Buon giorno Signore*.'

'Leonora, I told you that you can call me Papà.'

'*Sì Signore*.'

But she smiled. He loved her sense of humour and the way she had become familiar enough with him to take liberties. He supposed she was growing up – soon she would be a practised *coquette* of marriageable age.

'Did you bring me a present?'

'Well, now, let's see. Perhaps you can tell me how old you are today?'

More little digits pushed through the grille. Five, six, seven. 'Seven.'

'That's right. And haven't I always given you presents on your name day?'

'Always.'

'Well, let's hope I haven't forgotten it.' He made a pantomime of searching through his smock and all his jerkin pockets. At last he reached behind his ear and pulled out the glass heart. With relief he saw his measurements were correct as he pushed the gem easily through the grille and heard Leonora gasp as it fell into her hand. She turned it over on her little palm to admire the captured light.

'Is it magic?' she asked.

'Yes. A special sort. Come closer and I'll explain.'

Leonora pressed her face to the grille. The sun caught the gold motes in her green eyes and Corradino's heart failed him.

There's some beauty in this world I could never recreate.

'*Ascolta*, Leonora. I have to go away for a while. But that heart will tell you that I will always be with you, and when you look at that heart and hold it in your hand you will know how much I love you. Try it now.'

Her fingers closed round the heart, putting out the light.

She closed her eyes. 'Can you feel it?' Corradino asked.

Leonora opened her eyes again and smiled 'Yes,' she said.

'See, I told you it was magic. Now do you have that ribbon I gave you on your last name-day?'

She nodded.

'Well push it through the special hole I made and hang it round your neck. Don't let the Prioress see it, or Father Tommaso, or lend it to the other girls.' She clasped the heart and nodded again.

'Are you going to come back?'

He knew he could not. 'Someday.'

She thought for a moment. 'I'll miss you.'

He suddenly felt that his insides had been gutted, like the fish in the *Pescheria* market. He wished he could tell her of what he had planned – that he would send for her a soon as it was safe. But he dare not trust himself. The less she knew the better.

What she does not know, she cannot not tell; what she cannot tell, cannot not hurt her. And I know too well the poison that is hope, the waiting and the wanting. What if I can never send for her?

So he only said; 'I'll miss you too, Leonora *mia*.'

She pushed her fingers through the grille again in their acknowledged sign. He caught the message and placed each of his printless pads on her tiny finger tips, little finger to little finger, thumb to thumb.

Suddenly the door to the *calle* opened and the tonsured head appeared. 'Corradino, how many times do I have to tell you not to come sniffing round my girls? Is that not how this sorry mess came to pass in the first place? Leonora, return to the orchestra, we are ready to begin.'

With a last glance, Leonora was gone, and Corradino muttered an apology and made as if to leave. But when the priest had gone back inside the church, he stole back down the *calle* and listened as the music began. The sweetness of the harmony, and the soaring counterpoint, bled into his soul. Corradino knew what would happen, but he gave in to it.

For when she holds the glass heart in her hand she holds my own heart there too.

He knew he may never see Leonora again, so this time he leant against the church wall and let the tears flow, as if they would never stop.

CHAPTER 4

Through the Looking Glass

Still the music played.

Nora sat in the church of Santa Maria della Pietà and tried to think of a word for what she was feeling. Enchanted? Too reminiscent of old-world courtesies. Bewitched? No; the word seemed to imply an entrapment by a malign force.

But no-one has done this to me. I came here of my own volition.

She glanced left and right, at her unknown companions. The church was packed – her neighbour, an elegant Italian matron, sat so close that her red sleeve lay across Nora's forearm. But Nora did not mind. They were all here for the same reason, bound together, all – that was it; enraptured – by the music.

Antonio Vivaldi. Nora knew the soundbite version of his life – a red-headed priest, had asthma, taught orphans, wrote the Four Seasons. But he had never really troubled her musical radar until now. She had found him too clichéd for her art-student trendiness – music for lifts and supermarkets, done to death. But here, in the warmth of candlelight, she heard Vivaldi played by live musicians, in the very church where he had written these pieces, first rehearsed them with his orphan girls. The musicians were all young, studious looking Italians, all extremely accomplished, who played with passion as well as technical excellence. They had not pandered to tourist sensibilities by donning period dress – they let the music speak. And here, Nora heard the Four Seasons as if for the first time.

Oh, she knew that the church itself had changed – she knew from her pamphlet guide that the Palladian façade was late eighteenth century, added after the *maestro's* death, but she felt as if the priest were here. She peered into the candling shadows beyond the pillars, where keen locals stood to hear the music, and looked fancifully for his red head amongst them.

When Nora had arrived in Venice she felt unmoored – as if she drifted, loosed from harbour, flowing here and there on the relentless arteries of tourism. Carried by crowds, lost in babel of foreign tongues she was caught in a glut of guttural Germans, or a juvenile crocodile of fluorescent French. Wandering, dazed, through San Marco she had reached the famous frontage of the Libreria Sansoviniana in the *Broglio*. Nora fell through its portals in the manner of one stumbling into Casualty in search of much needed medical attention. She did not want to act like a tourist, and felt a strong resistance to their number. The beauty that she saw everywhere almost made her believe in God; it certainly made her believe in Venice. But the city had physically shocked her to such an extent that she began to feel afraid of it – she needed to find an anchor, to feel that she could belong here as a native. Here in the library she would search for Corradino. Kindly, tangible words, factual lines of prose scattered with dates would be the longitudes and latitudes to bring her into safe harbour. Here he would meet her like a relative at an airport. Let me show you around, he would say. You belong here. You are family.

The concierge at her hotel, a kindly, avuncular man, had recognized her mental state in the manner of one used to the effect of his city. It was he who had suggested the Libreria as a good place to learn of her ancestor, and of where she could view his work around the city. The short answer *Signorina*, he said, was 'almost anywhere'. Nora was cheered by his familiarity with the name of Corradino Manin; he spoke of him as a familiar drinking acquaintance. But as to what to see in the city itself his advice was simple. He waved his hand expansively. '*Faccia soltanto una passeggiata, Signorina. Soltanto una passeggiata.*' Just walk, only walk.

He was right of course. From her pleasant hotel in Castello, she had wandered the *calli*, losing track of time and direction, and caring not at all. Everything here was beautiful, even the decay. Rotting houses stood next to glorious palaces, squeezed on either side by grandeur, their lower floors showing tidemarks of erosion where the lagoon was eating them alive. The stained masonry crumbled into the canal like *biscotti* dipped in Marsala but this seemed only to add to their charms. It was as if they submitted with pleasure to the tides – a consummation, one devoutly to be wished. Nora wandered the bridges, as enchanted by a string of washing hanging from window to window across a narrow canal, or by a handful of scruffy boys kicking a football in a deserted square, as she was by the delicate Moorish traceries of the fenestrations.

Nora resisted the notion of planning her direction. In London her life had been mapped out for her, signposted and marked down. She had not been lost, properly lost, for many years. She knew exactly how to get around her capital, aided, if need be, by the regimented, colour coded tube map or the A-Z. Stephen, always a mine of information, had told her that when the tube map was designed, the artist deliberately kept the distances between the stations constant, even though in fact they were widely different. This was an attempt to make the citizens of the metropolis feel safe, to accept this weird, subterranean mode of transport; to feel that they could move through exceptionally well-marked out quadrants of the city with ease and security.

But here in Venice Nora's desire for spontaneity was aided by the city itself. She had a map in the back of her hotel guide – it was useless. Only two directions were posted on the walls of the *calli* in ancient yellow signage – San Marco, and Rialto. But, as the S-shape of the Grand Canal dictated, these were often in the same direction. She actually arrived in one *piazza* where a wall bore two yellow signs for San Marco, each one with an arrow, each one pointing in the opposite direction.

I am Alice. These are directions designed by the Cheshire Cat.

Her image of life through the Looking Glass became even stronger, when, as the sun began to set, she decided she really had better try to reach San Marco. But as she attempted to follow the signs, they enticed her farther and farther away, leaving her at last at the white arch of the Rialto.

Nora stopped for a restorative coffee under the bridge. She watched the tourists swarm across, anxious for news like the merchants of old, clutching guidebooks and copies of Shakespeare. She mentally removed herself from these crowds.

I am no tourist. I am here to stay, to live.

Her life was packed up and held in storage crates in the unlovely shipyards of nearby Mestre, waiting on the mainland, paid up for a month – the time she had given herself to get an apartment and a work permit.

She watched the *vaporetti* chug by, and thought of her father. As a crowded boat stopped at the Rialto *fermata* she watched a young man in the customary blue overalls leap to the dock, coil the tow rope and pull the boat into its mooring with the ease of long practice.

My father.

The idea was alien to her. The idea of her mother doing anything so free as coming here and falling both in love and pregnant, was also alien to her. She turned her thoughts from her mother. She did not want to acknowledge that she had been there first. She wanted this to be *her* odyssey. 'I'm not my mother,' she said aloud. Instantly, the waiter was at her elbow, with a friendly questioning air. She shook her head, smiling; paid, tipped, and left.

This time, she borrowed her strategy from the Red Queen of the Looking Glass. She went the *opposite* way from that instructed by the San Marco signs, and soon, sure enough, found herself entering what Napoleon had termed, inadequately, 'the finest drawing room in Europe'.

The sun was lowering, the shadows enormous. The Campanile loomed over the square like the giant gnomon of a sundial; the loggias housed elongated arcs of light. Nora gazed aghast at the opulent bronzed domes of the Basilica – such decoration, such grandeur, a trove of treasure looted from the east. Here Rome and Constantinople had mated to bring forth this strange and wondrous humped-backed beast, an entirely new creature, a dragon of coils and spurs to guard her city. And, in contrast, the exquisite wedding cake of the Doge's Palace, serene and homogenous, iced with a filigree of white stone. Only here would the Orologio, a clock made for giants, where golden beasts of the zodiac roamed across its face instead of numbers, seem fitting and in keeping. Nora felt as if she needed to sit down. Her head was spinning. She opened her guidebook, but the words made no sense – they swam before her eyes, the black and white facts an irrelevance when faced with this technicolour splendour. Besides, she had set herself apart from the tourists at the Rialto and had no wish to return to their number, guidebook glued to hand, eyes flicking from page to monument like an inept newscaster struggling between script and camera.

Why did no one warn me about this?

She had been told for years to come here by friends, art tutors, even by her mother. No one could believe she had never been before, as an artist, as a half-Venetian. But her coffee by the Rialto had given her a moment of clarity. She knew she had not been before *because* of her mother. Elinor had had the Venetian adventure, and been cruelly hurt. The *Serenissima* had thrown her back, found her wanting. Nora had not wanted to come here and make comparisons, find echoes of that story, stand in her mother's shoes. She had wanted to make her own discoveries of Italy – Florence, Ravenna, Urbino. All those champions of Venice amongst her friends had told her that it was the one place in the world that lived up to the hype. *They* had all told her.

But those she charged with her ill-preparedness were the artists, the writers.

Canaletto, why did you not adequately depict this place? Why were you, in all your mastery, not able to describe this to me? Why did you merely sketch, not capture the details of this beauty? Turner, why couldn't you capture the sun bleeding into the lagoon as I see it now? Henry James, why did you not prepare me for this? Evelyn Waugh, your passages of praise were faint insults when faced with the real thing. Thomas Mann, why leave so much out? Nicholas Roeg, even with your cameras and your celluloid, why could you not tell me either?

The young woman in the great reception chambers of the Library explained to Nora in her precise and perfect English that unfortunately she may not enter the inner sanctum of the building. Visitors without reader's cards were, however, welcome to use the reference section. Nora produced her passport and watched the girl write out a day-pass in her neat round hand, and followed her, tingling, through double doors to the left of the main doors, which whispered a greeting as they closed behind her. The books waited in the still and stuffy air, dust and warm leather welcoming Nora with the familiarity of her student days. An elderly man was her only companion. He looked up, nodded, then dropped his bright eyes to his texts. The girl offered a brief explanation of the catalogues and melted away.

Nora began her search among the yellowing cards of the catalogues. 'Manin' offered a bewildering number of entries, but she quickly realized that most of them pertained to a Doge – Lodovico; or Daniele, a revolutionary lawyer who had resisted the Austrian occupation of 1848. The sun moved across the great windows before she found the numerous references to Corrado Manin, and from a distant shelf hauled down a huge tome of the kind that adorns the coffee tables of the world, its photographs unloved and un-looked at from years end to years end. Seated at a leather covered table she leafed through its pages and was dazzled – even the faded 1960s photography did little to diminish what she saw there. Page after page of beauty, intricacy and sheer majesty, the work made her drop her head to her hands and prompted the old man to glance at her with concern.

I came here to find a city cousin to give me an entrée into Venice, and I find instead a Master – a Leonardo, a Michelangelo.

Nora felt humility, inadequacy and pride in equal measure. Her eyes rested at last on a chandelier of surpassing beauty and read the legend beneath. '*Candelabro – La Chiesa di Santa Maria della Pietà, Venezia.*' Memory prompted her – she had seen, pasted on the warm walls of the city, a bill which proclaimed that tonight saw the beginning of a series of concerts of Venetian music in their original settings. The church of the Pietà had been listed. Nora quickly replaced the book and headed out into the light, turning right to the Tourist Information Office in the Casino da Caffè. She bought her concert ticket and headed for San Zaccaria, stopping for a plate of pasta which she ate watching the sun dissolve into the lagoon.

Now, in the church of the Pietà, she knew she had made a good choice for her first night. The day had been such a revelation, such an assault on her senses, that she needed this time to just sit, to be forced into inertia for a couple of hours. She sat, let the music creep in her ears, and tried to collect her thoughts.

From the moment she arrived at Marco Polo airport she had felt a loss of control – as the motor launch whisked herself and her suitcase across the lagoon towards Venice she felt buffeted, physically by the wind, and mentally by her experience.

Since her waking in the small hours she had been in a kind of trance, automatically going through the well rehearsed motions of going abroad – taxi to the airport, checking in luggage. The feeling of lightness and of no return, as, unencumbered by bags, she wandered through the airport shops, all full of things she didn't need. In the bookshop she picked up a novel with a reproduction of Canaletto on the cover, and thought it strange that, by noon, she would be walking in the very precincts that he had painted. She put the book down – she had no need for fantasy. She was entering her own reality of Venice.

On the flight, she still felt in control. She accepted with thanks her food and drinks, her courtesy magazine, listened carefully to the safety instructions. But the moment she landed Nora began to feel this new, but not unpleasant, helplessness. She realized that, in her futile, ludicrous day-dreams, she had pictured the plane landing in Saint Mark's Square, on some futuristic runway. But the reality was almost as strange – Marco Polo seemed to be actually *on* the water, an island airport, surrounded by sea. She had not thought through the next stage either, but now realized that she would be taking a boat to Venice. Of course. As the driver handed her on board the rocking water taxi she contrasted the experience with the black cab and cheerful cockney driver that had taken her to Heathrow at six.

Something else she had not realized. The boat soon reached a landmass and began to chug along a narrow canal. Nora knew at once this was not Venice itself, but heard a strange distant chime, like the fading resonance of a bell, calling to her. As if he read her thoughts the driver jerked a thumb at the ancient buildings and shouted briefly above the wind '*Murano.*'

Murano. The home of Glass. The workplace of her ancestors. She felt a jolt as she passed the *fondamente* crowded with glass factories. The same *fornaci*, in the same places, housing the same skills that they had for centuries. She knew that the next day she would be back, to enquire about work. Instead of feeling afraid of her mad scheme, she felt suddenly sure. This was real, and she was going to make it work. The word destiny came into her mind. A silly, romantic word, but once there it would not leave. She clasped the glass heart around her neck and felt suddenly theatrical. She wanted to make some sort of gesture. She began to unplait her hair, and let the mass of it blow in the wind. She meant to salute Murano, but knew that, in truth, the gesture was for Stephen.

She regretted the impulse when she had checked into her hotel, trying to comb the tangled mess into some sort of order in the mock rococo mirror in her bathroom. She looked so different to the way she had looked in her own mirror at four in the morning. She looked at her Venetian self in the Venetian glass. Her hair was wild, her cheeks ruddy from the sea breeze, her eyes shining with a zealot's light. The glass heart was the only constant, as it still hung from her neck. She thought she looked a mess – even a little crazy, but at the same time, rather beautiful.

Someone else thought so too.

He sat across the aisle from her in the church. Probably

thirty or so, extremely well groomed like most Italian men, tall as his legs tucked uncomfortably behind the pew. And his face – before she realized, the thought had formed in her head.

He looks like he has stepped from a painting.

At once, she remembered her mother's story, was horrified that their thoughts had chimed in the same way thirty years apart. She turned away. But having thought it, she couldn't take it back. She looked again, and he was still looking at her. Her cheeks burned and she turned determinedly away once again.

The music sweetened her thoughts and Nora focused her eyes on what she had come to see; the great, decorative glass chandelier that was suspended high above her head, looming out of the dark of the roofspace like an inverted crystal tree. Numerous droplets hung from decorative branches which seemed so impossibly delicate that they could hardly support their diamond fruits. Nora tried to follow each arm of the glass with her eyes, to see how it curved and turned, but each time she lost her place as the design bested her. Each crystal teardrop seemed to capture the candle flames and hold them within the perfection of the prism. She could hear, ringing in her head, the resonant note she had heard earlier as she passed Murano, but in another instant realized that this note was real, tangible. The glass itself was sweetly singing, the timbre of the strings and their vibrations caused every branch and pendant crystal to sound their own, almost imperceptible counterpoint. Nora looked at her pamphlet for information on this miracle her own ancestor had wrought. There was nothing, but Nora smiled to herself with what she knew.

It was here when you were alive, Antonio Vivaldi.

Then, as now, you heard your own compositions echoing back to you in this crystalline harmony. In point of fact, it was here before you were even born. And it was made by Corradino Manin.

CHAPTER 5

The Camelopard

The great chandelier crossed the lagoon, hanging in the dark barrel. Submerged in water, swinging in complement to the waves, muffled from all sound and sense. The water that surrounded it was ink dark, but tiny motes of moonlight hit the prisms here and there, like single diamonds in pitch. The fluid was cushioning, safe, amniotic. Tomorrow the chandelier would be born into its purpose. Last night it had been completed. Tonight it waited. The barrel was lashed upright in the boat by so many ropes that the great dark mass looked to have been captured in a fisherman's net. The boatmen splashed and heaved their oars, singing an old song of the *Piemontese*. From inside the barrel, the chandelier began to sing too.

Corradino ached, but he would not stop. The chandelier hung before him on an iron chain in a near-finished state, shining gold in the flamelight from the furnace. Its crystal arms reached out to him in supplication, as if begging for completion. One of its five delicate limbs was missing, so for the final time Corradino reached in the fire. Pushing his *canna da soffio* rod into the heart of the melt he rolled it expertly, drawing out a gather of molten glass, which clung to the end of his blowpipe. He began rolling the glass against a hardwood paddle, marvering it into the correct shape to begin its transformation. Corradino thought of the glass as living, always living. He had made a cocoon from which something beautiful could now grow.

He took a breath and blew. The glass miraculously arched from his lips into a long, delicate balloon. Corradino always held the breath out of his lungs until he had made sure that the bubble, or parison, he had created was perfect in all dimensions. His fellows joked that he was such a perfectionist that, were the parison not perfect, Manin would never take another breath in, and expire on the spot. In truth, Corradino knew that the slightest winds of his breath at the crucial heat meant the difference between perfection and imperfection, between the divine and the merely beautiful.

He watched the glass changing, chameleon-like, through all shades of red, rose, orange, amber, yellow and finally white as it began to grow cool. Corradino knew he must work fast. He thrust the parison into the *forno* to reheat it briefly, then began to manipulate it with his hands.

Not for him the protective wads of cotton or paper that

others used to save their skin from shriveling and blistering with the heat. He had long since sacrificed his fingertips to his art. They had burned, scarred and eventually healed smooth with no prints. Corradino recalled the tales of Marco Polo who had said that the ancient T'ang dynasty of China used fingerprints as a means of identification, and the practice had endured in the Orient ever since.

My identity has become one with the glass. Somewhere in Venice, or far overseas, my own skin lies embedded in the hard silica of a goblet or candlestick.

Corradino knew that his glass was the best because he held her in his hands, touching her skin with his, feeling her breathe. He took up his *tagianti* shears and began to pull a delicate filigree of curlicues from the main cylinder, until a forest of crystalline branches sprang from the tube. Corradino swiftly broke the blowpipe free, and transferring the piece to a solid iron rod – the *pontello* – he began to work with the open end. Finally running out of time as the unforgiving glass hardened, he took it to the mother structure and wound the new arm round the main trunk, in a decorative spiral. There was no rough spot – no *pontello* mark – to remain, like an umbilicus, to betray the origins of the limb.

He stood holding the arm while the final hardening took place, admiring his work, then finally stood back and wiped his brow. Although shirtless, as the *maestri* always worked, he still felt the burning of the furnace fires on his skin from dawn till dusk. He wondered, looking at the diligent workers around him, whether this profession were a good preparation for hellfires. What was it that Dante wrote?

'. . . tall flames flowed fierce,
Heating them so white hot as ever burned
Iron in the forge of any artificers.'

Corradino knew the work of the Florentine well. His father had allowed all the family to bring one possession – one most precious thing – with them from the Palazzo Manin on the night they escaped. His father had brought a precious vellum copy of Dante's *Divina Commedia* from his library.

That was my father's choice. It's the only book I own. It's the only thing that remains of my father.

Corradino banished the thought of him and turned back to the punishing flames.

No wonder that, back in 1291, the Grand Council of Venice had decreed that all glass-making should take place on the island of Murano, because of the constant threat of fire to the city. A blaze begun by the furnaces had more than once threatened to engulf Venice. It had been a wise idea to move the centre of production, for just a few years back the English city of London had been all but destroyed by fire. Not, mind you, that it had been started by anything as artistic as a glass foundry. The latest rumour among the merchants on the Rialto had spoken of the blaze beginning in a pie-shop. Corradino snorted.

'Tis an English trait – always thinking of the stomach.

The London fire had meant good business here on Murano. The English King Charles seemed to want to create London anew, and fill his grand modern buildings with mirrors and glasswork. There was, therefore, much demand from that chilly capital for the work of Corradino and his comrades.

Although Corradino had finished the main frame of his chandelier there was still much to do. It was growing dark, and one by one, the fire-breathing mouths of the furnaces were extinguished, doors closed, and his fellows left. He called to one of the *garzoni* to a last errand, and as the boy ran through the *fornace*, jumping over iron pipes and dodging around buckets as the men worked, Corradino smiled and thought the apprentices' nickname '*scimmia di vetro*' – glass monkeys – seemed particularly apt.

The boy was soon back with the box. '*Eccolo Maestro*.'

Corradino opened the long rosewood box. Inside were 100 small square partitions, all numbered, all lined with a wad of flock wool. Corradino got to work. He took a small *pontello*, much smaller than his trusty blowpipe, and dipped it into the glass that lay, molten and unformed, waiting, at the bottom of his furnace. He pulled out the rod which now resembled a lit candle. Waiting a moment, he then plucked the glowing orb from the rod and began to roll the glass in his palms, and then more delicately in his fingers. When satisfied, he pulled out a string of the glass to form a teardrop, and fashioned a delicate hook on its end. He dropped the jewel he had made into the bucket of water that rested between his knees. After a long moment, he plunged his hand into the bucket and rescued the gem.

His action brought to his mind the stories of the pearl fishers of the East, stories that were brought back in the days of Venice's mastery over Constantinople, way back in the thirteenth century.

Do those boys who dive for pearls in the deep, striving for the oysters while their lungs burst, feel the same satisfaction I do? Surely, no: when they find a pearl, it is mere luck – a beneficence of nature. When their brothers in the Hartz mountains in Germany who mine for silver in the heat and dark of the hills, find a pure seam of silver, do they feel as if they have created this treasure? And you diamond miners of the Africas, as you prise a perfect gem from the rocks, can you feel the pride that I do? No, for I *have made these things of beauty. God made the others. And now in this world of men, in our seventeenth century, glass is more precious than any of* your *treasures; more than gold, more than saffron.*

Dry instantly in the heat of the flames, the droplet

Corradino had made was placed delicately in the compartment marked '*uno*' in the rosewood box. Even nestling in the wool flock its diamond-like purity was not dulled. Corradino sent up a silent prayer of thanks to Angelo Barovier, the *Maestro* who had, two centuries ago, invented this '*cristallo*' glass of hard silica with which Corradino now worked. Before then, all glass was coloured, even white glass had an impurity or dullness, the hue of sand or milk or smoke. *Cristallo* meant that, for the first time, full transparency and crystal clarity could be achieved, and Corradino blessed the day.

Corradino turned back to the making of his droplets. He still had ninety-nine to make before he would allow himself to return to his quarters for his wine and polenta supper. He could not entrust this work to one of the *servente* apprentices, because each one of the hundred droplets was different. In a move that had astounded his fellows, Corradino insisted that each droplet, because of its position on the chandelier, its distance from each candle, had to be a slightly different shape in order to transmit the same luminescence from every angle when suspended from the ceiling of a church or *palazzo*. The other glassmakers in the *fornace* and the boys used to gaze for hours on end at the contents of Corradino's droplet boxes, shaking their heads. They all looked exactly the same. Corradino saw them looking and smiled. He knew he had no need to hide his work – they could look all day long and would not know how he did it. Even he did not really understand what his fingers did as he thought of where this particular droplet would hang on the finished piece.

Corradino always went to look at the place where his chandeliers would hang. He asked his customers endless questions about how the room would be lit, he looked at the windows and shutters, he even considered the movement of the sunlight and the impact of the reflections from the water of the canal. And each time he noted down his calculations in a little vellum notebook, recording everything. This precious volume was now, at the height of Corradino's mastery, crammed with his ugly handwriting and his beautiful drawings. Numbers, forming intricate measurements and equations, also jostled for room on the page as Corradino believed in the power of the ancient science of mathematics. Thus, each piece that he made and each advancement in technique was documented so that he could develop his art by making reference to his previous pieces. Now, having finished the last unique glass drop, he took out his book. He found the calculations he had taken from Santa Maria della Pietà and made a quick quill sketch of his finished piece. Even on the page the chandelier seemed to stand out in a crystal relief.

Corradino guarded the book well, wearing it next to his skin at all times, but knew that even if his fellows could see it, they would not be able to decipher its secrets. He also knew that the other *maestri* laughed at him, and passed around the jest that Manin even wore his book when he pleasured a woman. He was truly an unusual man. But a genius, oh yes, truly a genius.

The testament to his genius was in every *palazzo* in Venice, every church, every grand eating house. It was in every shining chalice he made, every mirror smooth as the lagoon in summer, even every glass bubble or bonbon he made as *Carnevale* favours. They all had the same glow of an expensive gem. And now he knew that his newest work would illuminate the dark, vaulted ceilings of the Santa Maria della Pietà like no light they had ever seen. And it would sing, as many of his pieces spoke or sang. At the flick of a fingernail one of his cups would ring out the tale of the gold that painted its rim – of Samarkand and the Bosporus and the white hot days of eastern summer. This chandelier would echo the music of the girls that played in the Pietà. The girls that were orphaned, and had no one to love or love them, so poured their love into their music. His glass would sing back. It would tell them that at least one among them was loved.

The Pietà. Corradino smiled. Tomorrow he himself would go to the Pietà with the chandelier droplets. The chandelier itself would travel ahead of him in a special, flat-bottomed boat. Corradino had himself designed the packing system for his precious *candelabri* – they were suspended from the lid of a huge barrel filled with filtered lagoon water. This meant that the fragile design was cushioned from all knocks, and could survive all but a capsizement.

Then to arrive in Santa Maria della Pietà, to be winched from the barrel, water streaming from it in the godlight of the windows, like an extension of the exquisite glasswork. To fulfill its destiny, to light the church for perhaps centuries, to enable the girls to see the dark insects of the music notes as they raced across the pages of their scores, to enable the sublime noise that they made to the ultimate glory of God. And Corradino would complete the process as he painstakingly hung each drop in its proper place before the final piece was winched to the ceiling.

I myself will finish it, as is fitting.

It was the second greatest pleasure of this life of his. And tomorrow it would be married to the first – seeing Leonora. He began to make his final glass jewel, not heeding that all the slots in his rosewood box were already full. This was not to be a droplet for the chandelier – it was a gift for her.

Corradino knew that, when the glassmakers had been moved from Venice to Murano there had been another motive than that of civic safety. Venetian glass was the best in the world, and had been since eastern glassmaking techniques had been brought back from the fall of Constantinople. Such methods were honed and developed, techniques were passed from *maestro* to apprentice and a powerful monopoly grew for the Republic on the back of these secrets. One the Grand Council was reluctant to relinquish. Almost at once, for the glassmakers of Murano, the island became not just their living and working quarters, but something of a prison. The *Consiglio Maggiore* understood well the saying; 'He who hath a secret to keep must first keep it secret.' Isolation was the key to the keeping of these secrets. Even now, permission to go to the mainland was rarely given. And more often than not, the *maestri* would be followed by agents of the Council. Corradino, because of his talent, and his practice of taking careful measurements, and the necessity of placing final touches himself, was given more latitude than most. But he had, once before this time, abused this trust. For on such a mainland trip he had met Angelina.

She was beautiful. Corradino was no celibate, but he was used to seeing beauty only in the things that he had made. In her he saw something divine, something that he could not make. He met her in her father's *palazzo* on the Grand Canal. Principe Nunzio dei Vescovi wished to discuss a set of two hundred goblets that were needed for his daughter's wedding celebration. They were to match his daughter's wedding gown and mask. Corradino brought, as instructed, an inlaid box full of pigments and gems that he might use to achieve the colour.

All the great houses of Venice had two entrances, denoting their own unmistakable dichotomy of class. The water entrance was always fantastically grand, an imposing, decorative portal, with great double doors and part-submerged boat-poles striped in the colours of the household. The water door opened to invite the honoured guest into an enclosed pool, marble-walled, with a landing stage leading to the exalted reception rooms of the *palazzo*. The trade doors, opening into the *calle* at the side of the house, were more modest, for tradesmen and messengers and servants, opening directly onto the pavement. This distinction, this difference of doors, revealed much about the city – Venice owed everything to the water. The Lagoon was all. It was on the water, those shifting but faithful tides, that Venice had built her supremacy and her empire – how fitting, therefore, that the waterways of Venice were given precedence in this way. Corradino's gondola, on that fateful day, was waved to the water entrance. The great silver palace enveloped him and he was shown to the main apartments by a deferential liveried servant. As Corradino, in the humble leathers of a *soffiature di vetro* entered the beautiful salons looking out onto the water he realized that all had been done for him in deference to his rare talent. The Prince, a man with the long features and silver hair of nobility, received him as he would a kinsman. Corradino's place in the world seemed assured.

A servant was sent to fetch the Principessa Angelina, and the dress. The Prince discussed the pigments and their prices with Corradino over a fine Valpolicella, then as the old man looked up and said 'there you are my dear,' Corradino heard no more.

She was a revelation.

Blonde hair like filaments of gold. Green eyes like leaves in spring rain. And the countenance of a goddess. She was a vision in blue – the silks of her wedding dress seemed to have a hundred hues in the morning light and the dappled reflections of the canal.

As for the *Principessa*, she knew of Corradino by repute, and had longed to see the artist that all spoke of. She was surprised to find him so young – not more than twenty, she guessed. She was pleased to find him handsome, although not unusually so, with the dark eyes and curls of the region. His face – perpetually tanned by the furnaces – recalled the stern, dark, eastern icons that looked down from their jewel encrusted frames in the Basilica at Mass. In his person, he looked quite commonplace. But he was not. He was as priceless, she knew, as those icons themselves with all their jewels.

Angelina remembered being among the privileged company that had gone, the year before, to see an exhibition of a fabled creature at the Doge's Palace, the Palazzo Ducale. They called the creature a Camelopard, the fabled *Giraffa camelopardalis*, and it had been loaned by a King of the Africas. The name meant nothing to the *Principessa*. But when she saw the animal she felt an almost feral excitement as she watched from behind her mask. Enormously tall, chequered like a Harlequin, and with an impossibly long neck, the creature strode slowly around; its form slicing through the sunlight shafts that flooded in through the *palazzo's* windows. The great chamber of the *Sala del Maggior Consiglio*, cavernous, gorgeously painted in red and gold frescoes and with the highest ceilings in Venice, seemed the only room fitting for the display of this fantastical beast. From the ceiling, seventy-six past Doges of Venice, rendered by the great Veronese, looked down unmoved at the sight. Their living successor looked on in wonder from his throne, crowned with his *corno* hat, whispering to his consort from behind his beringed hand. Meanwhile, the alien silent creature paused to examine a high scarlet drapery with a snake-like black tongue, eliciting delighted gasps from the audience. It lifted its tail and expelled a pile of neat droppings onto the priceless floors, treading in its own excrement. The ladies giggled and squealed while the men guffawed, and Angelina pressed a floral posy to her nose. But her excitement remained. She felt herself in the presence of something truly unusual, something unique. She did not ask herself if the Camelopard were beautiful or not. That question was an irrelevance. If the beast had been for sale she would have had her father buy it.

She looked now at Corradino and felt the same sensations. It mattered not if he was young and handsome, only that he was truly unusual, something unique. She felt the need to possess him. When Angelina dei Vescovi smiled at him all thought of the pigments went out of Corradino's head.

He soon remembered them though, oh yes. In fact, he found it necessary to make many trips to the Palazzo Vescovo in the months before the wedding, to discuss those all-important pigments. Sometimes he saw the Prince as well as his daughter. But mostly he saw the *Principessa* alone. These were very important matters, you understand. It was crucial to get such things absolutely right.

A week before her wedding it was discovered that the Principessa Angelina dei Vescovi was with child. The *Principessa's* tiring maid, a tool and spy of the Prince, observed her mistresses' linens, which remained a blanched white throughout the time of her monthly courses. The wench reported the *Principessa's* pregnancy to the Prince almost before Angelina knew of it herself. The betrothal was broken on grounds of ill health, and Angelina was spirited away, in the utmost secrecy, to her father's estates in Vicenza for her confinement. In an effort to salvage his daughter's reputation, the Prince threatened his servants with death if any word were breathed back in Venice of Angelina's disgrace. Corradino, in a clandestine visit to the palace to see Angelina, found himself met by two of the Prince's gentlemen and carted upstairs to the Prince's study. There he had a brief and bitter interview with Nunzio dei Vescovi in which he was told in no uncertain terms that it was more than his life was worth either to attempt to contact Angelina again or to remain in the city. So harsh were the Prince's words, so belittling of Corradino's status, that he instantly lost all semblance of the nobility he had regained when he had first been received at the palace. He felt, now, that his talents were no match for the riches and the standing of the Prince, which he had once had and now lost. In years to come his mind would not let him remember many of the Prince's bitter words, but one exchange would not leave his memory.

After Nunzio had spent his rage he turned his back on Corradino and looked out over the lagoon. In a soft, defeated voice, he had said; 'Sometimes, Signor Manin, even by *touching* something beautiful, we ruin it for ever. Did you know that a butterfly, that most wondrous of insects, can never again fly once her wings have been touched by the fingers of man? The scales of her wings fall away, and they are useless. This you have done to my daughter.'

This sentiment, and the notion that Corradino was capable of destroying the beauty he had always striven to create, somehow frightened him more than anything else the Prince had said. For the second time in his life, Corradino fled in real fear back to Murano.

Corradino blamed the *Libro D'oro*, The Book of Gold. In 1376, in recognition of the skill of glassblowers and their value to the Republic, it had been decreed that the daughter of a glassblower could marry the son of a noble. But no such dispensation was given for the daughter of a noble to marry a humble glassblower, even one that came from noble stock. There was no future for Corradino and Angelina. Corradino returned to Murano with no idea of how the affair had been discovered, or of the child that he had fathered. He confided only in his dearest friend and mentor, who advised him to stay on Murano lest the Prince should make good his threat to seek revenge.

For two years Corradino heard nothing of his lover and worked as if a demon rode his back. Then he was given a dispensation to go into Venice to make a reliquary for the Basilica of San Marco and deemed it safe to return at last. On his first day in the city for two years he contrived to see Nunzio dei Vescovi.

His entry into the Palazzo dei Vescovi was quite different this time. The grand doors to the water stood open as Corradino's gondola drew near – one partly unhinged and hacked for firewood. The great salons stood empty; looted of all their riches, the rich draperies rat-nibbled or torn down. No servants remained, and as Corradino mounted the rotting stairs he began to guess why.

The stench of the sickroom brought bile rising to Corradino's throat. Twisted on the bed lay Nunzio dei Vescovi, cocooned in his vile coverlet, half his face eaten by the '*male francese*' – the 'French Disease'. Syphilis. The man was dying. But the thing on the bed – once a Prince – began to gasp at Corradino and it was long moments before Corradino understood. Nunzio's face was twisted meat, the disease had eaten large portions of his lips, and the sibilants and plosives of speech were denied to him.

'*. . . ino.*' A claw-like hand extended to the table by the bed. On it sat a flask of wine and a goblet, dusty with the syrup of an ancient draught slick in the bottom. God only knew how long it had been since the man had been tended by another human soul.

Corradino crossed himself and poured the wine. A dead wasp fell into the glass, but it did not seem to matter. The Prince eased himself onto his shoulder with palpable agony, and drank, the wine dribbling like blood from his roofless mouth. Corradino knew he did not have long – he asked the only question he had. 'Angelina?'

'. . . ead.'

Corradino turned to go. He had expected as much. He would send a priest for Nunzio, but he could do no more.

'In . . . hildbirth.'

The hideous whisper halted him. Corradino turned.

'There's a child?'

'In . . . ietà. . . . ell o-ne . . . onour of family. . . . o-one.'

Very well. He could grant this last thing. He nodded, in an unspoken agreement to keep the secret.

'And her name?'

'. . . eonora. . . . anin.'

The supreme irony.

She has my *name.*

Corradino watched Nunzio die, the moment after the wretch had unburdened his heart. He shed no tears for the Prince and was no more than momentarily saddened about Angelina – he had done his mourning for her in his two years on Murano. And he had not loved her. Corradino had never been in love. But he went to see the two-year-old Leonora Manin at Santa Maria della Pietà and fell in love for the first time in his life.

On the dock of San Zaccaria, at the entrance to the Piazzetta di San Marco, there stand two tall white pillars. They hold aloft the statue of Saint Theodosius of Constantinople, and the chimera of the winged lion, adopted and bastardized by the city as the Lion of St Mark. The Lion's paw rests on a book, the pages of which read '*Pax Marce in Tibia*' 'Peace be with you Mark' – the fabled greeting of the Angels as they dubbed Mark the Saint of Venice. Three pillars were looted from distant Tyre to stand here, but the third toppled into the sea while being unloaded, and still lies at the bottom of the lagoon. At the instant that Corradino first laid eyes on his daughter, the Camelopard – thin and weary from its three year progress around the great courts of Milan, Genoa and Turin – was being loaded onto a ship bound for home. A mass of ropes encircling its long neck, it was but two short steps from the vessel that would carry it back to the African potentate who had lent it to the north. But the planks that ramped to the ship were glassy with rain; the creature reluctant to walk into the heaving sea. Like the pillar centuries before, the Camelopard pitched forward into the lagoon as its handlers leapt clear. Its enormous height meant that the noble head could be seen above the water, liquid brown eyes rolling, black tongue lashing, as it swallowed salt water. A gathering crowd pulled at the slippery ropes, but the creature's gawky limbs were too ungainly for rescue and, within an hour, the Camelopard died. It sank to the bottom of the lagoon, in silent peace, and in a last motion of grace the long neck and heavy head sank to rest over the lost pillar of Tyre.

CHAPTER 6

The Mirror

Nora looked at her reflection and knew she had made a horrible mistake. She should never have come. There was none of the resolve in her eyes that had been there earlier.

I see the portrait of a blinking idiot.

It was her second day in Venice and she was on a trip to Murano, organized by her hotel. Thousands of tourists every year were shuttled over to Murano by the boatload, cameras in hand. Ostensibly they had come to have a trip around the glass factories and marvel at the glassblowers' skill. In actuality, such trips were little more than a shopping expedition for wealthy Americans and Japanese. The highlight of Nora's trip had come earlier – a five minute tour around the factory floor. She watched the men at work, blowing and shaping the glass, some with serious intent, some with crowd-pleasing theatricals. She looked at the building and the furnaces, and knew they had hardly changed in four hundred years. She wanted very much to be a part of it, knew she could do a little of what these men did. She stood, rapt, and was jostled by a crowd of impatient Germans eager to get to the point of sale.

So that they could buy a conversation piece for their Hamburg dinner table, and say to the Helpmanns over coffee; 'Yes, we picked this up in Venice, genuine blown Murano glass, you know.'

This was *their* endpoint – this large shopping area, well lit, whitewashed, and bright with glass of every sort. Goblets stood in regimental ranks on the shelves, their orderly lines belied by the spectra of coloured helixes that twisted through their stems. Chandeliers and *candelabri* of astonishing baroque detail hung from the ceilings, crowding each other like the branches of some fantastical forest. Beasts and birds seemed moulded from volcanic larva of all hues of orange and red. Subtle pieces with the clarity and texture of cracked ice jostled with hideously ugly nineteenth century work; fat birds trapped in perpetual song by trellised cages. And the walls were crowded with mirrors, of all sizes, like a collection of portraits which featured only their admirers. I will frame your face, was their fickle promise. You are my subject. I will make you beautiful. Until you pass me by and the next face stares into my depths. Then only that visage will be my concern.

Nora looked now into one such.

Little wonder that a mirror is known as a looking glass. We're all looking for something when we gaze into one. But I am not looking at myself today, but the glass itself. The glass, the glass is what matters.

A mantra which was meant to make her brave again. She looked to the mirror's frame for reassurance. Weaving around it were glass flowers of such delicacy, such colour, that she felt she could pluck one and smell its scents. Such artistry convinced her – not to go on, but to go back.

I am crazy. I will look round a little more and then go home, all the way home, to London. I must have been mad to think that I could come here and expect an entrée into one of the oldest and most skilled Venetian professions. Just on the basis of my name and my own small talents.

She clutched the A4 black portfolio which she had brought with her. It contained glossy photographs of the glasswork she had exhibited in Cork Street. She had been proud of it, until she saw this room.

Mad. I will go.

'*È molto bello, questo specchio; vetro* Fiorato. *Vuole guardare la lista dei prezzi?*'

The voice came close to her ear, shocking her out of her dismal reverie. It belonged to one of the smooth, well dressed gentlemen that helped the customers with their purchases. He looked elderly, proprietorial, kind. He could see that he had surprised her, and looked regretful.

'*Mi scusi, Signorina. Lei,* è *italiana*?'

Nora smiled, in apology for her reaction.

'No, not Italian.' Now was not the time to explain her pedigree. '*Sono inglese.*'

'I apologize,' said the gentleman in perfect English. 'But truly, you have the look of an Italian. A Botticelli,' he smiled with great charm. 'Would you like to see our catalogue, our price list?'

Nora screwed up the last of her resolve. His recognizing her for an Italian seemed an invitation into the last chance saloon. 'Actually, I wanted to enquire about a job.'

Instantly the man's demeanour changed. Nora had slipped, in his eyes, from wealthy customer to worthless backpacker. He had such enquiries for shopwork daily. Why couldn't they all go to Tuscany and pick grapes? '*Signorina*, I regret that we don't take foreign nationals to work in the shop.'

He made as if to leave her. She said, with desperation, 'I don't mean in the shop. I want to work in the *fornace*. As a glassblower. *Una soffiatrice di vetro.*'

She wasn't sure if the request sounded more ridiculous

in English or Italian.

The man laughed with derision. 'What you suggest is impossible. Such work takes years of training. It is a highly skilled profession. A Venetian's profession. And,' this to her blonde tresses, 'a man's profession.' He turned from her to a German couple arguing loudly over a goblet set.

'Wait,' Nora said in Italian. She knew she had to leave, but not like this. Not with this man thinking her an idiot, a nuisance. She could not be dismissed this way. 'I wish to buy this mirror.' She wanted the mirror of flowers to take back to London. She had gazed into it while her dream died, and the flowers would serve to remind her of what a beautiful dream it once was.

Seamlessly, the man altered his manner again. With smooth charm he gave orders for the mirror to be packed, and took Nora downstairs to the shipping desk. He asked for an address in England and Nora, on an impulse, gave her mother's. The mirror could stay with Elinor until Nora sorted herself out. She despondently wrote out her own details and signed the Amex slip, while the man checked her signature with a cursory glance.

She was actually walking down the staircase before he called her back.

'*Signorina*?'

She returned to the desk, now weary of the trip. All she wanted now was to be able to leave, to get back on the boat with all the rest of the tourists, for that was where she now belonged.

'Is there some problem?' she asked.

The man was looking at her mother's address, and back to her Amex slip.

'Manin?' he said. 'Your name is Manin?'

'*Sì*.'

He took off his half-moon glasses as if dazed. In Italian, as if unable to compute his English anymore, he said, 'Are you – do you know . . . have you heard of Corrado Manin, known as Corradino?'

'Yes, he is my direct ancestor. He is the reason I wanted to come here, and learn the glass.' She suddenly felt tears pricking her eyes. She was an abject failure, failed mother, failed wife, failed adventurer on a fool's enterprise. She wanted to go, before she cried in front of this man. But, surprisingly, he stayed her by holding out his hand. 'I am Adelino della Vigna. Come with me for a moment, I'd just like to check something.'

Nora let him steer her by the elbow, not down the main staircase but through a side door marked, forbiddingly, '*Privato*.' The Germans looked on with interest, sure that the *fraulein* had been caught shoplifting.

Nora followed Adelino down an iron staircase, until the smell and heat told her they were approaching the factory floor. He led her through a heavy sliding door, its materials warm from the temperatures within. She felt the full blast of the *forno* for the first time.

Like the fifth of November when your front is toasted by the bonfire but your back stays cold.

Adelino led her to the flames, answering in swift Italian the whistles and teases of the *maestri* who made predictable comments on old Adelino entering with a young blonde. The old man stripped off his jacket and reached for a blowpipe. Nora began to proffer her portfolio, but Adelino waved it away. 'You may as well throw that on the fire. Here we begin all things new.' He pushed the blowpipe into the fire, raddling the coals till they spat. 'I run this place. All I deal with now is point of sale and shipping, but I used to work the glass, before my lungs went. Show me what you can do with this.'

Nora took off her coat and slung it behind a pile of buckets. She took the rod gingerly, knowing she had only one chance.

Help me, Corradino.

Nora collected the gather from the *forno* and began, gently, to blow the glass. She rolled it, reheated, shaped and blew, holding her breath out until the parison had formed. Only when satisfied did she breathe in again. Corradino had heard her. It was perfect.

Nora drank the evil, dark espresso Adelino had poured her while he hunted round his chaotic desk for a pen.

'I'm taking you on as an apprentice, for one month, on trial. The pay is low, and you'll just be a *servente* helping the *maestri*. No finished pieces. You understand?'

Nora nodded, incredulous. He handed her a form, covered in his inky scrawl.

'Take this to the *Questura* – the Police Station – in Castello. It's on the Fondamenta San Lorenzo. You need to get a residency permit and a work permit. This will take a while, but it should help that your father is from the city, and that you were born here.' For now Nora had recounted her history to Adelino. 'Meantime get this form franked by them and you can work here while the paperwork is being processed.' He shrugged expressively. 'This is *Venezia*, and she takes her sweet time.'

Nora put down her cup gently on the desk, afraid that any sudden moves would break the spell; that she would wake and find herself back though the Looking Glass again, staring at her reflection in the shop. Adelino caught her eye.

'Understand this. You have a small talent for this work, which may grow. But I'm hiring you solely on your name, and my respect for Corradino's art. Try to live up to him.' He rose dismissively. 'Be here on Monday at 6am sharp. No lateness, or you'll be fired before you are hired.' He allowed himself a smile at his small witticism, which lightened the asperity of his speech. 'Now I must get back to the shop.'

Nora stumbled into the daylight, dizzy with disbelief. She looked at the long low red building that was her new workplace, at the small ranks of red houses by the canal, and the faded street sign on the wall. She stared.

The Fondamenta Manin. Manin Street. The main street of Murano is named for Corradino. For Daniele. For me.

The spires of San Marco spiked in the distance, a tiara of piercing beauty crowning the lagoon. Nora had never seen Venice from such an aspect before. She jumped as high as she could and screamed with joy, and went to join the baffled Germans on the waiting boat.

From his office window, Adelino watched her, and narrowed his eyes meditatively in an unfathomable expression which his late wife would have recognized as a danger sign. His gaze lighted on the same street sign that Nora had just seen. The Fondamenta Manin. The whole place was named for her. Her family *is* glassblowing, time out of mind. She had talent – talent that would quickly grow. She had the great Corradino on her team. And she was certainly beautiful.

He turned his back on the vista and faced his office and reality. This was not the seventeenth century. No longer did this foundry, or this city, hold the monopoly on glassmaking. Murano and San Marco were crammed with glass factories and gift shops selling gew-gaws and bon-bons of glass, confections for the tourists to take home. Competition for the patronage of the wealthier tourists, those Americans or Japanese who would invest in a larger piece, was fierce. Adelino was forced to make ruinous deals with the more exclusive hotels to run glass tours, and more often than not in these times the tourists would take photos and get back in their boats having ordered nothing from his shop.

He sat down heavily at his desk. His business was in trouble, so why had he just hired a green girl, whom he would have to pay a wage? Why were his fingertips damp with perspiration? Why did his heart quicken? Adelino began to tingle, as the age-old mercantile tides ebbed and flowed in his veins. A lovely girl, a famous genius of an ancestor, and his own struggling glass factory. They all added up to one word; Opportunity. It was one of his favourites.

Four days later, Elinor Manin received a well-wrapped parcel at her Islington home. It was a Venetian glass mirror of great beauty, sprigged with glass flowers so delicate it seemed as if they lived. There was no note. Elinor sat at the kitchen table, looking in the mirror resting on the debris of its wrappings, at her sixty-year-old face. She began to cry, her hot tears splashing the cool glass.

She felt as if somehow, from beyond the grave, the mirror was from Bruno.

CHAPTER 7

The Lion and the Book

The *Questura* in Castello was an attractive building. Like many municipal offices in Venice, the Police Station had a past life as a *palazzo* and its former existence was betrayed by the Moorish mullions of its windows. Even so, Nora would have been happy to visit it just the once.

This was not to be. The slow workings of Venetian administration meant that this was her sixth visit in four weeks. She had filled in form after form, all with incomprehensible names or numbers. She had produced every single paper or certificate that had documented her life, from birth certificate to driving licence. And each time she had dealt with a different policeman, recounting her tale from the beginning, dealing with reactions that ran the gamut from frank incredulity to plain indifference. This English *Signorina* had somehow been given an apprenticeship with the *maestri* on Murano, and now needed a living permit and a work permit. Each official had a different take on her plight.

The *Signorina* must have a rental address in Venice, then after she had attained her living permit, or *permesso di soggiorno*, she would then apply for the *permesso di lavoro*, or work permit. No, said another, she must be given her *permesso di lavoro* first, then have it ratified by her employer, then she would qualify to take rental quarters in the *sestiere*, then she could apply for a *permesso di sogiorno*.

I want to scream.

Nora's manner had metamorphosed over these visits from the friendly, slightly ignorant blonde demeanour that she had found all her life to work well with officialdom, to the hard-nosed, demanding manner of a harridan. The progress of her application, however, had stayed exactly the same, retaining its state of complete inertia.

I have a recurring dream where I'm floating underwater in the lagoon, gasping for breath, but unable to swim to the surface because I'm bound with reams and reams of red tape.

Today, a peerless autumn day, she entered the door of the police station with steely determination, her features brittle with counterfeit smiles.

I have been in Venice for a full month. I need to get this sorted.

The last month had passed with that strange elasticity which characterizes significant periods of life. On the one hand, the time had slipped by with a rapidity which surprised Nora. On the other, she could not believe that it was only four weeks ago that she had been living at Belmont, amid the detritus of her dead marriage. She had worked hard at the furnaces from that first Monday, when she had entered the *fornace* with an air of one going to school for the first time. She had bound her hair in a scarf and worn her oldest jeans in an effort to blend in as much as possible. It had not worked. The heat was such that in the space of half an hour she had shed the scarf and was working in jeans, bare feet and a vest top, to predictable comments from the others.

But all in all, Nora's first day at the *fornace* was both exhausting and exhilarating. Most of the men were guardedly friendly, in a manner which made her suspect that they had been given instruction by Adelino. Two of the younger glassblowers, a goodlooking pair who seemed to be somewhat of a double act, were friendly and helpful and watched her progress with dark, appraising eyes. She left when the others did, congratulating herself on having made no major mistakes that day, and was gratified when her two young colleagues asked her to come for a drink with the others. Adelino was not with them, but thinking herself safe in numbers Nora followed gratefully along the Fondamenta Manin to a warmly-lit welcoming bar. The *maestri* were clearly regulars, as their 'usual' ten Peroni beers sat ready on the bar like the green bottles of the song. Nora collapsed on the bar stool chivalrously proffered by Roberto and rolled her head around on her aching neck. She heard some of the gathered men joking about offering her a massage and she smiled along.

I must get used to barracking and locker-room jokes; I must not be phased by it all. This is a man's world – always has been – and I have to learn to fit in. No princess behaviour.

She pressed the cold bottle of Peroni to a forehead still hot and flushed from the furnace's kiss, and felt the welcome chill of condensation dripping to her cheek. She took a long cool slug of the beer and, as her lips touched the bottle and her teeth chinked the glass she thought of the continuity of the glassmakers' art. Here in her hand was the equivalent of the wares produced by Corradino and his colleagues, but now mass-produced, recycled, soulless and utilitarian. Above the bar MTV blared, interrupting her thoughts, and Roberto beckoned her to a small corner table which Luca had already secured. Nora sat, smiled, and answered their questions about London, Chelsea FC and Robbie Williams in that order. In turn, she discovered that both men were the sons of glassblowers.

'In fact,' said Luca, 'Roberto here has the longest glassblowing history of all of us here, even though he's the youngest.'

'But the most talented,' put in Roberto, his white grin mitigating the boast.

'Actually, that's annoyingly true,' countered Luca. 'Old Adelino is always blowing smoke up your arse.'

'He says I've inherited the family "breath",' Roberto explained modestly to Nora.

'Yeah,' said Luca holding his nose, 'I think I know what he means. You stink.'

Roberto cuffed Luca and they both roared with laughter. Nora shifted in her seat and suddenly felt very old. These boys were charming, but a bit . . . immature? She dragged the conversation back to her point of interest and addressed Roberto. 'Your family? They've always been in the trade?'

'For ever. Right back to the seventeenth century, in fact. My ancestor, Giacomo del Piero, was the foreman of our very *fornace* back then.'

The seventeenth century! Corradino would have been here too! Could the two men have known each other?

'I suppose,' Nora began nonchalantly, suppressing her excitement, 'that there were many different *fornaci* here then?'

'No,' said Luca, who seemed slightly more intellectual than his colleague, 'in those days, there was only one glass foundry on Murano. Venice was still a Republic so it was easier to control the monopoly that way. All the glassmakers in Venice lived and died here after the foundry was moved in 1291; actually they were threatened with death if they tried to leave, and if anyone escaped their families were imprisoned or murdered to force the fugitives to return.' Luca paused to emphasise this ghoulish fact and took a swig of beer. 'After the city state fell many more factories grew up here; there were about three hundred factories in the city then. But then Murano declined once the glass monopoly was lost and other nations learned how to make good glass. In 1805 the glass guild was abolished, the furnaces shuttered and the artists scattered throughout Europe.'

'It's a very different trade now,' put in Roberto. 'In Giacomo's time, all kinds of glass were made here, from the humblest bottle,' he waved his Peroni in an echo of Nora's own thoughts, 'to the finest mirrors. Now, everyday glassware is made in huge bottle plants in Germany, or at Dulux in France or Palaks in Turkey. Our only lifeline is the quality market – the "art" if you like. Tourists are our only buyers, and our foundry only gets a small part of that market. Competition is fierce now. In fact,' here he looked speculatively at Nora, 'you were lucky to be taken on.'

Nora lowered her eyes as Roberto took a slug at his beer. She felt uncomfortable, almost slighted, but Roberto carried on.

'So you could say Giacomo was the best back then,' he concluded, 'as he was the foreman of the only factory.'

She noticed how Roberto talked of ancient history as if it were no more than a heartbeat ago. 'You speak of him as if you knew him,' she said, recognizing something of her own sentiments.

'All Venetians do that,' said Roberto smiling. 'Here the past is all around. It happened only yesterday.'

Nora recognized the connection to his ancestor that she felt for Corradino, and this decided her; she would share her history. 'This is all really strange, because *my* ancestor worked here too, around the same time. He must have known Giacomo. His name was Corrado Manin, known as Corradino. Have you heard of him?'

Roberto's face went suddenly still. He exchanged a look with Luca. 'No,' he said abruptly. 'Sorry. Another Peroni?' He rose at once and headed to the bar without waiting for a reply.

Nora sat stunned, her face tingling as if from a slap. What was bothering the man? She turned to Luca who bathed her in a charming smile. 'Don't mind Roberto. He's a bit funny about his ancestor. Thinks he owns the *fornace*. He's always trying to get Adelino to raise his profile, and sell the glass on the del Piero name. Probably thought you were trying to muscle in.'

'But ... I wasn't ... I didn't ...'

'Really, it's cool. Forget it. Here he comes.'

As Roberto returned with three more Peroni Nora did her best to be particularly charming, flattering him with questions about glassblowing in an effort to atone for her gaffe, although she was still not entirely clear what she had done wrong. Roberto unbent and showed some signs of being mollified, but there was something else there too – as time passed he was getting heavily drunk. The hour was becoming late and Nora began to fret about her boat back to Venice, when it suddenly occurred to her that Luca had gone to the toilet about twenty minutes ago and not come back. She glanced around the bar but he was nowhere to be seen, and moreover, all the other *maestri* had gone too. She recognized no one.

Oh Christ.

Nora sighed gustily. She was suddenly transported back ten years to St Martin's, when it had been her unhappy duty to shepherd maudlin friends home when they had had a skinful. Surely she did not have to do that now, at her age, for this drunken boy? She swore under her breath and took Roberto's arm, helping him to stagger outside. He swayed gently at the canalside, and she wondered if he was going to be sick, but then he smiled unsteadily and lunged towards her, planting his mouth roughly on hers.

Nora's response was so Victorian it surprised her. She pushed him roughly away and fetched him a stinging slap which nearly sent him into the canal. That sobered Roberto up. His good looks disappeared as the handsome mouth curled into a sneer, and Nora suddenly felt afraid. 'Come on,' he said, moving in once more. 'You owe me something, you Manin slut.'

Nora turned and ran.

She didn't stop until she came to the *Faro vaporetto* stop, but the thought occurred that Roberto too would make his way here, as it was the nearest *fermata* on the island. Shaken and edgy, aware that she was the only one waiting, she hailed a passing water taxi and spent far too much money getting back to her hotel.

The next day and for many others she reaped her reward. Roberto had done his work – none of the men talked to her at all now. She wondered what he had told them all about her that was so bad that even the affable Luca barely acknowledged her. Roberto either ignored her, or attempted to make her life difficult with little shows of petulance or spite. Her tools would go missing, her own small experiments in glass would be found broken. With growing incredulity Nora realized that she was being bullied. She began to feel the same dread that she had felt at school when she encountered the sixth form girls with too much eyeliner who called her 'hippy' because of her long hair. She had never dreamed that a man could be so vindictive to a woman who had turned down his charms – she had assumed that after the incident she would merely drop off Roberto's radar. Sometimes she would feel a chill on her neck and turn to find him staring at her with such freezing hatred that she felt sure that there must be something wrong with him

– something that drove him to hate her over and above sexual rejection.

But what could it possibly be? I hardly know the man. Is he unbalanced?

Now she had no-one, except a gentle soul called Francesco who would occasionally, unsmilingly, show her the proper way to do her work and then respond to her thanks with a shy nod. She knew they were all waiting for her to give up and go home. She saw Adelino occasionally when he came down to the factory floor, and welcomed his presence as she used to welcome the appearance of a teacher in those long breaktimes at school – she knew that, in his presence, the bullying would stop. She knew he checked up on her progress, but so far he had had no cause to speak to her about it.

But in her lonely bubble, her own hermetically sealed vessel of silence, she knew her work was improving. In the absence of company or conversation the glass became her friend. She began to understand its ways in a manner she would not have done if she had been distracted with banter and conversation. Her duties at this stage were no more than to melt the gather, clear any impurities, and blow the occasional parison. She had no shaping or moulding duties beyond the most rudimentary, but did some cooling and reheating. Yet she began to see this compound of silica and sand as something living and organic. She understood that it breathed – taking in oxygen as hungrily as any living thing. It had moods – from the hot red, to the honeyed gold, to the crystal white. It had textures, sometimes as flowing as sweet syrup, sometimes as hard as tempered steel. She could well believe that in Corradino's time they made knives of glass – deadly, silent, clean.

Corradino. She thought of him often. She felt as if the glass connected them, that it was drawn out between them until the connection were as thin and stretched as a cello string, yet it still resonated with a low, long note across the centuries.

He is my companion while the others talk around me. I talk to him.

By osmosis, Nora's Italian, already good, quickly became excellent. When her month's trial was complete she went to Adelino, who expressed pleasure at her progress and her wish to remain. But he was concerned that she had not yet obtained her work permit, and seemed particularly insistent that she get one, as if he himself was working to some undisclosed timetable.

So back to the Police Station Nora went. As she entered the lobby she determined not to leave without her permit. She waitied patiently in the designated area reading endless leaflets and posters about the dangers of drugs, guidelines for motorized boats and street crime. When she was finally shown through to an inner office Nora sighed as she noted that the smart young officer that came to attend her was unfamiliar to her, and she prepared to repeat her entire saga again.

This young man, however, despite his abrupt manner, seemed to have more of a clue than those that had gone before. He seemed fairly well acquainted with her case. She was so taken aback by this that it was fully half an hour before she realized that she had seen him before.

Years later she could remember exactly the moment when she realized this. He was looking through her documentation and seemed to spot a discrepancy. He looked from her birth certificate to her application for a work permit and frowned slightly.

'*Signorina.*' He shuffled the papers again. 'Here on your application you have named yourself Nora Manin.' He stumbled a little over the foreign name. 'But on your certificate of birth from the Ospedali Civili Riuniti here in Venice you are named as Leonora Angelina Manin. Can you explain this to me?'

'It's an abbreviation. Because I was brought up in England my mother gave me the English version of my Italian name.'

The officer nodded, his eyes on the forms. 'I see. But you understand, I will need you to fill in this form again with your given name.' He stood and pulled a fresh buff form efficiently from a nearby filing cabinet.

Nora attempted to keep her rage in check. 'Can't I just correct *this* form?'

In answer the young officer located his pen, unscrewed the cap and laid it definitely in front of her.

Nora seethed as she filled in the form yet again, calculating that it must be the fourth time she had done so, each time because of a trifling error such as this. Even worse, this form had already been signed by Adelino, so now she must ask him to do it again, which meant at least one more trip back here. Nora silently cursed the form, cursed the city, cursed the officer with the clean fingernails who was such a jobsworth that he had made her jump through this hoop. Finally done, she watched him check it through meticulously, hating him.

'*Bene*,' he said finally. He handed the form back. As he did so he said, with his first hint of friendliness, 'You know, Leonora is a much better name than Nora. And it is the right name for a Venetian. See,' he pointed to the Lion of Saint Mark, which adorned the top of Nora's form. 'The Lion. *Il Leone*. Leonora.' He raised his eyes to hers for the first time, and she placed him at last – he was the man from the Pietà, the one that had glanced at her in the Vivaldi concert.

She wondered if he had recognized her too, before she registered what he had said about her name. It struck her that it was the exact opposite of what Stephen had said to her - that Leonora was pretentious and affected. Here it was not. Here it fitted. Here Nora was the strange name, an English name, a cause for comment. She was becoming a Venetian. She looked at the man who had invited this epiphany, and smiled.

He returned the smile, then instantly the professionalism was back. He looked down at the forms again. 'You are still living at the Hotel Santo Stefano?'

'Yes.'

The officer took a sharp intake of breath, making that peculiar sound that, in any language, denotes great expense.

'I know. I'm looking for a flat at the moment.' Nora felt the urgency better than anyone. The money from the sale of Belmont was fast disappearing, and a month in a hotel hadn't helped.

The officer looked thoughtful. 'I know someone who could help you. My cousin is an agent for a number of apartments in San Marco. If you want, I could show you some. Maybe at the weekend? I'm off on Saturday?'

Nora felt doubtful, memories of the evening with Roberto and Luca fresh in her mind. But this man was a public official. And she did need a flat. She was determined however, to plan future meetings in the safety of daytime.

'What about 3 o'clock?'

He nodded.

'Where?' she asked.

He got up to open the door for her. 'How about the Cantina Do Mori? The Two Moors? In San Polo?'

Where else. A little known, ancient, steadfastly Venetian drinking place. To a tourist, he would have suggested Florian's. She felt flattered. 'Perfect.'

He held out his hand as she made to leave, and as she shook it he said, 'I'm Officer Alessandro Bardolino.'

She smiled again. 'At the Do Mori, then, Officer Bardolino.'

And Leonora Manin walked out of the *Questura*, once again without her *permesso di lavoro*.

CHAPTER 8

La Bocca del Leone

The first time Corradino fled for his life to Murano went like this.

The Manins were a powerful and wealthy family. They accrued a significant fortune from their mercantile interests along the Black Sea to the Levant and Constantinople. By the mid-seventeenth century they had attained considerable political power to match.

The head of the family, Corrado Manin, lived with his twin younger brothers Azolo and Ugolino, in a grand *palazzo* in the Campo Manin, a square named in the family's honour. Corrado took a wife, Maria Bovolo, a woman of good character and even better connections. They had a son, also called Corrado, but known as Corradino, the diminutive form which distinguished him from his father. The family adored each other and the house ran like the well appointed merchant ships that had made the Manin fortune. There were many servants, a French tutor for little Corradino, and the Manin men were free to pursue their interests in the political sphere.

One summer, when Corradino was ten, and becoming a well-formed intelligent boy, the Manin fortunes changed.

Corrado was elected to the Council of Ten, the close-knit junta that ran the Republic of Venice. Azolo was also elected in the same year. Ugolino was excluded from office by an ancient edict that stated that no more than two members of any one family could serve at the same time. This stricture was designed to avoid familial corruption, but merely fostered it. Embittered by his exclusion, for Ugolino was actually a half-hour older than his twin, he continued to assist his brothers in their clandestine objective – to secretly win friends among others of The Ten in order to depose the Doge and replace him with Corrado. Corrado and his brothers loved their *palazzo*, but how much better to live in the Doge's Palace, and protect the family interests with the Dukedom of Venice? In this Corrado took his great love for his family to its natural conclusion. He wanted everything for them.

But Venice was ever a place of duplicity. Like its revellers the city also wore a mask. Beneath the beauty and artifice of its surface ran the deep waters of deceit and treachery. This ever present threat was embodied in the *Bocca del Leone* – the Lion's mouth.

In deepest precincts of the Doge's Palace a stone Lion's head waited, carved into the wall in sharp relief. As the inscription below the dark slit invited, those who had information on another citizen of the Republic were to write down their suspicions and feed the document through the Lion's mouth: '*Denontie secrete contro chi occvltera gratie et officii o collvdera per nasconder der la vera rendita d'essi.*' The *Maggior Consiglio* would deal with the matter, swiftly and thoroughly. Many such letterboxes adorned the walls of the city, their inscriptions specifying the type of denunciation with which they dealt – tax evasion, usury, bad trading practice. But here in the Doge's Palace the Lion dealt with the highest of crimes – political treachery against the State. And on the day of *La Festa del Redentore* in high summer, when the cool chambers were empty and quiet as the crowds shouted and cheered far away, a hand fed a letter through the Lion's mouth into the infinite blackness within. The letter bore Corrado Manin's name. The Lion consumed him. And the hand belonged to Ugolino Manin.

The second Ugolino's hand let go of the paper he wanted it back. He actually contemplated reaching into the dark to try to retrieve it, but the baleful stone eyes of the Lion warned him. He felt that his hand would be bitten by unseen teeth. He could ask for it back, but from whom? The denunciations were secret – he knew not where the slit led, or to whom. Admission into that inner sanctum might mean his own death. He knew only that every name swallowed by the Lion soon reached the ears of The Ten, and, as all Europe knew, a word to The Ten was a death sentence. Ugolino stumbled out of the palace, down the Giants' staircase, feeling sick at heart. Mars and Neptune, great stone sentinels of the steps, judged him with their blank white eyes. As his own sight was blasted by the daylight Ugolino ran, blinded, through the Piazza San Marco. The great square was empty this day as he had known it must be. He had calculated that this was the only day on which his crime would go unseen, as all citizens of Venice crowded the banks of the Giudecca canal on the other side of the city. He knew that the crowds would be watching the spectacle of the bridge of boats, built over the width of the canal to the door of the church of the Redentore. Ugolino pictured the faithful walking to church over the water as Our Lord had done, to give thanks for their redemption from the Plague.

Redemption. He needed it now.

He felt his knees give way in an involuntary genuflection, his knees cracked on the hard stone, and he knelt for a moment. But he could not pray until he had made all things right. He rose and began to race through the sunlit square, and even in the dark narrow *calli* he still could not see, this time because his eyes were flooded with tears. He thought of his brothers and sister Maria, and most of all of little Corradino. He had now bought their deaths. Unless . . . . He knew what he must do.

★ ★ ★

Corradino felt cold lips pressing his warm cheek. He woke to see his father's face illumined by a single candle. All else was blackness. His father was smiling but looked strained. 'Wake up, Corradino *mio*. We are going on an adventure.'

Corradino rubbed his eyes. 'Where to, Papà?' he asked, his ten year old mind consumed with his characteristic curiosity.

'To the *Pescheria*.'

The Fishmarket? Corradino rolled out of bed and began to dress. He had been to the Fishmarket on the Rialto before, but always with Rafealla, the maid. Never with his father.

But 'tis true that you must visit early – the catch comes in at dawn.

'Quickly, my little monkey. *Presto, piccola scimmia*.'

As they were about to leave the chamber Corrado said: 'Wait, *scimmia*. You can choose one thing from your room to take with you. It should be the thing you like the best, Corradino.'

Corradino was puzzled. 'Why?'

'Because we may be away for a little while. Look – I have my choice.' Corrado opened his coat and Corradino saw the shadowy shape of a book.

It must be that book by the Dante fellow. The one about comedy.

Father loves it. Perhaps it makes him laugh?

Corradino began to search his chamber in the lowlight. Corrado stood waiting, not wishing to alarm the boy, but knowing they must hurry. Ugolino had come to him at sunset with the worst news – he had been watching the Redentore and had got wind of a plot to denounce Corrado to the Doge. Their scheme was undone and they must flee at once.

'Found it!' Corradino clasped his favourite possession in his hand. It was a glass horse, a delicate replica of the bronze horses on the Basilica di San Marco.

Corrado nodded and led his son quickly out of the room and down the staircase. Corradino noticed the eerie shapes the candle cast on the walls – strange dark phantoms chasing him and his father. The portraits of his ancestors, usually friendly with their Manin features, looked down now with the malevolent envy that the long dead reserved for the living. Corradino shivered, and fixed his eyes on the new painting hanging in pride of place at the foot of the stair. It was a family group, painted on his tenth name-day, picturing himself at the centre of his father and uncles. Behind the family was an allegorical seascape, in which the richly appointed Manin fleet avoided stormy clouds and fantastical sea snakes to come safely home to harbour. He remembered that his costume had itched and his ruff scratched at his ear – he had fidgeted and been reprimanded by his father. 'Be as a statue.' Corrado had said. 'Like the

Gods in the courtyards of the Doge.' But Corradino had not – in his mind he had become one of the horses on the top of the Basilica. He and his father and uncles formed the great bronze quartet in his head – noble, all-seeing and so so still. Now, below the painting as if they had stepped from the frame, he saw his mother and uncles waiting at the foot of the stairs, masked, cloaked and booted – ready for travel also. Corradino's fear grew and he flung himself into his mother's arms, something he usually thought he was too old to do. Maria held him tight and kissed his hair.

Her bosom smells of vanilla, as it always does. The spice merchant comes to her once a twelvemonth and sells her the pods for the essence that she makes. They look like long black shriveled slugs with seeds inside. How can something so ugly smell so beautiful?

Quite different smells awaited them at the *Pescheria*. Corradino sniffed the saltiness in the grey dawnlight as they left their covered gondola at the Rialto. The white bridge loomed out of the morning mists – a ghostly sentinel that bid them halt and go no further. Corradino followed held his mother's hand tight as they wove through the mass of maids and merchants to the vaulted arches of the market. His father disappeared at once behind a pillar and, by craning round the edifice, Corradino saw that he was speaking to a hooded figure. As the figure turned its head as if hunted, Corradino could see it was Monsieur Loisy, his French tutor.

Monsieur Loisy? What does he here?

The conference went on for some time, and Corradino distracted himself by looking at the mass of fish spread on the wooden trestles before him. There seemed an infinite variety, smooth silvered shoals and spiky, dangerous-looking crustaceans. Some tiny as a glass sliver, some so huge and weighty it seemed a miracle they could ever swim the seas. Usually Corradino loved to look at the alien fish on these outings, ducking under the trestles and losing himself in the fabulous strangeness of the market. Raffealla always lost her patience and the maid allowed herself to use some of the words that were familiar enough to the fish-vendors, but with which the mistress didn't wish Corradino to become acquainted. Today though, the eyes of the fishes seemed to hold a threat, and Corradino went back to be close to his mother. He knew of the Venetian saying 'healthy as a fish', but these fish weren't healthy. They were dead.

His father and Monsieur Loisy were now joined by a third man. He was not masked and cloaked, and by his dress and scaly hands Corradino knew him for a fisherman. The three men began to nod and a leather purse changed hands. Corrado beckoned and led the family to the dark recesses of the covered market. There lay a large fishcrate, and, incredulously, Corradino watched his mother lie in the bloodied straw.

'Go on Corradino,' urged his father. 'I told you we were going on an adventure.'

Corradino lay down in his mother's arms, and soon felt the heavy press of his uncles and father by his side. He thought of the fishes that he had seen packed into their boxes, their silver shapes straightened and compressed.

We are fishes too.

Corradino saw his tutor's face through the wooden slats as the lid closed. '*Au revoir petit.*'

Corradino was cheered by the form of words. He loved his tutor and his French was excellent for his years. Surely if Monsieur Loisy meant never to see him again, he would have used the more final form '*adieu*', rather than, 'I'll see you again?'

Corradino settled into his mother's arms and smelt the essence of vanilla again. He felt a lifting and a rocking as if on water. Then he slept.

He woke with a sharp pain in his side and shifted with discomfort. Soon a heavy jolt told of their landing and the lid of the crate was prised loose. Disheveled and stinking, Corradino clambered out, blinking in the early morning light. He looked about him at the small ranks of red houses by a canal, and behind him, the spires of San Marco from what seemed a great distance. He had never seen Venice from such an aspect before. The water on the lagoon was dappled silver like the skin of a fish, the smell of which remained in his nostrils. He watched as his uncles Azolo and Ugolino paid the boatman. Uncle Ugolino looked ill. Perhaps the odour of fish, thought Corradino. But now there was a new smell – a sharp, astringent, *burning* smell. 'Where are we?' he asked his mother.

'Murano,' she said. 'Where they make the glass.'

Then he remembered. Corradino reached into his jerkin to find the place where he had felt the pain. He drew out his glass horse – it was in pieces.

* * *

I am sick of this house.

It seemed to Corradino that he had been inside for years, though he knew it had only been two days. The house was a tiny, whitewashed shack, with only two floors and four chambers, not what a little princeling was used to. Corradino was wiser than he had been two days ago. He had learned much. Some he had been told, some he had worked out.

I know that this house belongs to the fisherman father met in the Pescheria *and he was paid to bring us here in the crate and keep us hidden and my father is in trouble with the Doge and uncle Ugolino found out in time and warned him we must escape. Also Monsieur Loisy has helped us – he made the contact at the Fishmarket and suggested that we come to Murano because glass deliveries go from here to France and Monsieur Loisy has friends in France that could help us and we must hide on Murano for a time until we can be smuggled out. To France.*

Corradino knew little of France, despite Monsieur Loisy's enthusiasm for his homeland. He had even less desire to go there.

My father and uncles have told me that I must not leave the house where we hide, even for a moment.

But as the days went by they all began to feel a little safer, and Corradino felt his legendary curiosity begin to surface.

I want to explore.

So, on the third day, Corradino waited till his mother was at her toilet and unbolted the rickety wooden door. He found himself in an alleyway and made his way down to the canal, which he could see at the end. He wandered by the waterway, meaning only to look at the boats and throw stones at the gulls. But soon he began to smell the aroma that he had detected when he arrived, and followed his nose until he came upon a large, red building on the waterfront, facing into the lagoon.

There were sluicegates leading into the building, smoking with steam. Doorways opened into the fresh air and in one such, a man stood. The man was about the age of his father. He wore a pair of breeches and no shirt and had a thick bracelet of hide on each arm. In one hand he held a long pole on the end of which there seemed to be a burning coal. He winked at Corradino. '*Buon giorno.*'

Corradino was not sure that he should be speaking to the man – he was clearly a tradesman. But he liked the man's twinkly eyes.

Corradino bowed as he had been taught, '*Piacere.*'

The man laughed. 'Ah, *un Signorino.*'

Corradino knew he was being mocked, and felt that he should walk away, head high. But his curiosity won – he badly wanted to know what the man was doing. He pointed to the coal. 'What's that?'

'It's glass, Your Majesty.'

Corradino heard the tease, but the voice was kind.

'But glass is hard.'

'When it is grown up, yes. When it has just been born, it looks like this.'

The man dunked his coal in the water of the canal, where it hissed viciously. When he pulled it out it was white and clear. Corradino looked on with great interest. Then, remembering, 'I used to have a glass horse.'

The man looked up. 'But you don't any more?'

Corradino felt suddenly as if he were going to cry. The glass horse, and its loss, felt all of a piece with the loss of his house, of Venice, of his old life. 'It broke,' he said, and his voice did too.

The man's eyes softened. 'Come with me.' He held out his hand. Corradino hesitated. The glass-maker bowed formally, and said, 'My name is Giacomo del Piero.'

Corradino felt reassured by the formality. 'Corrado Manin. They call me Corradino.'

Corradino put his small soft hand in the man's big rough one and was led inside the building. He was astonished by what he saw.

There were fires everywhere, banked in iron holes with doors. At each doorway at least one man worked, shirtless, with rods and coals like his new friend. They put the rods to their mouths as if drinking, but seemed to blow.

I remember a painting I saw when me and my father were guests of the Doge in his palace. It showed the four winds of the earth with their cheeks puffed out as they blew a fleet of Venetian ships into safe harbour at the Arsenale. These men look like that.

As they blew the glowing coals of glass grew, and changed, into shapes Corradino recognized – vases, *candelabri*, dishes. Some worked with shears, some with wooden paddles. Everywhere there was steam as the shapes were cooled in water. Everywhere small boys ran, fetching and carrying, boys not much older than he. They were shirtless too. Corradino began to feel hot.

Giacomo noted this.'You should take off your coat. It looks expensive. Your Mamma will be angry if you burn it.'

Corradino's coat was the worse for his journey. It was dirty, it had lost more than one of its opal buttons and it smelt of fish. But it would be a stupid man who did not see at once that it was highly valuable. And Giacomo del Piero was not a stupid man.

Corradino took off the coat, and his silk undershirt and cravat too. Feeling much better as he slung them behind a pile of buckets, he turned to face the glare of the fire and felt for the first time in his life the bone-bending heat of a glass *forno*. Giacomo pulled a blob of orange glass from the fire with his rod. He rolled it on a wooden paddle and Corradino could already see its colour change to a dark red. Giacomo waited for a moment. Then took up a small pair of iron shears and pinched and worked at the glowing material. Before Corradino's eyes his horse was born again – with arched neck like the horses of Araby, delicate hooves and flouncing mane. Amazed, he watched as Giacomo set the little creature down, and it gradually cooled to a clear, crystal white. 'Pick it up. It's yours.'

Corradino picked up the horse. 'Thank you. I love it.'

He looked regretfully to the doorway, at the midday sunlight. 'I should go.'

'As you wish,' said Giacomo. 'Perhaps you will visit again.'

I may not get a chance. I am going to France, any day now.

'Perhaps I could stay a bit longer? Just to watch you work?'

Giacomo smiled. 'You can. But only if you keep out of the way.'

Corradino promised.

For the rest of the day Corradino watched as Giacomo worked what seemed to be miracles in glass. To take an unformed lump of matter and change it, like a conjuror or alchemist, into such works of art seemed to Corradino almost magical. He watched carefully each heating and reheating, each spin of the rod, each tender breath filling the belly of the red glass. He broke his promise many times as he crowded Giacomo, until the kindly man began to give him errands, and soon Corradino was as dirty as the other boys. Soon, too soon, the shadows began to lengthen in the doorway, and regretfully, Corradino supposed that he must go. But just as he was about to voice his thought a terrifying shape filled the doorframe.

It was a tall figure, black-cloaked and hooded, wearing a black mask. But the figure held none of the jollity of the *Carnevale* festivities. And when it spoke, its chilling tones seemed able to freeze the furnaces themselves.

'I seek a noble boy. Corrado Manin. Is he here?'

Giacomo alone stopped his work, as the nearest to the door. Glass-work was too precious, too easily ruined, to stop and stare. Even at this man, who was clearly someone of importance. And so it proved.

'I am an emissary of the *Consiglio Maggiore*. I have a writ to search for the boy.'

Giacomo subtly put his bulk between Corradino and the figure. He scratched his head and spoke, to belie his intelligence, in the wheedling tones of a peasant. 'Gracious *Signore*, the only boys we have are the *garzoni*. The *scimmia di vetro*. There are no nobles here.' From the corner of his eye Giacomo could see the opal buttons of Corradino's coat winking in the furnace light, as if to betray their young master to the dark phantom. Giacomo turned away from the coat, hoping to draw the dark eyes of the mask with him.

Sure enough, the chilling orbs held his gaze. 'If you see him, you have a duty to the State to inform the Council. Is that clear?'

'*Sì Signore*.'

'Just the boy, you understand. We have the rest of the family.'

They have my family?

Giacomo heard the boy gasp and step from his shadow. Instantly he turned and cuffed Corradino to the ground, a stinging blow that burst his lip and gave him reason for his tears. 'Franco, for the last time, go and draw some water! *Che stronzo!*' Giacomo turned back to the figure. 'These boys, I tell you. I wish The Ten *would* send us some nobles to work here. More brains, less thickheaded.'

The eyes in the masked face looked from Giacomo to the boy on the floor. Filthy, shirtless, bleeding, snivelling. A mere glass monkey. With a flounce of the black cloak, the agent was gone.

Giacomo picked up the tear-sodden boy and cradled him in his arms while he wept. Not just now, but for years later, as his apprentice, living in his house, when Corradino woke at night screaming.

In my dream my mother smells of vanilla and blood.

Giacomo never told the other *maestri* where his new *garzon* was from. And he never told Corradino what his neighbour told him of the fisherman's house where the Manin family had been found. It was left as a warning – empty, no bodies, but its white walls slick with blood from floor to ceiling, like the scene of a butchery.

Of course, they found Corradino eventually. But it took five years, and by that time Giacomo, now foreman of the *fornace*, was able to plead for his apprentice's life in front of the Council, in the *Sala del Maggior Consiglio* of the Doge's Palace. He stood, tiny in the cavernous rooms, beneath the riotous frescoes of red and gold, and argued Corradino's case before The Ten. For the boy, at the age of fifteen, was almost preternaturally talented.

He could already work with glass like no-one Giacomo had seen.

The Council was disposed to keep Corradino alive. The Manin family was no threat any more, it was practically wiped out, and Corradino would be kept, like all other *maestri*, a prisoner on Murano.

How were any of those gathered on that day, when Giacomo pled for Corradino's life, to know that they were wrong about the fortunes of the Manin family? How was poor dead Corrado Manin to know that his family would rise at last to greatness, and that one of his descendants *would* occupy the throne of the Doge? And how were any of them to know that Lodovico Manin would be the last Doge of Venice who would, in that very chamber, sign the death warrant of the Republic? That when he put his hand to the Treaty of Campo Formio in 1797 the city would be sold to Austria, and Manin's signature would sit below that of Venice's new ruler, Napoleon Bonaparte?

If the Council had known, they would not have spared Corradino Manin. But they did not know, and they did spare him.

Not through the quality of mercy, but because of the mirrors that he made.

CHAPTER 9

Paradiso Perduto

Leonora got to the Cantina Do Mori at a quarter to three on Saturday. As she looked at the frontage of the café with its distinctive bottle-glass doors she wondered if she had been the victim of an elaborate joke. Perhaps Officer Bardolino was laughing at her with his workmates. Leonora gave herself a little shake – this wasn't primary school. She had been so affected by her situation at work that the shoots of her paranoia were taking hold. The man seemed to be in earnest – no doubt he would like to find a tenant for his cousin. She would just go in and wait.

It was raining so the café was quite busy. But despite the crowds Leonora found a quiet table at the back under a huge double mirror. She admired the workmanship, and the slightly greeny-gold look of old glass in its gilded baroque frame. The bevel seemed perfect to her although she knew the work must be centuries old. She ordered an *espresso* and looked around at her leisure. The clientele today were clearly Venetian – the waiter had addressed her in Veneziano, and she had surprised herself with the force with which she replied in her fluent Italian, echoing his local accent with her own. Once again she felt pleased that Officer Bardolino had suggested this place. It was still a secret well kept from the tourist hordes. Then it occurred to her that he was, in a courteous way, attempting to give her a treat.

If he shows up.

But she need not have worried. On the dot of three, with the characteristic efficiency he had shown in her interview, he walked through the doors. She was taken aback by the fact that he was now in jeans and a smart jacket – more as she had first seen him in Santa Maria della Pietà. Leonora had somehow, ridiculously, pictured him turning up in uniform. But he still recalled the painting – what was it? – and turned the heads of a group of lunching ladies. With a sort of shock, as he brushed the raindrops from his black curls, Leonora faced the facts.

He's a very good-looking man. They all see it too.

She felt a whisper of fear.

He greeted her, sat, and summoned the waiter with practised ease. He shed his jacket, and settled back on the bench comfortably. He seemed to have a certain elegance coupled with an ability to be instantly comfortable, like a cat. Leonora smiled and waited for their discourse to begin. She felt suddenly confident. Would he enter straight into the business of the day or engage in pleasantries first?

'Why are you drinking coffee?'

Leonora laughed. His question seemed so incongruous that it caught her by surprise.

'You are laughing at me,' he said, caught between amusement and annoyance.

'A little. Why shouldn't I drink coffee? Have I made some sort of social *faux pas*?'

'No, no. I just wondered if you were . . .' he searched for the word, 'teetotal. Such a strange English word. I always thought it meant one totally drank tea.'

Leonora smiled. 'No, no, I drink. A lot. Well, not a *lot*. But I do like my wine.'

'Good.' He grinned. '*Due ombre, per favore*.' This to the waiter who hovered at his shoulder.

'What's an *ombra*?'

Officer Bardolino grinned again. 'A shadow.'

'I know what it *means.* But what is it when it's a drink?'

'Don't worry. It's just a little cup of house wine. The name is centuries old. There used to be wine carts in San Marco in medieval days, and the wine merchants would slowly move the carts all day to stay in the shadow of the Campanile. To keep the wine cool.'

The waiter set down the cups on the dark wood board. Leonora tasted the wine and felt that its flavours were enhanced by the story. 'I love tales like that. But I've not been able to read a guidebook since I got here. It's almost like I'm too busy seeing, and living, to read.'

Her companion nodded. 'You are right. Better to find these things out as you go, from those that live here. Guidebooks are full of soundbites.'

She smiled to hear his opinions chiming with her own. 'Tell me more about this place.'

He returned the smile. 'In a soundbite? Casanova used to drink here.'

'Is that why you brought me here?'

I shouldn't have said that. How presumptuous and . . . clumsy. I'm behaving like a schoolgirl.

'You thought that was a line,' he said, with a perception which surprised her. 'I actually brought you here because of the glass.' He indicated the mirror. 'It is unique. This double-looking glass is famous because it was the largest mirror made of its time in which the panes are perfect twins. I thought it might interest you, as you work on Murano.'

I've misjudged him. Have I ruined the day by being flippant? Should I tell him about Corradino?

'Officer . . .'

'Please, for God's sake, call me Alessandro.' The humour was back, thankfully.

'I love it here, thank you.'

He smiled again, then resumed his businesslike mask. 'Did your *fornace* fill in the counterfoil of your form for you?'

'Yes.' Adelino had obliged again.

'Then bring it by next week and we should be able to wrap up this work permit. Then if you get a flat too, you can get your *permesso di soggiorno*.' He waved away her thanks.

After a pause, Leonora spoke. 'Can I ask you a question?'

He nodded.

'It seemed to take you less time than the others. How come?'

Alessandro stretched. 'I detest paperwork, so my only solution is to cut through it as quickly as possible. My colleagues – they hate paperwork too, but their solution is to bury it with more paper, to hope that it goes away. See,' he dug out some papers from his pocket; 'more efficiency.' He spread the papers on the table for her. She could see they had photocopied pictures of houses and details below, much like the information from an estate agent. 'My cousin, Marta, has given me the keys to these four. We'll go and see, and if you like any, you can move in tonight.'

'Tonight?'

'You are surprised?'

Leonora shook her head, bemused.

'It's just that I've been trying to see apartments for a month and there have always been delays, or problems, or paperwork . . .' This extraordinary man seemed to cut through all of Venice's sedentary rhythms.

'Ah, that's what comes of knowing a local.' Alessandro smiled. 'Here's the one I think you should see first. It's quite close to here.' He pointed to one of the four, two rooms in a beautiful three storey house. She followed Alessandro's finger. The address was printed clearly – Campo Manin.

It was a top floor flat in a large, shabby, once-grand house. Though modern in all other respects, she was intrigued on entry by the original staircase that formed the axis for all the apartments, now with ugly modern fire doors. It was grand and beautifully worked. Leonora put out a hand and touched the flaking, turquoise paint. When it and the gilt was new, did family portraits stare down from these walls, to watch the servants and masters mount and descend? As if catching an echo she said, 'Corradino?'

Alessandro was struggling with the latch of apartment 3C. 'What?'

'Nothing.' It was too early to confess that her best friend in all of Venice was a ghost. 'I just wondered if any other Manins had lived here.'

Alessandro shrugged, his mind on the door. 'It's possible.

Very possible. Ah . . .' This as the door gave way and Leonora followed him into the flat. It was plain, sparsely furnished, but with two enormous windows which looked out onto the campo, and best of all, a rickety spiral stair of wrought iron which led onto a flat terrace, and the crazy rooftops of Venice all around. Leonora leant on the crumbling balustrade and gazed at the Campanile in the distance. She could hear bells.

I want to live here. I knew as soon as I walked in the door.

Alessandro's no-nonsense approach to practicalities continued to astonish Leonora for the rest of the day. She presumed her choice would result in a further couple of weeks of negotiations, followed by a protracted moving-in period. But Alessandro was on his mobile phone to his cousin at once, speaking in rapid tones. They had barely completed the tour of the rudimentary bathroom ('don't expect hot water all the time; not in Venice,') when the cousin – Marta – appeared. She was a businesslike, friendly woman with glasses, short hair and none of the physical beauties of her cousin. She sat with Leonora at the well scrubbed table, on one of the odd chairs. By the time Leonora had signed the twelvemonth lease, Alessandro had contacted the storage company on Mestre and arranged for an unheard-of Sunday delivery of Leonora's belongings for the next day. Both cousins offered to be present to help with the furniture, Leonora was given the key, and she and Alessandro went to her hotel to pack and check out.

He seemed in no hurry to be elsewhere, nor did he seem overly friendly in the odious way she had detected in her colleagues – the friendship of men who want more. They talked constantly as they walked and worked, mostly of that holy Italian trinity – art, food and football. Once her luggage was installed in her new flat, together with some essential supplies for morning, she began to feel, incredibly, that he was enjoying her company. Her pleasure and confusion grew, as with the arrival of dusk he said, with the brusque, no-nonsense manner she now recognized as characteristic: 'Shall we get a drink? We should celebrate. I know a good place.'

Leonora raised a brow. 'As good as the Do Mori?'

He laughed. 'You can't get better than this place I'm thinking of. It is, quite literally, Paradise.'

She looked carefully at him. His eyes did not look calculating, or lustful. They looked frankly back at her. He looked thirsty.

I know I shouldn't go. I know that I'm going to.

Paradise on a Saturday night was a noisy place. Leonora, crushed against Alessandro at the bar, had to scream her order for a Peroni directly into his ear. He emerged from the crush with four bottles ('to save time') and led her to the end of one of the long refectory-like tables crowded with flamboyant young bohemians. Alessandro secured them two seats opposite each other in a dark alcove illuminated by the inevitable candle stuffed in a wine bottle. Gouts of multicoloured wax masked the bottle completely and told the story of the candles that had gone before. As was her habit, Leonora began to pick at the solid mass. By her side, sitting close, a youth with multiple piercings rattled rapid Veneto to his equally punctured girlfriend opposite. Alessandro took a long drink and Leonora looked at him. The noise had abated a little, but she still had to bellow. 'What *is* this place?'

He smiled. 'I wasn't wholly truthful with you. This isn't Paradise, it's *Paradiso Perduto* – Paradise Lost. It's just about the only late bar in Venice – always full of students. It's a bit of a crush, but at least you can get a drink past midnight.'

Leonora smiled wryly into her beer. Paradise Lost.

Have I lost my Paradise? Was Stephen, and Belmont and St Martin's my Paradise? Or have I come to find a new one here?

As if reading her mind Alessandro asked, quite suddenly: 'Why did your husband leave you?'

Leonora nearly choked on her Peroni. She was daily surprised by the forthrightness of the Venetians. She expected them to be as winding and circumspect as the secret alleyways of their city, or as circuitous as their bureaucracy. But they were neither. Only this morning the lady serving her in the café where she took breakfast had asked her whether she had a special *amore* back home. The receptionist at her hotel, that avuncular, kindly gentleman, had already identified her marital status and her lack of children. And now, here was this unfathomable man asking her the most personal of questions. It seemed that Venetians had an ability to cleave to the point as cleanly as the prow of a boat slicing the waters of the canal. She played for time, holding the glass heart at her throat to steady herself.

'How do you know he left me?'

Alessandro sat back in his chair. 'You have a tan line where your wedding band once was. And your finger has changed shape somewhat, receding towards the knuckle, which means you were wearing the ring for some years, not just a short engagement. And you are sad. And you are *here* – I think if *you* had left *him* you would have stayed at home?'

Leonora looked up from her hand and saw a sympathy in the intelligent dark eyes which twisted her gut. Stung to a crushing retort, her own reply surprised her.

'He chose a golden casket.'

'How come?'

'*Merchant of Venice*? Portia's suitors had to choose between three caskets of silver lead and gold. Happiness lay in the lead casket, not the gold.'

Alessandro smiled, 'I know. I *live* here. D'you think you

can grow up in this city without knowing the story? What I meant was, in what sense did he choose gold?'

'I think he fell for the packaging. Such as it was.'

'Don't do that.'

'What?'

'"Such as it was." You're very beautiful.' He stated it baldly, not as a compliment but as a matter of empirical fact.

She twisted a golden rope of hair around her hand. 'Once, perhaps. But misery and loss seem to drain it all. I feel black and white now, not colour.' She dropped the skein of hair. 'I was an artist then, a creative, a bundle of emotions, rather than the . . .' she searched for a phrase, 'synaptic circuit of chemical reactions which made Stephen. I think he fell for the opposites in us. But once he opened the casket he realized that what he really wanted was something practical and scientific, exactly like himself.'

'And did he find it?'

'Yes. It's called Carol.'

'Ah.'

Leonora took another slug of beer, and it began to warm her. At that moment she knew that she wouldn't mention her infertility to Alessandro. Some small primal voice prevented her – she didn't want this man to know that she was not complete.

At length he spoke, but not of her. From now on it was clearly *quid pro quo*. 'But you know, it's possible to be *too* alike. I had a girlfriend till last year who was pretty much my twin. We grew up together, we liked all the same things, we were both ambitious, we even supported the same football team. But then she was offered a promotion based in Rome. She took it. Left. *Finito*. Her ambition separated us in the end.' He drank.

Leonora was stumped. She didn't see this man as vulnerable – but he too had been left. She said gently, 'Was she in the police too?'

'No. A journalist.' He seemed reluctant to say more, and Leonora let their personal silence fall amid the universal chatter. At length, though, he continued.

'Until then we were happy. There didn't seem to be any problems. No . . . bones of contention.'

Leonora was struck at once by both the story and his articulation, and saw a way to divert the course of their conversation.

'Where did you learn such good English?'

'London. I went there for two years after my military service, while I was deciding what to do with my life. I worked in a restaurant – with Niccolò, another cousin. I spent my time between a Soho kitchen and the London Hippodrome, picking up terrible women.' He grinned. 'I learned the swearwords first.'

'Where?'

'Both places. Then I came back to the Police Academy in Milan, and then home to Venice when I qualified.'

Alessandro expertly tapped out a cigarette, and offered

her one with that international symbol of the raised eyebrows and questioning grunt. When she waved it away, he lit his own and took a long draw. She thought of what he had said. Home. Venice.

My home too now.

'So you made your decisions, then, in London?' she asked.

'Not really. There was never really a choice. My parents were indulging me with those two years, giving me a false sense of autonomy. But I was always going to be a policeman. They knew it and I did too.'

'Why?'

Alessandro shrugged expressively. 'Bardolino tradition. Father, uncles, grandfather . . . .'

'But you're happy?'

'I will be, if I pass for Detective. That's what I'm training for now.'

'Well. The Mystery of the Missing Wedding Ring was all pretty convincing.'

He laughed, not displeased. 'Sherlock Holmes, eh? We'll see. It depends if I pass the exams. But being a beat cop in Venice is not much fun, unless you can take your nourishment from the views alone. It's all stolen cameras and lost luggage – tourist teething troubles. And we have a terrible reputation for stupidity – have you heard the one about why Venetian policemen always go around in twos?'

Leonora shook her head.

'One can read and one can write.'

She smiled.

'You think that's bad. The fire service have it even worse – they say the fire station in Venice has an answerphone for their emergency number, and a recorded message tells you that they'll attend to your fire in the morning.'

Leonora laughed. 'Is that how you lost the Fenice?' Venice's jewel of a theatre had burned to the ground ten years before.

'No, that was the city's fault. The canal to the Fenice was so silted up that the *pompieri* boats could not get through in time to stop the blaze. Civic irresponsibility, I'm afraid. This place is falling apart.'

'And sinking?'

Alessandro shook his head. 'None of the locals really believe that the city is sinking. But one thing they do believe is that lots of people are making money out of perpetuating the fear that it is. There are plenty of so-called funds collecting to save the city, but most of the money just lines the pockets of the officials. No, the tourists are more of a problem than the water.'

Leonora was at once surprised at this statement and gratified that Alessandro did not seem to include her in his definition. 'The tourists?' she queried. 'Aren't they the lifeblood of the city?'

Alessandro shrugged expressively. 'Yes. But if blood pressure gets too high it can kill, you know. There are about a hundred tourists for each native Venetian now. That's why all the locals know each other. We stick together. And the city will survive. Venice has been here for centuries, and she'll be here for centuries more. There's a certain ... continuity.'

Leonora nodded, while her fingers plucked at the wax. 'I know what you mean.' Then, as if taking a step towards intimacy, she admitted, 'When I first saw you, I thought you looked like a painting. I don't know which one though.'

'I do.' He smiled, but did not elaborate. 'It's common here. You see the same features walking around that have been here for hundreds of years. The same faces. The only face you never see is that of Venice. She always goes masked, and beneath the mask she's always been corrupt.'

'Plenty to do for a Detective then, with such widespread corruption.'

Alessandro gave a wry smile. 'Yes, actually. High Crime in Venice is as interesting as the petty crime is tedious. Art theft, property fraud, smuggling. Boys' own stuff.'

She could sense that he wasn't entirely joking. 'And when are the exams?'

'In two month's time. If I pass those, I'll be happy.' He finished his beer and regarded her over the empty bottle. 'And you? What will make you happy? Are you looking for a lead casket? A new Paradise?'

Leonora dropped her eyes. Again his thoughts had chimed with hers – plucked out the heart of her mystery. She looked at the candle between them and realized that she had picked off every vestige of wax from the bottle that held it. The glass stood as green and smooth as when it had first held wine, freed from its wax prison. As she watched, fresh clear wax spilled from the pool below the wick and assumed a milk-white solidity as it fell on the virgin glass. She answered at last. 'No. I'm not looking.'

I believed what I said . . . then. I went on believing it right up until the moment that he leaned over and kissed me. Hard stubble, soft mouth, and a fire I had forgotten about.

They walked in silence through the empty streets. San Marco was deserted, a yawning space like a roofless cathedral. Only the crystal stars formed the crossribs and bosses overhead. The night was chill but Leonora burned. The pigeons now roosted but her thoughts flew.

With an impulse she could not explain she turned perfect cartwheels across the square, stars wheeling over her feet, hair sweeping the stones. She could hear Alessandro laughing as she span. She did not know the meaning of the kiss, but she knew what she was feeling.

It feels too much like joy, senseless joy.

CHAPTER 10

Rendezvous

Corradino stared into his double mirror with satisfaction. It hung, in pride of place, on the back wall of the Cantina Do Mori. He knew he had done good work – the surface was smooth as the lagoon on a spring day and the bevel was perfect – even his eye could see no flaw. He averted his gaze before it could meet itself and sat at the couch beneath his mirror to wait. Corradino had never met his own eyes in a mirror. He barely knew his own image. He always looked at the glass – his vision stopped at the surface and looked no deeper to peruse his own visage. Perhaps he feared what he may find there, or perhaps he had no interest in his own features, but only those of the glass. He never asked himself these questions.

He only knew that Signor Baccia, the *proprietario* of the Do Mori, would be pleased with this mirror. He wondered though, why he had been summoned again – the walls of the Cantina were now completely clothed in paintings or mirrors. Such opulence reflected the prosperity of the place, a thriving watering hole for two centuries now. Baccia no doubt had more money to spend, and was about to overdo it. Corradino winced – more mirror work would throw off the beautiful lucent balance of his unique double mirror, shining in its twin loveliness – like Castor and Pollux – a constellation of perfection. Part of Corradino's disgust was reserved for this new brew, coffee, that he was sampling as he waited. He had never really formed a taste for it.

It rots my guts. Give me a good goblet of Valpolicella any day.

At length Signor Baccia emerged from the back of the busy café. Rotund and richly dressed in the latest French-style chemise, he stopped to talk to a group of gaudy Venetian matrons who were participating – a little self consciously – in this latest of fashions.

Baccia looks a little strange today.

Normally the *proprietario* was affable, avuncular, jolly. Today he was all of those things, but seemed nervous, as if today his demeanor was little more than an act. A heavy man, he nonetheless sweated too copiously for the cool of the day, and cast darting glances from side to side, as if followed. Corradino wondered if he had got himself into some kind of trouble with The Ten, and was under the eyes of an agent. Corradino had no such doubts about himself. He had the relaxed air of someone who *knew* he was constantly being followed.

He had seen eyes staring at him from masked darkness for years now. The man leaning at the *traghetto* stop. The bonbon trader in the street who looked a little too hard at him. The courtesan on the Ponte delle Tette with a warm smile but eyes of flint. A thousand different guises in a thousand different places. Always discreet, but over the years Corradino had learned to identify them in a moment. Each time his eyes fleetingly met those of these spies, whether tall or short, male or female, he had a sick fancy that each pair belonged to the same agent – the dark phantom that had followed him to the *fornace* all those years ago.

The man that murdered my family.

But surely Baccia had nothing to fear? He was a man of the State through and through. Corradino knew that the Council subsidized the rents of this plot, and that much of the Republic's business was conducted at the Do Mori under the mask of sociability. And yet Baccia did look – yes, definitely, he looked ill at ease. The *proprietario* made his way at last to Corradino and, at the greeting kisses, Corradino could feel the film of perspiration on Baccia's cheeks.

'Antonio?' said Corradino interrogatively as Baccia sat heavily on the brocade couch opposite. 'What's the purpose of this meeting? Not more mirrors to tip your *caffè* into the realms of a brothel?'

Baccia looked positively ill as he leaned in to Corradino, his breath heavy and laced with wine. 'Corradino. Listen well. Lean back in your seat for me.'

'What? . . .' Corradino was perplexed, but at a fervent nod from his friend he did as he was bid. He pushed his shoulders back, further, further, until at last they met other shoulders – of the patron sitting back to back with him on the other side of the settle. At once Corradino made as if to address the man, to excuse himself, but a voice stopped him which was not Baccia's.

'No. Don't turn around. Eyes are upon us.'

The Italian was perfect, but had the Frankish accent that took Corradino back twenty years to his French tutor. His childhood flooded into his head like a blush as the blood thrummed in his ears.

'Monsieur Loisy?' It was all he could do not to turn and throw himself into the man's arms.

'No. My name is Duparcmieur. Gaston Duparcmieur. We have never met. But in time you shall know me better.' The voice had an authority, but was warmed with a touch of amusement.

Corradino felt irritated at his mistake – as if he had given himself away. He clothed his discomfort in anger but something, still, kept him from turning round. With his eyes on the discomfited Baccia he said sharply, 'What's this about? I will not place myself in danger.'

He felt the shoulders shift, and again, the amusement and authority married in the voice of the Frenchman. 'Corradino, you have always been in danger. Since the day that your uncle Ugolino betrayed you to The Ten and you and your family flew for your lives. Did you know too that it was your uncle who betrayed your family's whereabouts to the agents of the Republic? He sold the death of your mother for his own safety, but in this he was deceived – they took him too and left only you, my little glassblower.'

Corradino leapt from his seat, and was immediately encircled firmly in the bearlike arms of Baccia. The *proprietario* clasped him and kissed him again on both cheeks. Loudly he bellowed; 'That's settled then. Two more mirrors for the salon. And they shall be works of art, just as you have made before.' He drew Corradino close and Corradino felt warm breath on his ear as Baccia hissed; 'Corradino, you must listen to this man, do not rise or turn, do not give in to your passions. This man can help you, but we are watched. Be still. Sit and talk to him, as if you talk to me.'

Corradino sat slowly and tried to collect himself. What did this mean? Could it be true of his uncle Ugolino, who had loved him so well? That he was a traitor? A thousand questions crowded his brain. The only one he could articulate was; 'Who are you?'

'If you would know me, you may gaze into your own mirror. But be swift, and secret.'

Corradino slid his eyes left and met those of the man

who sat behind him. He was dressed in wine velvet, in the style of a doctor of Padua, and a long nosed, white, *medico* mask lay in his lap. But the pointed beard and curled moustaches were those of a French dandy. His eyes, as they steadily held Corradino's, were of the grey slate that he powdered and added to his marver for the semblance of pewter. The Frenchman looked young, not much beyond his middle years. Perhaps thirty like Corradino himself.

'You see, you and I are of an age,' said the Frenchman, as if reading thought. 'But our differences are more marked. I love my country, as you have ceased to love yours. And you can work the glass like an Alchemist trained by Angels. And that is why I am here.'

'How do you know of my family?'

'You mentioned a man of my country that you loved well. He is known to me also.'

'Monsieur Loisy? He lives?'

'He does not.' The voice was brief. 'He was betrayed and the assassins found him. But not before he could tell us of his extraordinary pupil. You see, he never lost his concern for you and your well-being. He made enquiries and found that you lived, and were working on Murano. He followed your progress, as did we. But those who seek can also be found. His tracing of you led to the tracing of him. He was found, and poisoned by The Ten as he visited these shores hoping for sight of you.'

Corradino's head throbbed with his pulses and he could barely draw breath. Sadness for Loisy, and love for his loyalty, could not be given space here as the questions succeeded one upon the other. 'How do you know this?'

'Because I was one of those that aided him.'

'And stood by as he was murdered?'

'Loisy was warned not to return here. He did not heed my advice. You should not emulate him.'

Corradino held the eyes of the silent Baccia as his stomach lurched. The treacherous coffee beans ground the humours in his stomach and left a residue in his mouth – he tasted them and this evil news together. His searching brain at last found the needful question. 'What do you want of me?'

'We want your skills. What else?'

'And who is We?'

'Myself, of course. But more importantly, His Majesty King Louis XIV of France.'

Corradino choked. He stared into Baccia's bloodshot orbs, traced the map of capillaries he saw there as if perusing the royal bloodlines of France.

'What can you mean?'

'All will be told to you in time. But know this. We can help you; give you the life you deserve, in Paris. You will be feted as an artist, celebrated as a genius, not treated as a menial slave as you are here. We can give you riches, and nobility. Think of it – your country of Venice has used you for her ends, to augment her beauty, but has given you nothing. She has enslaved you – you, of the noble line of Manin. Not only that, but she has taken your family from you,' the voice paused, 'nearly all your family.'

Corradino's head snapped left and again he met the pewter eyes. What followed was little more than a whisper from the Frenchman.

'You could bring her too.'

Leonora. He knows of Leonora.

'Don't decide now,' said the voice as Corradino turned away in sick turmoil. 'You must not tarry here or we will be discovered. Stay and talk with Signor Baccia. He will make all seem as usual – he will order somewhat of you, and you must take the measurements and write them in your vellum notebook as you always do. Then leave, go back to Murano, and do nothing. Presently your foreman will tell you of a commission at the Old Theatre, and that you are to come to Venice to meet with a Maestro Domenico about a candlebra. If you come to this meeting you will see me again – I will be Maestro Domenico, and I will tell you of the King's desires. If you decide you want no more of this, plead of sickness and send another in your place. We will not trouble you again.'

Corradino felt the shoulders shift as the Frenchman rose. As Duparcmieur adjusted his cloak and mask he said, in a final undertone, 'Think on this, Corradino. What do you owe your Republic of Venice? Why not begin again, in France, with your daughter?'

Then, with a flourish, he was gone.

Corradino sat, as if stunned, as the *proprietario* went mechanically through his instructions for a mirror that would never be made. Then he made his way through the crowds of San Marco as if sleepwalking, while his ever-present shadow followed him. In his stupor he almost wandered towards San Zaccaria, to the Pietà, to tell Leonora. But he checked himself. He must not risk it, not when the footsteps were following. He must not spoil it now.

Not now that there is a way for us to be together.

CHAPTER 11

The Merchant of Venice

As soon as Leonora entered Adelino's office, and took the proffered seat, she could tell that something was afoot. For one thing, there was a large white flip chart obscuring the beloved view across the lagoon. For another, two extra chairs held a pair of fairly unusual and wholly unfamiliar individuals. Adelino introduced them as 'Chiara Londesa and Semi, from the Attenzione! Agency in Milan.' On hearing the word 'agency', Leonora knew she had not imagined that exclamation mark. They were in advertising.

Warily, she eyed the strangers, as they eyed her back in the manner of a couple examining a cut of meat before purchase. Chiara Londesa sported a cropped t-shirt featuring a near-pornographic manga design. Her swarthy colouring and calculating sloe eyes were offset by a shock of brutally short peroxide hair. Her colleague Semi, who seemed to boast no surname, was even odder. From top to toe he was dressed as the perfect English gentleman – Norfolk jacket, severely knotted tie, and polished Lobb shoes. As he leant forward Leonora could see – surely not? – the glint of a fob watch and chain peeping from his pocket. She fought the urge to laugh.

In the prolonged silence Semi rose and circled Leonora's chair, stroking his chin in an affected gesture straight from a James Mason movie. With the air of one selling his daughter to white slavers Adelino said, 'see? Didn't I tell you?'

Semi, still circling, nodded. Expecting cut-glass Brideshead tones, Leonora found his perfect Italian an audible shock. '*Sì. Perfetto.*'

Perfect for what?

Semi and Chiara, now ignoring Leonora, began to converse passionately in urbane Milanese. Through the frantic hand-gestures and rattled speech Leonora picked out a number of ominous words. Press ads. Interviews. Local, then national. Flyers to hotels for their hospitality packs. Photoshoot. Storyboard. At this last Chiara crossed to the flip chart and revealed an image which seemed to depict a blonde Botticelli Angel blowing a trumpet at heaven's gates. Leonora rose and looked closer. She had been mistaken. The angel was wearing jeans and a tight fitting vest. The trumpet was no trumpet but a blowpipe. The bell of the trumpet was an exquisite vase. The angel was blowing glass. The image was beautiful and terrible, and now at last Leonora did laugh. She turned back to three totally serious faces.

'Let me be clear about this. You're proposing to run some sort of ... advertising campaign ... on the back of, well, *me*?'

'Not just you, Signorina Manin, but your exalted ancestor.' With a practised flourish, Chiara turned the page. 'May I introduce: The Manin range.'

Oh no.

Visuals and slogans shouted at Leonora. Photos, mock-ups for packaging.

More pages with copy lines writ large: 'The Glass that built the Republic.' 'See the real Venice through our Glass.' 'Manin Glass, made by true Venetians for 400 years.' 'Manin Glass, the original Venetian Glass.' Over and again there were images of the blonde Botticelli (presumably herself) and a dark child in a frock coat and ruff.

'Unfortunately, there is no adult portrait of Corrado Manin. He fled his family home aged ten, so there is just this which we took from a family group.' Chiara's shrug expressed regret for this personal tragedy – not for the little boy's loss, but that she herself was inconvenienced by the lack of an adult image. Leonora studied the closed, serious face of the little boy who had grown into greatness.

The designers had excised him from the painting, separated him from his family once again to stand alone. She had not known of this portrait, or even this part of his history, and felt ashamed.

How is it that these grotesques straight from the Commedia dell'Arte know more of Corradino than I do myself? Because they bothered to find out. I must know more about him.

Chiara's pitch continued apace. 'Our campaign depends on two major elements – Corrado Manin, the Mozart of glassmaking, gives this foundry's output the continuity of long history – the solid, antique image with an impeccable *Venetian* pedigree. And you *Signorina*, are his ancestor – and the only female glassblower on the islands. We can sell the *modernity* of the latest designs on your image – the contemporary, the avant-garde, but always with the weight of your family history at your back.'

I feel sick.

Leonora turned to Adelino and spoke urgently in *sotto voce* Veneziano. 'This is obscene!'

Adelino rose and took her to the window. '*Scusi*,' – this to the Milanese who had gone into a huddle over a layout pad, clearly planning their next assault on the Manin name.

Adelino weighed in with a pitch of his own. 'Leonora

mia, calm down. It has always been like this. The Rialto tradesmen of the Renaissance, and Corradino himself, would have done anything to rise above the competition. They had no artistic sensibilities. They were businessmen – just as I am.' Seeing her resistance he took her hand in a final appeal. 'Leonora, I am overstretched. I have offshore interests; have borrowed widely to prop up the business. The *fornace* is struggling.'

Leonora looked across at the spires of San Marco; the view that had delighted her just a few short weeks ago when she had been given this job. Now the beloved towers seemed a bed of nails, a nest of swords where she would be impaled as a public spectacle. The lagoon was still and serene today, but her mind felt buffeted by tidal winds.

My mind is tossing on the ocean.

'What will the *maestri* think? I am a newcomer, a novice.' Leonora thought of Roberto's chilling antagonism, and the dislike of her that he had spread like a virus through the *fornace*. 'I can't put myself forward in this way. It's unthinkable.'

'On the contrary,' countered Adelino. 'Your family have been here longer than any. Corrado Manin built this industry. And you yourself have a talent, a precocious talent. Don't worry about the *maestri*, they will be grateful. If you improve business, they will do well, and keep their jobs. Maybe even receive bonuses. Their families will thank you too.'

It was the irresistible argument. If she could do anything to help the *maestri*, she knew she would do it. If the prosperity of the *fornace* turned around, would not even Roberto, in time, be forced to acknowledge her uses and forget their unfortunate start? Moreover, Leonora knew the unsaid truth: if she did not do this for Adelino, what good was she? Why did he need an extra worker, a beginner at that?

I am to be the pound of flesh.

'Do I have a choice?'

In answer Adelino turned back to the Milanese. 'She agrees. Set it all up.'

Chiara and Semi looked up from their pad with expressions of faint amazement. They had never felt that Leonora's compliance would be in any doubt.

Adelino was alone at last. His head ached after a protracted discussion in which the advertising team had been forced to make several concessions to Leonora in the battle for good taste. He glanced at the screen of his ancient computer, where the portrait of a ten-year-old Corradino sat, still and silent under glass. He addressed the long dead boy.

'What can you do for me, Corradino?'

Catching himself, he turned to the window. The flipchart had gone back to Milan, so he could gaze out to sea unobstructed, like a merchant of old waiting for his argosies to richly come to harbour.

CHAPTER 12

The Dream of a King

Corradino clutched at the heavy velvet curtains, feeling the sweat from his printless fingertips soak into the nap of the fabric. For a moment he felt a fear that was so palpable it sent a chill through his stomach and bowels, and muddled his senses so that he could barely remember what he must say.

'Maestro Domenico?' At last the name that he had repeated in his head like a catechism for the last month returned to him.

He had gone back to work after meeting Duparcmieur and tried to live as normal. But normality had left him now, seemingly forever. He recalled the conversation constantly in his head, remembering every word, every look, every nuance. For days he lived in the dread and excitement of hearing the summons of Maestro Domenico. In his dreams this alias had assumed an identity of its own, a ghostly, terrifying shade who removed his mask to reveal the rotting countenance of his uncle Ugolino. Ever present, too was the mortal fear that The Ten would discover that he had attended a clandestine meeting and at last seek his life. Corradino even considered denouncing the Frenchman to the Council – he could take an agent to the next meeting and have Duparcmieur put to death, and prove himself a loyal member of the Republic. Three things stayed him from this course.

Firstly, he felt a natural resistance to taking the path of his uncle and denouncing another man through the Lion's mouth. He had long thought it odd that in Dante's *Divina Commedia* – the book he read now as his bible – the lisping, hapless traitor that suffered the torments of the Inferno was called Ugolino, like his beloved dead uncle. Now he knew how fitting it was that his uncle shared a name with this unfortunate Florentine.

For my uncle was the worst kind of traitor; one who betrayed his family.

Betrayal of the State was but a small sin next to this. Which brought Corradino to the second reason.

Duparcmieur's words rang in his head: 'What do you owe the Republic, Corradino? She has enslaved you.'

It was true. He loved his work – lived it even, but he knew that only his skills kept him alive. If for any reason he ceased to be able to do his work, he would be lost. And they had done worse, much worse . . . 'Taken your family from you . . . nearly all . . .' Aye, that 'nearly' was what stopped him betraying Duparcmieur. The third reason.

Leonora.

As the days turned to weeks of waiting – to the point where Corradino asked himself if he had dreamt all – he had the overriding desire to find out more of the Frenchman's plan. Was there a way he could begin a life overseas with Leonora? She whom he loved as he had loved no one else since his own mother?

Over the weeks his fears receded and were replaced. He now felt a hunger, an impatience to be contacted. Would the summons ever come? Had the Frenchman been denounced by another – perhaps Baccia – and even now lay tortured, dying, dead?

Yesternight, though, the summons had come at last. Giacomo, with the air of one who knew nothing beyond his words, had passed on a message that Corradino was to meet Maestro Domenico of the Old Theatre at noon of the next day. Corradino had given a disinterested nod while his stomach lurched. He excused himself, went outside, and vomited into the canal.

Here, now, at the Teatro Vecchio, the maze of stairs and corridors had brought him to this curtain. He knew not where it led, only that once he drew its folds aside, there could be no return.

Or I could leave now.

In tones hoarse as a crow, he spoke the name, and there was silence. With a mixture of disappointment and relief he wondered if there were no one there. But those accents he remembered so well spoke from beyond the arras.

'*Sì. Entrate.*'

With a shaking hand, Corradino drew the heavy drape aside and entered into he knew not what. Like the Dante of his book – of his father's book – he entered on a new path, with a new guide, midway through the journey of his life. He knew naught of where the road would lead, or the one who would lead him.

'So, you have come, Corradino.'

Corradino's ready reply died on his lips. He could not see the one who spoke, only the spectacle below.

He was standing in a box-like extrusion above a dark and cavernous space. But at the fore of the space was a shining arc of gold, a baroque riot of giltwork crowning a stage that was brilliant with the light of a thousand candles. On the stage were characters – such characters! Not the pantomime costumes of the *Commedia dell'Arte*, or the gaudy garb of the *Carnevale*, but players dressed in cloth of gold, jewels, and tissue of silver. One such princess stood with the company grouped around her in the attitude of an antique painting, and she sang with such passing beauty that Corradino all but forgot his fear and trouble. But this was not the holy beauty of the Pietà choir, but a secular, joyful song in a language he did not know.

'Monteverdi,' said Duparcmieur's voice. 'This is an aria from *L'incoronazione di Poppea*. Claudio was considered to be somewhat of a genius, but, as with most of that type, a deeply irritating man. You have not been to the opera before?'

Corradino shook his head, dazed.

'These and other delights await you when you enter Paris, an even greater city of culture. Close the drapes behind us, and we may have our conference while we enjoy the song. It is, of course, vital that we are not seen. This is why we meet as these players rehearse.'

Corradino did as he was bid, and as his eyes adjusted to the darkness of the box he could at last make out the figure of his conspirator.

'Do sit down, my dear fellow. There is a chair behind you.'

As Corradino sat, he peered at Duparcmieur through the gloom. Gone were the doctor's weeds, and in their place the flamboyant garb of a theatrical impresario. The hair and whiskers were unstyled today, and silvered to give an aged artistic look.

'Well. And to our business. I think our best approach is for me to put our proposal to you, and then you may question me. Agreed?'

Corradino nodded faintly in the dark, but the movement was caught by the Frenchman.

'Good. Then I will begin, for our time here is short. You have heard, I suppose, of His most illustrious Majesty, King Louis XIV of France.'

Another nod.

'Indeed. Who has not. In reflection of his glorious reign and great wisdom, the finest architects are even now building what will be the most magnificent royal palace in the known world, in the lands of Versailles near Paris. Greater than those of the ancient Roman or Egyptian peoples, than those of the Nabobs and Maharjees of the Indies, than the antique and noble Greeks. Greater even than those strange and wonderful mansions of the Chinois in the Orient that your own countryman, Marco Polo, lately found. And yet, in order to do this, and set such a place apart, His Majesty has himself had a notion which will have men wondering for centuries.'

Corradino found his voice. 'And what is his notion?'

'He wishes to construct a great chamber entirely out of mirrors.'

Corradino was silent. The song from below drifted through his brain as he imagined such an audacious thing.

'How interesting.' The amusement that he remembered well returned to the Frenchman's voice.

'What interests you?' asked Corradino.

'That you did not say at once that it could not be done.

This convinces me even more that you are the man for the task.'

'Why must the King build such a thing? The expense will be very great, the work difficult and long.'

In the gloom Corradino could see the expansive wave of the Frenchman's hand.

'These things matter not to His Majesty. What matters is the show and pomp of royalty. Such a palace, with such a hall, will make other great men esteem him greatly. Politics hang upon magnificence, Corradino. We are esteemed by our person, and our possessions. Such a place could become a centre of policy for centuries to come. Great councils will be held there, and great deeds done.'

'I see. And you want me to help you.'

Now was Duparcmieur's turn to nod.

'We wish you to come to Paris. We will quarter you in comfort and luxury in the lands around the Palace, and you will superintend the mirror and glasswork. After a time, when all is safe and the work progresses well, we will send for your daughter.'

Corradino started 'She cannot travel with me?'

A shake of the perfumed head. 'Not at once. The danger is great for one, much greater for two. It is much safer that she stays here for now. You must tell her nothing of this, for her own sake, even when you take your leave.'

'But Monsieur, there is no possibility of my being able to leave the city alive. I am watched at every turn and under great suspicion for reasons of my family.'

Then Duparcmieur leaned close, so close that Corradino could smell the pomade of his hair, and feel the warmth of his breath. 'Corradino, you will *not* leave the city alive.'

CHAPTER 13

The Cardinal's Nephew

The house at least, is mine. I am the tenant. I will make it a home.

Discomfited by the developments at the *fornace*, dreading the photoshoots and interviews she knew would come, Leonora had two comforts: her work, as the glass began to answer to her hand and breath, and the little flat in the Campo Manin. When she returned home in the amber light of the evening – for there were to be no more invitations from her colleagues to keep her out after dark – she felt her heart lift as she got her first glimpse of the old building, sleeping in the evening sun, bricks the colour of a lion's pelt. Her eyes raised automatically to the two uppermost windows – *her* windows.

This was the first home that was truly hers. Here she was answerable to no-one, not her mother with her academic books and fine prints, not her student housemates with their hippy artschool chic, and not Stephen with his solid, unoriginal antiques and magnolia walls. She would create the home that *she* wanted – surround herself with the colours and textures and *things* that she wanted to see every day, to offset her own new self.

She began to spend her weekends wandering the markets of the city – alone but not lonely, picking up fabrics and objects that spoke to her of Venice. She rooted through the little dark and secret shops of the Accademia on her own private treasure hunt. She returned home triumphant with her booty like a latter-day Marco Polo. The darkwood bowl she had found in the Campo San Vio was placed on the kitchen table and filled with a pyramid of fragrant lemons from the San Barnaba fruit boats. The enormous stone toe, hewn from some statue (where? And when?) which was so hefty she had had to have it delivered, now propped open the kitchen door. She poured over paint charts and spent long hours covering the walls – her living-room-bedroom she painted the sea-turquoise she had seen in the stairway, a colour she hoped had bled through time from Corradino's age, which she garnished with gilt edging and gold sconces. She found an enormous old mahogany box bed, which had to be hoisted through the window with the help of her enthusiastic and voluble neighbours. She made it up with soft pillows and bedspreads of creamy Burano lace, tatted by the old women who sat in the doorways of their coloured houses, warmed by the sun as their fingers flew in their laps. The kitchen she painted a glowing blood red, and collected little tiles the colour of stained glass, to mosaic above the sink. She found a block of ancient wood at a house clearance – huge and dark, it had the vestiges of carving which suggested it had been hewn from a palace door. It served perfectly for a chopping board.

The roof terrace she swept and tiled with terracotta slabs from Florence. She wired the balustrade for safety and bought numerous pots to fill with plants to give day-colour and night-scent – dotted around the terrace like portly little men. Many were filled with herbs to pinch for cooking – the basil she took downstairs to the kitchen windowsill, as the herb she knew she would use the most.

Leonora and the pot of basil. I remember from school that ridiculous poem about Isabella – she hid her lover's head in her pot, under the herb. Perhaps Keats' mad bad and dangerous pal had more of a clue about love – Byron lived here, loved here. Mind you, he threw his mistresses into the grand canal when he tired of them. Have I been discarded too? Will I see him *again?*

Leonora's Cork Street glassware languished, carefully packed, stowed in the kitchen cupboard. It seemed to her now too sterile, clever and over-worked. Instead she chose some of the more amateur, earthy pieces she had blown on Murano

– squat, shallow hurricane lamps in primary colours – and ranged them along the balustrade. Tealights flickered inside, warming the glass as the dusk fell. She decided against any patio furniture – she had no expectation of guests – but bought luxurious, fat cushions in jewel coloured silk, on which she lounged on sunny evenings with a glass of *prosecco*. Sometimes she sat on until the night chilled and the stars came. They seemed larger here. In London, even on the Heath, the stars seemed distant; refracted through a dusky prism of smog and dust. Here the stars stooped close – she felt she could reach up her hand and pluck one of the burning orbs like a celestial fruit. The sky was the dusky blue of the Virgin's cloak.

Marta, her landlady, came round now and again, on little matters to do with the house, and had begun to stay for a glass of wine. She had become a tentative friend, and once brought round a fragrant Venetian stew of fish and beans in a warm stone pot. As the two women shared the feast and a bottle of wine, it was Marta who told Leonora the secret to Venetian cooking. 'Simplicity,' she said briefly. 'Here we have a saying: "*non più di cinque*". Never more than five. Venetians say that you should not use more ingredients than you have fingers of one hand.'

Leonora nodded but her thoughts were elsewhere. She steeled herself not to ask about Alessandro.

Alessandro.

She told herself, as the flat took shape, and as her work improved at the *fornace*, that she was happy. She was a glass-blower. She lived in this gem of a flat in this jewel of a city. But on the Saturday that she found the final piece to complete her home, she was brought face to face with the truth.

She had gone to a shop she knew, behind the Chiesa San Giorgio by the Accademia Bridge, to find something to hang in the empty space above her bed. It was there, hanging on the back wall, behind the armoires and busts and lampshades – an icon of Our Lady of the Sacred Heart. The Virgin held the burning heart in her hands, her face serene, the heart a visceral beating red against the cerulean cloak. Leonora bought it at once, took it home and hung it. Perfect. Then she understood.

My *heart burns too.*

It was one kiss, and he had never called her, never come round in four weeks. On subsequent, necessary trips to the Police Station she had, as before, seen a new officer each time. Yet she yearned for Alessandro, even to catch a glimpse of him. Leonora had never read Dante but recalled one of his lines (from – of all things – *Hannibal*) 'He ate that burning heart out of her hand.' Another Beatrice, namesake of Dante's great love, had spoken of eating a man's heart in the marketplace. Leonora felt the description to be apt – she felt, in a muddle of Dante and Shakespeare, that those poets had spoken of exactly how she felt – that she had eaten a burning heart which was now lodged in her chest. She felt none of the serenity of the Blessed Virgin. She wanted Alessandro, pure and simple. She thought her heart had cooled and set for ever after Stephen, hard and cold like the glass heart she wore.

But no, for even this heart that I wear, after four hundred years, would be melted again if I placed it in the fire.

And then, into her completed house, he came. That same Saturday, in the evening, an unfamiliar rasping brought her out of her reverie. She realized it was her own doorbell, and opened her door to Alessandro, smiling, brandishing her work permit, her residence permit and a bottle of Valpolicella. He made no reference to his absence, but came characteristically straight to the point.

'Shall we get some dinner? I know somewhere you'd like.'

Leonora felt shocked, and breathless. Vanity made her grateful that she was at least in the right clothes – she had put on a white crochet dress for the heat of the day. Determined not to be won over immediately she raised a brow. 'Another cousin?'

He laughed. 'Actually, yes.'

She looked carefully at him. He proffered her white permits like a flag of peace.

They walked abreast through the narrow *calli* to the trattoria, neither one ahead or behind. Their knuckles grazed one another's and before Leonora could register the pleasurable shock of the touch she felt her fingers clasped firmly in his warm hand. Since childhood, when her hand had been held, whether by her mother or later Stephen, Leonora had felt awkward – always waiting for the moment when she could comfortably let go without giving offence. Now, for the first time, she let this virtual stranger hold her hand in comfort, only breaking away as they arrived at the trattoria and began to weave through the crowded diners.

Alessandro was greeted by the *proprietario* like a long-lost and much missed brother. 'Niccolò, my cousin,' explained Alessandro from the corner of his mouth, as Leonora found herself on the receiving end of two effusive kisses – not the air-kisses of the English vicarage tea-party, but well-planted, warm salutes. Niccolò, a similar age but twice the girth of Alessandro, led them to the best table, with a peerless view of the twilit Campo San Barnaba, with the fat, full moon rising.

'The moon shines bright . . . On such a night as this . . .' No, I must not get ahead of myself. Take everything as it comes.

As they settled themselves at the red-chequered cloth Niccolò appeared unbidden with two menus, a pair of glasses and a bottle of wine. He plonked the bottle in front of Alessandro, gave him a wink and a clap on the shoulder, then melted away.

As Leonora studied the menu she felt suddenly shy and discomfited. Their conversations had always been so direct and easy before that the silence troubled her. Her eyes scanned the Italian type, looking for comfort. She seized on two familiar words in her panic. 'Minestrone and lasagne.'

Alessandro shook his head. 'No.'

'What!' she was briefly incensed.

'That stuff is for tourists. You *live* here. You should have this.' He rattled off two dishes in Veneziano so rapid that even her attuned ear didn't catch the words. 'Polenta with calves liver and risotto *d'oro*. Both delicious, both Venetian specialities. You'll love the risotto, it's made with tiny flecks of gold leaf. Truly a dish of the *gran signori*.' He dropped his voice 'You're not . . . vegetarian are you?' as if enquiring after a delicate medical condition.

She shook her head emphatically.

'Thank God. All the English are. Niccolò!' Alessandro's cousin appeared from nowhere and took their order before Leonora could protest. She sat back, befuddled, and began to munch on a breadstick to buy some time. She had been furious when, in the past, Stephen had overruled her choices with his superior culinary knowledge. Why wasn't she angry now?

Because, you little fool, you're being introduced to Venice by a

Venetian; you're being included, treated like a local, just as you wanted.

As if to reflect her thought, Alessandro spoke again. 'You know, there's a story that breadsticks come from Venetian ship's biscuits, the food that built our trading empire. The recipe was handed down by mouth over the generations until the end of the eighteenth century, when it was lost forever. But then in 1821 someone found a whole batch of them in a bricked-up Venetian outpost in Crete, and reconstructed the formula from there.'

Leonora smiled, relaxed, and took another. 'It's strange to think of my ancestors munching on these very same biscuits, tasting what I taste, feeling them crumble in the mouth like I do. The Manins had quite a shipping empire at one time. And my ... father ... he worked on the *vaporetti*. So I guess the sea is in the blood.'

'It's in everyone's blood here. Your father ... is he still alive?'

'No. He died when I was very little. My mother took me back to England. So though I was born here you are right to call me English – it's what I am really.'

Alessandro shook his head. 'No, you are a Venetian. Do you have any other family here?'

'I remember my mother saying my Italian grandparents are dead. And I think my father was an only child.' It was on the tip of Leonora's tongue to tell Alessandro about Corradino, but something stopped her. It was he, and not

Bruno, to whom she felt the connection of family, but didn't know how to adequately explain that she felt far more curiosity about the long-dead glassblower than she did about her own father, the man who broke her mother's heart.

'It would be interesting to find out more about him – now you're here. Give you some history. I could . . . help . . . if you let me? I've got contacts through the *Questura*.'

Leonora smiled. 'Perhaps.'

But it's Corradino who calls to me.

When the food arrived, it was indeed delicious. She ate heartily, but with nothing of the relish and concentration that Alessandro afforded to his meal, head down, spooning up his dishes. She watched him indulgently, and he caught her at it.

'What?'

'You eat with such . . . not appetite, not hunger, not lust, but a bit of all three.'

'*Gusto*?'

'Yes, exactly! It means all those things and more. I guess we don't have an equivalent word in English.'

'The English don't need one,' he said, including her again. And then he smiled.

And that was that.

Gusto. The word stayed in her head for the rest of the night.

Gusto, she thought, as he kissed her hungrily on the Ponte San Barnaba.

Gusto, she thought as they drank Valpolicella straight from the bottle on the balustrade of her roof garden, their feet dangling perilously over the canal far below.

Gusto, she thought as he took her by the wrist and led her, unprotesting, to her bed.

Gusto, she thought, as he took her loudly in the darkness.

In her dream they were in bed; Leonora's blonde hair tumbled on Alessandro's chest. But when she woke he was gone. Light from the canal played on the ceiling of her apartment, and illuminated the icon above her bed, with the heart burning still. Brighter today.

Leonora smelled coffee and padded through to the kitchen. The pot was on the stove, still warm, with plenty left. She poured herself a cup, concentrating hard on not feeling hurt.

He owes me nothing, has promised me nothing, why should he stay?

When she went to the fridge for milk she saw it. A postcard stuck under her fridge magnet. She recognized the style of Titian; a picture of a cardinal flanked by two young men. The man on the right, also in priests' robes, was the image of Alessandro. Leonora read the back; Tiziano Vecelli, portrait of Pope Clement X with his nephews, Niccolò and – surely not! – Alessandro. 1546. Beside the legend there was something else too. A hasty scrawl which read: '*Ciao bella.*'

Leonora sat heavily at the table, heart thumping. What did it mean? Was the postcard something he carried around with him, a device for susceptible foreign girls? What did '*Ciao bella*' mean? It had a terrible ring to it, the tacky sign-off of a lothario from a hundred movies. Even '*bella*' in this context held no weight. It was all of a piece with the offhand phrase – it did not denote beauty. She tortured herself over the semantics of the phrase. She knew that *Ciao* came from '*ci vediamo*'. The same meaning as the French '*Au revoir*' – I'll see you again. She did not know the Italian for '*Adieu*'.

Leonora shook her head. She did not want to plan, or flagellate herself with these thoughts. She did not know what Alessandro wanted from her, if anything. She watched the water on the ceiling, listened to the cries of children playing outside and two old men having a shouted conversation with each other across the *campo*. Sunday stretched ahead, yawning empty. She must busy herself; find something to do, something to think about, before it was too late.

It's already too late. I'm in love.

CHAPTER 14

A Rival

It was Monday. Leonora was on the roof, leaning on the balustrade, looking over to the lagoon and wishing she were on the boat to Murano. But today Adelino had insisted that she stay at home, to be interviewed by a journalist from *Il Gazzettino*, the foremost newspaper of the Veneto region. She had dressed carefully in a white linen dress she had found on the Rialto, and bound her abundant hair with lace ribbons. She knew that today there was to be no photographer, but she was under instruction from the Milanese advertisers to appear as feminine as possible at all times. They didn't want to sell their campaign on the back of a tomboy – the whole point of Leonora's appeal, apparently, was that she was a girl in a man's job. Oh well. If she could project an image of womanly vulnerability she might appeal to the journalist's better instincts.

If he has any.

What she really wanted to do was don her usual uniform of old jeans, vest and ancient army jacket, put up her hair and take the number 41 to work. She was sick of being primped and posed – the last few weeks had been a test of her endurance as she had been photographed at work, at home and even in period costume. She had to grudgingly admit that the resulting print adverts and posters did make her look ... well ... pretty, and they were certainly more tasteful than what had first been proposed. They had centred on placing Corradino in modern environments and Leonora in ancient ones. Leonora had balked at the idea of sharing a frame with her dead ancestor, but the results had been interesting, even intelligent. One featured a modern café with a couple enjoying wine from a pair of exquisitely modern goblets from the newly launched 'Manin' range.

The scene was determinedly contemporary, but a careful look in the 'Manin' mirror beside their table showed a reflection of the interior of the Do Mori, circa 1640, with patrons in period costume and a composite of the young Corradino standing at one of the tables. Leonora found it quite ghostly, but intriguing in the manner of The Marriage of Arnolfini: the image in the mirror was the point of the piece. Her role was to bring modernity to the Antique end of Adelino's business. In modern day dress she was placed in classic Venetian paintings which featured glasswork and mirrors. In the main image she was computer manipulated to match the colour and style of paint and brushwork. She was dressed in seventeenth century costume of golds and greens, her hair flowing in the golden ripples of the most desired courtesans, her ivory skin given the craquelure of ancient tempera. Once again, in the image in a mirror – antique Manin this time – she was reflected in her work clothes, holding the tools of her trade instead of a fan or flower. But however tasteful the ads, Leonora felt increasingly uncomfortable as the huge machine of the campaign swung into motion. She knew that Adelino had poured all the money he had into the enterprise, borrowing against collateral he no longer owned, plunging deeper into debt on this one desperate chance. She felt too, the growing contempt of her colleagues – her face burned as she posed in front of the furnace – not from the heat but from the glances of her colleagues who, watching, worked around her. At the centre of the antagonism Roberto was ever present, his resentment and growing hatred palpable on his face. It was clear that, at the same time that he thought Leonora unworthy of such attention, he thought himself very much worthy of it. She knew that he had approached the Milanese with his own family history; by chance she had heard Semi and Chiara laughing about him. Roberto did not enjoy being laughed at.

Leonora felt a chill as a breeze reached the balcony. Autumn was coming, and the tourists would soon be gone. She looked down into the *campo* and noticed that already the steady stream of tourist traffic had abated as, swallow-like, they prepared to move south to warmer climes. Firenze, Napoli, Amalfi, Roma.

Not me. This is my home.

She looked fondly down at the square, her square, which shared her name and Corradino's too. It occurred to her for the first time that this place she had chosen was the architectural embodiment of past and present, of herself and Corradino, of Adelino's cross-centuries campaign. Along one side, Luigi Nervi's vast modern bank, the Cassa di Risparmio di Venezia. On the other, the beauteous historical houses where she now lived. And in the middle (she had been delighted to learn) a statue of another Manin: Daniele, the revolutionary whose past she had glimpsed in the library that day. An unknown kinsman who came between herself and Corradino on the timeline of centuries. An upstanding lawyer who had resisted the occupation of the Austrians with as much conviction as Doge Lodovico Manin had sold the city to them. Rewarded for his loyalty he stood upon his plinth, the winged lion of Saint Mark crouching at his feet, one hand tucked Napoleon-style into his waistcoat with unconscious irony. But his sacrifice and struggle had been corroded to comedy by the passing years, as the dignified copper of his likeness had oxidized to bright jester's green.

As she watched, her attention was caught by a sharply

dressed woman crossing the square with purpose, her stiletto heels clicking on the stone.

No tourist she: clearly a local.

She wore a navy suit which screamed designer tailoring, with a nipped-in waist and a skirt with a length just the right side of trashiness. Her hair, razor cut to skim her shoulders, flashed blue-black in the sunlight. She wore the inevitable sunglasses, which only gave greater emphasis to her glossy red lips. Her sexy confidence allowed her to acknowledge but at the same time ignore the vocal admiration of a handful of masons working on the bridge. She was clearly accustomed to such tributes.

A woman like that would tell Semi and Chiara to go to hell.

She watched the woman with admiration until she disappeared from sight, and seconds later heard the now familiar rasp of her own doorbell. Leonora ran down her spiral steps, heart thumping. She would not admit that each time the doorbell rang she hoped for Alessandro.

But it was not Alessandro. It was the woman from the square. She held out her hand.

'Signorina Manin? I'm Vittoria Minotto.' Such was the force of her personality that Leonora reached out to shake her hand, and moved aside to give passage to the apartment. She clearly looked as confused as she felt, for in explanation the woman said, 'From *Il Gazzettino*.' She flashed a press card in the manner of a member of the FBI.

Leonora attempted to pull herself together and offered a chair, but the journalist was off, stalking around the house, peering at the furnishings, picking up objects and putting them down again. With a practised gesture she pushed her shades into her raven hair and peered at the view as if making mental notes. Her one word '*bello*' at once praised the décor and condemned it. 'This will do for *you*,' it seemed to say, 'but it is not in *my* taste.' At close proximity her confidence and sexuality were almost tangible. Her style and poise, her sharpness of dress, made Leonora feel blowsy and badly put together. Her dress and the twisted locks of her loose hair, with which she had been pleased as she looked in the mirror that morning, now seemed messy and amateur.

I'm behaving like a sixth-former with a crush. If she's having this effect on me, *what must she do to a man?*

With an effort that she was afraid was visible to her guest, Leonora pulled herself together, trying to regain her composure, and with it, the ascendancy. 'Can I offer you a drink? Coffee?'

Vittoria turned and favoured Leonora with a smile of immense charm and startling whiteness. 'Please.'

The journalist sat, this time unbidden, at the kitchen

table and snapped open her briefcase with the sound of a cocked gun. She took out an innocuous notebook and pen, and something else – small, silver and threatening, it squatted on the table. A tape recorder. Vittoria took out a third item, a pack of cigarettes, shook one out and lit it. Both the brand and the way she lit the thing reminded Leonora sharply of Alessandro, with a brief stab of pain. Vittoria made a waving gesture, and the smoke wreathed around her blood-red nails. 'You don't mind?'

Leonora was unsure whether the journalist was referring to the tape recorder or the cigarette. She minded both, but shook her head.

Click. Vittoria's thumbnail depressed the button and the tiny spools began to cycle. Leonora brought the coffee from the stove and sat opposite the journalist, feeling the air of contest. The recorder whirred like the timer of a chess match.

'Can you tell me a bit about yourself?'

'What do you want to know?'

'Perhaps a little background for our readers?'

'Starting in England? Or here? I'm sorry . . . I'm not used to this. Perhaps . . . could you . . . I think I'd find it easier if you asked me direct questions.'

A sip of coffee. 'Fine. What made you come to Venice?'

'Well, I was born here, even though I was brought up in England. My father was Venetian. And I trained as an artist, was always interested in glassblowing. My mother told me the story of Corradino, when she gave me this heart which he made.'

Vittoria's eyes narrowed and she reached out to grasp the trinket. Her fingers were cold, and smelled of nicotine. '*Bello,*' she said, with exactly the same inflection as before.

She released the heart as Leonora went on, 'and I was intrigued. I wanted to come and see if I could carry on the family trade.'

Family trade. That was good. Chiara and Semi will be pleased with me. Now please let's get away from England, I don't want to talk about Stephen.

'Just like that? Wasn't it hard to leave family and friends? Boyfriend? Husband?'

Damn.

'I . . . was married. He . . . we divorced.'

A drag of cigarette. A nod of the head. 'Ah I *see*.'

Leonora felt that somehow Vittoria had divined her whole sorry history.

This woman has never been left by anyone. She has always been the leaver, and pities women who have been abandoned. Women like me. Even Alessandro didn't come back for more.

'And once here, you went to Signor della Vigna for work?'

'Adelino. Yes. I was very lucky.'

A raise of the eyebrow. 'Indeed. When you got the job, how much d'you think was down to your talent, and how much was down to your famous ancestor, Corrado Manin?'

Leonora would not rise. 'If I'm honest, I don't think I would have gotten the chance that I got if it weren't for Corradino. But then again, Adelino would never have employed me if I couldn't actually blow glass. He'd be a fool to, and he's no fool.'

She was reminded of all those interviews with budding young actors from theatrical dynasties, who always protested that being a Redgrave, or a Fox, was actually a hindrance to their careers. She and Stephen always used to scoff at the TV. She was no more convinced by her own answers than she was by theirs.

Vittoria nodded, in retreat, but the next attack was close. 'And your colleagues? The *maestri* that have been blowing glass for years? What do they think of you?'

Leonora shifted, thinking of Roberto. 'They were very welcoming, on my very first day.'

That at least, was true. It wasn't till we all went to the bar that it went sour.

'I think they had . . . reservations . . . when the whole Manin line and the ad campaign was first mooted. But, after all, if it does well, things will improve for them . . .

for all of us.'

'But what do they think of you personally?' persisted Vittoria. 'Are they your friends?'

'You'd have to ask them.'

Vittoria's lips curled into a sleepy smile. 'Perhaps I will.'

A mistake.

The journalist began to tap her biro against her perfect teeth. It was a technique she employed to good effect in her interviews with male officials. She did it to draw attention to her mouth – white even teeth parted slightly over her pink tongue between a slick of red lipstick. Her subjects usually forgot what they were about to say, and were led to commit some indiscretion. Leonora wondered what was coming.

'And how about the personal angle? Have you found any romance here in the city of love?'

Leonora could hear the heavy cynicism which underlay Vittoria's question. She was not about to admit her feelings to this woman – this woman who clearly did not believe in love – at least, not the romantic kind.

'No, there's no-one.'

Vittoria lowered her eyes and made as if to pack up her paraphernalia. It was another favourite trick of hers – they always started to relax. She shot Leonora a look of pity. 'It sounds very lonely. No friends, no boyfriend, just a long dead ancestor.'

Leonora was stung. Vittoria had already made her feel inadequate – she could not handle pity too. She rose to the bait. 'Actually there is someone. But it's all very new, so I'd rather not say anything more till I see how things pan out.'

This time both dark brows shot up. 'Could you give us anything? A tiny hint?'

Leonora smiled to herself in a private joke. 'He looks like he has stepped from a painting.'

Vittoria shrugged and snapped off the recorder with finality. 'Who doesn't?'

But as Vittoria passed the fridge on the way out she caught sight of him, staring out of the Titian postcard. The Cardinal's Nephew. Alessandro Bardolino. She'd seen the painting before, of course, in his house. His mother had bought a Titian print for him as part of a family joke. It had hung in his kitchen, and Vittoria had passed it a hundred times a day, before, of course, she had been promoted to Rome. And then, last month, been promoted back to Venice. She had seen the picture every day for the three years they had lived together.

Vittoria turned to Leonora and took her leave with such warmth and good manners that Leonora began to think she had imagined the needling of the interview. She was amazed that Vittoria seemed so upbeat – she had been careful to give little away, and the interview had been ...

well, quite boring?

But Vittoria Minotto crossed the Campo Manin with a spring in her step. The interview had been an undoubted success. She had several promising leads. Not least that the little *vetraia* was dating Alessandro. How amusing to take him off her.

How *interesting* life was.

CHAPTER 15

Treachery

It was late, and Leonora was alone at the *fornace*. She had stoked and stacked all of the furnaces and left them sleeping for nighttime, except the one solitary firehole at which she worked.

She had seen little of Alessandro, but he had, at least, telephoned her only last night. He was in Vicenza, on a course to complete his promotion to Detective, provided that he passed the stringent exam paper that he would sit at the end of it. For the duration of the course Leonora had vowed to stay on at the *fornace* late into the evening to work on her glassblowing skills, so that she would not yearn for the chimes of doorbell or telephone. In this new bubble of love in which she lived, she was afraid that she would lose her motivation, and that the glass, like a neglected friend, would turn upon her. She knew also that she needed to keep this strand of her life going as there was no knowing when the vessel that held her happiness would crack or burst under the intensity of her new passion.

For her fire for Alessandro still burned bright. She had been in her new apartment for just over a month, and there were just a handful of days when they had seen one another, and yet she thought of him constantly. His concentration on his promotion, his absence in Vicenza, all absolved him from any charges of neglect in her eyes. She made excuses for him. She comforted herself with the intimacy of the moments which they did spend together, and lived on daydreams of those times. She learned more about him, in snatches of conversation. He told her of his parents – his father a retired policeman, his mother a retired nurse, who had moved to the Umbrian hills to escape the relentlessness of Venice's tourism. She clung to these details, hoping that they brought him close, and tried to ignore the fact that she had never once been inside his house.

But now his physical distance gave her the chance she needed to clear her head and justify her position at the centre of the Manin advertising campaign. She tirelessly worked on her glass, while the moon rose outside over the lagoon. Her aim tonight was simple, and, at the same time, difficult. She wanted to learn to make a glass heart, such as the one she had been given that Corradino made. She still wore it, always, around her neck. Now, she undid the blue ribbon from which it hung and laid the heart tenderly on her *banco* – near enough to see for her comparisons, but far enough away from the blistering heat that would damage it. She recalled, in her first week here, attempting to make one, expecting it to be fairly easy compared to the wonders that the *maestri* wrung from their hands daily. But the kindly Francesco, her one ally, gently laughed at her – the heart of glass, he said, was one of the hardest things to make. Particularly one of such absolute symmetry, with a perfect, spherical bubble trapped at its centre, such as the one she wore.

Resolutely, she began. She took a small blob of gather from the fire, spun it for a second then transferred it deftly to a smaller blowpipe than she normally used. She took a short breath and exhaled, gently, as the parison grew like a water drop. Quickly she twisted off the bulb and began to marver it with her *borselle* tongs, making the creased depression between the two ears of the heart. But it was too late – the interior bubble had collapsed and separated, the lugs were different sizes. Leonora cooled the heart, and dropped it into a bucket at her feet, to be re-melted later. She began again. This time, she breathed the parison quickly, like a gasp, and had better success, but still this second heart joined the first in the bucket. She worked on, for perhaps an hour, oblivious to the sounds of the staff leaving the showroom, to sounds of cashing up, locking up. She was genuinely startled at a tap on her shoulder.

It was Adelino. 'Leonora *mia*, it is time for *me* to go home, therefore I'm damned sure it's time for *you* to go home.' He spoke in his usual, half-gruff, half-affectionate tones.

But his voice warmed as he saw the task she had set herself. 'Ah, the elusive glass heart. *Molto difficile, vero*?'

Leonora nodded ruefully. Adelino crouched and began to sort through her bucket of rejects – now full. 'Yes, as you see, very difficult. But these are not bad. What did you find wanting about this one?' He held up her last attempt. It seemed to him perfect, but Leonora had seen some anomaly in it. It was strange – with Alessandro, she wanted to believe that all was right; endlessly she made excuses and allowances to preserve her hopes. At the *fornace* she sought perfection and accepted no less. Even if everything looked in order, but her eyes were seeking hidden fissures, imperfect reflections, skewed illumination.

'It's not right,' she said stubbornly.

Adelino smiled, and stood. 'Always the perfectionist, eh? Actually, I'm glad you're here. I wanted to show you this.' He proffered a glossy photo. 'It's the first press ad. It's due to run on Monday.' Leonora, with studied nonchalance, closed the *forno* door and turned off the gas feed. Mentally she was preparing herself for the image – the picture that would launch her on the public. She took the print and perused it carefully. It wasn't bad. Ironically, they had gone with a Titian image first – a mock-up of herself dressed as Titian's famous Woman with a Mirror. One hand clasped a bundle of her flowing hair and the other held a glass orb. The image in the mirror showed the busy *fornace*, with her modern self stooping over the furnace. She looked at the picture for a long moment. Adelino took her silence for disapproval.

'Leonora,' he seemed to hesitate. 'I'm not a bad man. This is a tasteful, classy, campaign. It will benefit all of us. And besides,' she met his eyes at last 'I think you are ready to be a *maestra*. I think you are ready to make the pieces that we sell.'

Leonora felt numb, searching his eyes to detect a joke. She had been here a mere four months. Surely that was too soon to metamorphose from apprentice to *maestra*.

'Adelino, how much of this is to do with the Manin campaign? I want to earn promotion on my merits, not on the back of these ads.'

Adelino took back the picture. 'Look. Obviously it helps the campaign if you are a *maestra* here and not just a *servente*. But I wouldn't be offering you the chance unless I thought you were worthy. If these past few weeks have taught you anything about me, you'll know that I prize the reputation of my business above anything. I wouldn't let substandard glass be sold from this foundry.' Adelino bent to pick from the bucket the last heart she had made. 'This is true, and clear. It's good. Don't be so grudging. It's an excellent chance for you.'

Leonora relented. 'I am grateful. Thank you. I won't let you down.' As she turned to pick up her jacket Adelino surreptitiously put the heart she had made in his pocket.

'Now, please, clean up this God-awful mess. And clear off, so I can lock up.' They shared a smile at his affected gruffness.

His secret rescue had come just in time. For Leonora, before she shut the last firehole door, threw the bucket of imperfect hearts onto the dying heat of the coals, to melt down for gather the next day. She grabbed her bag, said a last 'thank you' to Adelino, and ran for her boat, tying Corradino's heart around her neck as she went.

Adelino felt the solid shape of the heart in his jacket pocket. Then without knowing why, he opened the door of the firehole to watch the crystal hearts bleeding and dying on the red coals, melting down into one mass. He had spoken the truth. He knew the girl *was* good enough to be the first *maestra* on Murano, but he hoped the men would accept this. He closed the door and shivered. Like Leonora before him, he had stared into the flames and looked for trouble.

It soon came, and from a not entirely unexpected quarter.

'What?' Roberto del Piero's shout sounded unnaturally high. The glassblower snatched up his latest piece – a beautiful *pasta vitrea* vase, clear glass with bright beads of colour trapped inside – and threw it against the furnace where it smashed into a million gems. Adelino had gathered the *maestri* together in the morning and made a short announcement of Leonora's promotion. There had been a stony silence from all the men – save one.

'You can't do this. You can't make this *puttana* a *maestra*. First those ridiculous adverts and now this. We'll be a laughing stock,' spluttered Roberto.

Leonora reacted instantly to the insult, and, as the whole the room froze following the smash of the vase – even as Adelino's white eyebrows drew down into a frown – she crossed the floor and landed a stinging slap on Roberto's face for the second time in their short acquaintance. 'Not so much of a *puttana* that I would sleep with a man like you. *That's* what's bothering you – you got turned down.'

Adelino intervened at last, grabbing the two of them like brawling cats. 'In my office, both of you.' With a strength that belied his years, he carted them off to his inner sanctum, an iron grip on their upper arms. Once inside and released, Leonora and Roberto eyed each other, she with anger, he with a malice that chilled her bones. She could hardly believe that such hatred had been engendered by a brush-off outside a Murano bar.

Adelino sat behind his desk, with a deep sigh. The trouble he had foreseen had come to pass. He knew of their altercation in the bar – staff gossip always reached him – but he sensed too that Roberto's hatred ran much deeper, and hoped to God he could be silenced before the truth, whatever it was, emerged. 'Roberto,' Adelino began, 'that vase would have fetched three hundred euros. That amount will be taken from your wages.'

'Take what you like,' the man sneered. 'But I will not work with this, this . . .'

'Don't say it again,' Leonora interjected, deadly serious.

Adelino broke in. 'Leonora. *Silenzio*. Now, Roberto, am

I to understand that you are giving me an ultimatum? That if I make Leonora a *maestra* you will go?'

Roberto, cooling, nodded. Adelino sighed again, refusing to meet Leonora's questioning eyes. She couldn't believe what was about to happen. Last night she had thought hard on the boat home and concluded that, whatever the state of play with Alessandro, she had achieved a great thing – she was the first female glassblower on Murano, a *maestra*. She had what she came to Venice for. She at last had the job that she wanted – an outlet for her creative and artistic passions.

And after one short night it is to be taken away, I'm to be pushed back down to servente, *through the malice of a man I hardly know. For Adelino will never get rid of Roberto. He is the best glassblower on the island.*

At length Adelino spoke. 'This is very difficult for me.' He raised his eyes, but met those of the man not the girl before him. 'Roberto, you are the best *maestro* here, but your head is as hot as the furnace. You can collect your money from accounts and go. The vase was on me.'

Leonora gasped, and turned to Roberto, almost expecting him to strike Adelino. But the *maestro* turned on her instead. Before Adelino could stop him, Roberto had Leonora against the wall, his hand cruelly twisted at her throat, holding the glass heart in his palm, the blue ribbon twined round his hard fingers. Their pose held a cruel echo of his amorous advances outside the bar, but his words were very different.

'Yes, you have wormed your way in here, *puttana*, but I bet they haven't told you that you are the spawn of a traitor? That your precious ancestor betrayed mine, and sold the secrets of the glass to France, where he died a rich man? Your grand ad campaign is a joke, based on a lie.'

'It's you who lies!' Leonora spat in the leering visage. 'Corradino lived here, worked here, and died here.'

'Little idiot. He died in France.'

Adelino, galvanized at last, hissed, 'Roberto, let her go, and get out of my sight.'

Roberto, as if spent by his revelations, released Leonora, and slammed out of the room.

The girl sank into a chair, as if dazed. Adelino fussed around her, appalled by the scene he had allowed to take place. He gave her water, and, as she waved his attentions away, sat down again, shaken himself. At last she looked up. 'What did he mean, about Corradino? How could he be a traitor? And how did he harm Roberto's family?

Adelino shook his head, bemused. 'Roberto is a del Piero. All those centuries ago, his ancestor Giacomo was a great *maestro*, and the mentor of Corradino. As far as I know they were the best of friends.'

'Then why would Roberto say what he said? Why would he hate Corradino and me? And what did he mean about treachery – and about France? I thought Corradino died here?'

Adelino nodded. 'Certainly he died here, of mercury poisoning, so the history books say.'

Leonora tried to absorb this, the threads of a hundred half-remembered tales of Corradino spinning webs in her addled brain. She soon realized that she was nodding her head repeatedly. 'Yes,' she said, 'that must be right . . .'

Adelino crossed the room and took her by the shoulder. 'Look. Why don't you take the rest of the day off? I'll smooth things over here. Come in tomorrow as normal and this will all blow over. Big day tomorrow, the first press ads go out. Get some rest.'

Leonora registered his kind tone but her stomach shrivelled at the thought of the ordeal to come. She stumbled thankfully out into the sunlight and turned to walk to the boat along the Fondamenta Manin. This time the familiar street name gave her no comfort. Instead she looked up at it and addressed the faded sign. 'Corradino, what did you do?'

CHAPTER 16

A Knife of Obsidian

And now, to make a knife.

The glass blades that Corradino made for The Ten's assassins, those deadly points which entered the skin with barely a whisper, they would not do for his purpose. Such knives hung, glittering, on racks on the walls of the *fornace* – ranked like so many chilling icicles that brought the cold winter of death. They were made here in great number for good reason. They could be used but once. Each knife was designed to snap at the haft after the fatal wound had been delivered. The wound would close and heal in death, concealing the manner of the victim's leavetaking. But for those friends or families that sought a *post-mortem* for their dead beloved, the glass blade served as the ultimate warning from the Council. Corradino knew that his blades were the most favoured by the dark shades that reaped for The Ten. When he honed their deadly points he sometimes thought of the men that would meet their ends as these blades entered their flesh, separating muscle and sinew, rending artery and vein. He felt haunted by the cries of their women and children; keening, bereft of their men and fathers, as he himself had wept for his dead parents. But he dismissed the thought with another:

If I refused to make these knives, my own life would be forfeit.

Corradino mitigated his guilt by making the blades as thin, strong and clean as his skill allowed. Like a surgeon, if he had to assist such butchery, he would make the passing as painless as possible.

The *fornace* was empty – all the *maestri* had gone, even Giacomo, whose age was beginning to tell. Corradino was alone with the glittering blades, the half-finished *candelabri* standing like amputees waiting for their missing limbs, and the shining goblets singing almost imperceptibly as they cooled. He looked around the cavernous space that had been his home for twenty years, cool now that the fires were dead. He checked that every last soul had gone and then lit a single candle. He turned to the door of a disused furnace that was set back into the wall. He opened the door and entered the gaping maw, his feet crunching on the detritus of old goblets and candlesticks that had been littered in here like damaged treasure, since the furnace had been stopped up many years ago. Corradino felt for the blackened brickwork at the back of the firehole, felt expertly for the metal hook and pulled. An inner door silently sprang open and he stepped inside.

Instantly he was at home. He lit from memory the candles on the many branched stick inside the door and the room that warmed into light resembled not a place of work but an attractive Venetian salon. A velvet chaise lounged in the corner. A firehole, dominating one wall, burned as merrily as a nobleman's hearth. And on the walls, reflecting heat and light, hung some of Corradino's most treasured pieces; the pieces that he knew would have to be released for sale one day, but not yet – not quite yet. Great mirrors spanned from floor to ceiling, making the room twice as large. Sconces, reaching out from the walls in a heartbreaking arabesque, rivalled the beauty of the flames they carried. Picture frames that held no image, but that would diminish any portrait in the world, no matter how celebrated the beauty of the subject. Only the centre of the room belied the appearance of a luxurious *palazzo* for here stood the tools of Corradino's trade – long water vats and silvering tanks, vials of multicoloured pigments and limbecs of evil-smelling chemicals.

This chamber is mine. Secret, safe, and the right place for the office which I carry tonight.

Corradino knew what was needed – a knife of his own design, called a *dente*, or tooth. It was well named; not slim and deadly like the assassin's knives that he was charged to make, and not designed to break off at the haft like them. Short but sturdy, made of dense dark glass and with a wicked point, the *dente* would do well for cutting and digging alike. He was still for a moment, surveying his benchful of powders and unguents, thinking of the type of glass that was needed. Then he knew.

Obsidian. The oldest glass in the world.

He stripped off his jerkin and went to work. The heat of his chamber was intense, as the firehole was large and the room – though sizeable enough for its purpose – heated quickly. Corradino thrust a handful of ash-like pumice from Stromboli into the fire instead of the customary sand. Then followed a handful of sulphur which burned his nose and made him tie a kerchief about his face. His task tonight was to recreate the hard black natural glass that spewed forth, time out of mind, from the volcanoes of the south. The kind of glass which set like stone. The kind of glass which had entombed the poor dead souls of Pompeii and Herculaneum, trapped like flies in amber – first liquid, then diamond hard. With a firehardened paddle he mixed the powders with a fiery blob of gather which had been heating in the fire all day like a sleeping salamander. He mixed and reheated the glowing orb, adding more pumice and a little pitch, until the glass was as dark and sluggish as treacle. Only then did he take his *pontello* and shape the knife, rolling the handle on the wood and leather *scagno* saddle which stood by the fire. When he was happy – for there must be no error tonight – he took the handle to the fire again and flamed the blade end for a long moment. When the dark handle glowed at the haft he brought it out and set it in a vice, blade end down, and watched as the rosy tip of the handle grew downwards with the force of gravity, and the molten glass dripped like a fiery stalactite into a wicked point. Corradino had invented this drip method, finding that it yielded a more perfect point than any amount of grinding or polishing after the fact. This way, the glass made its own edge. The glass must best decide how its enemies were to be dispatched. He counted his heartbeats and, at exactly the right moment and not before, he turned the vice so that the cooling blade turned, curving and hardening into the fang of the beast. Small and stubby, black and pin-sharp, the evil point glinted in the firelight

Yes – this should serve. The blade and handle are made all of a piece, so there is no weakness in the knife.

As Corradino sat and watched his black knife cool, he looked his last around the chamber. Known to no other save Giacomo, the room had been made for Corradino the day after he had discovered the secret of how to make his mirrors. All his most private work was done here. This salon kept the secret.

The secret, which lay buried in the art of glassblowing.

The secret that he merely stumbled upon when a vase that he was making went wrong. The secret which saved him from death at the hands of his greedy masters, The Ten. The secret which had freed him from the prison of Murano and given him the status to walk about Venice almost as other men, and thus give life to his greatest creation, Leonora. The secret which was not written anywhere, even in his vellum notebook, and was known to no man but he. The secret that was coveted by the foreign king who had brought him to this pass.

The secret which I swore to take to my grave. I did not know how true I spoke.

CHAPTER 17

Dead Letter Drop

Vittoria Minotto was intrigued. It was not a state of mind she experienced often, and in order to revel in the sensation fully she had suggested Florian's as a meeting place. If one was to put in for expenses, one might as well enjoy the experience.

The day was fine but there was a breath of Autumn in the breeze, so Vittoria chose a table just inside the famous green and gold salon, where he would easily be able to find her. There were no strains of string quartet or piano today. Many of the tourists were now gone – Venice was preparing to enter her period of hibernation before Carnevale. It was interesting to note – and as a local she had become aware of it over the years – that the thronging school parties and coach trips of summer gave way, in the winter months, to quiet weeks with the 'city break' couples dotting the *piazza* for the four days from Thursday to Monday.

Vittoria ordered her ruinously expensive *caffé americano* and lit her cigarette. She looked out into the square, to see if she could spot her date arriving. Ah, there he was. Young, good-looking, walking with a purposeful stride which scattered the pigeons. Better and better.

He found her at once. 'Signorina Minotto?' It was the voice from the phone call. Low, driven and agitated.

She inclined her head and blew out smoke. '*Sì*.'

He sat and, unbidden, took a cigarette and lit it. She liked him at once.

'I think I might know something which might interest you. About Leonora Manin. Actually no, it goes further back than that. About Corrado Manin. It might make quite a good story.'

That was it. He had said it. The word that she loved, that she lived for. The word that had captured her attention from being a little girl at her father's knee, holding her breathless from the words; 'Once Upon a Time'. How she had begged to stay up, to hear more!

A Story.

'Go on.'

CHAPTER 18

Non Omnis Moriar

Giacomo del Piero looked from his window over the Murano canal. He was sure he heard something stir without and carried his candle high, peering through the narrow quarrels of his window. He saw nothing, but the flame of his candle illuminated only his own reflection, fractured by the leadings of the panes. He saw an old man.

Giacomo turned from his image and thought of what he would do now. He supposed he must eat – there was some fine Bolognese sausage in the pantry, and a jug of wine to go with it, but somehow he had no appetite. He felt he needed to eat less as his age advanced – other things nourished him now. His books, his work, and his friendships. He thought of Corradino in particular, and that the boy had become as a son to him over the years. Perhaps he should go down the path to Corradino's lodgings, and share the wine with him? No, the boy was exhausted with this commission for that mysterious client, Maestro

Domenico of the Teatro Vecchio. Giacomo had never met the man, but he knew that the work kept Corradino at the *fornace* at all hours. Perhaps Corradino was even yet not at home to receive a visit.

Giacomo took up his ancient viol instead and his bow and fingers, unbidden, found a melancholy folk song of the Veneto which matched his mood. He felt a foreboding, a heaviness of heart which he could not explain. It was this feeling that had made him go to the window repeatedly since he had returned from the *fornace*.

So the muffled knock at the door when it came did not surprise him, as he had felt expectant all evening. As he set down his viol carefully on the trestle, he had a horrid fancy that he would be opening the door to Death itself, come at last to claim him. But the figure who stood there was not Death. It was Corradino.

They kissed each other heartily, although Giacomo thought at once that his friend looked agitated. Once inside he could not seem to sit or stand, and waved away the offer of wine, before accepting and downing the cup in one swallow.

'Corradino, what ails you? Have you a fever? Is it the mercury?' For Corradino had suffered much from a hacking cough of late – a sign which could indicate a corruption of the lungs from the mercury used to silver the mirrors. Only last week Giacomo had insisted that his friend place four peppercorns under his tongue to ward off the lung sickness – like all Venetians Giacomo had an enormous respect for the mysterious spices of the east. But even spices could not prevent mercury poisoning. The silver devil brought most of the glassblowers to their deaths – their art consumed them in the end. Corradino shook his head fervently at Giacomo's diagnosis, but his eyes burned in his head. 'I came to . . .' he began, and stopped abruptly.

Giacomo grabbed Corradino's arm and pulled him down on the trestle beside him. 'Compose yourself, Corradino *mio*. What is it you would say? Are you in trouble?'

Corradino laughed, but shook his head again. 'I came to say . . . I know not what . . . I want you to know . . . there is so much I cannot tell you!' He took a breath. 'I wanted to tell you that I owe you everything, that you are a father to me, that you saved my life over and again, that I can't ever repay you, and that, whatever may befall me, I wish you to try to think well of me.' He clasped the old man's hands fervently. 'Promise me this – that you will try to think well of me.'

'Corradino, I will always think well of you. What *is* this coil?'

'One more thing. If you should see Leonora, if you should ever see her, tell her that I have always loved her, and love her still.'

'Corradino . . .'

'Promise!'

'I promise, but you must tell me what you mean by all this. What has become of you tonight? What are you planning?'

Corradino reacted instantly. 'I am planning nothing. Nothing. I . . .' he laughed and dropped his head into his hands, his fingers parting the dark curls. Then, in more normal tones he said, 'Forgive me. It is some mood, some fancy. Dark humours come from the gibbous moon, which shines tonight.'

He motioned toward the window, and Giacomo saw, sure enough, that the moon was almost full, and had a strange hue. Perhaps that accounted for his own melancholy. 'Aye, I felt somewhat of the same mind myself. Come, let's drink this folly away.'

Corradino waved away the wine jug. 'I must go. But remember all I said.'

Giacomo shrugged. 'I will. But I'll see you at the *fornace* tomorrow.'

'Aye, tomorrow. I'll see you then.'

The hug was fervent and prolonged. Then Corradino was gone, and Giacomo was once again alone. As he stared out into the night, he wondered if he had really seen tears shining in his friend's eyes as he turned away. Despite the talk of tomorrow, the whole interview had the manner of a leavetaking.

A leavetaking indeed. When Corradino did not arrive at the *fornace* in the morning, Giacomo's foreboding reached its peak, awful voices clamouring in his head. He went at once to Corradino's lodgings, running as fast as his old limbs would carry him. He entered the little cot without knocking and headed to the second room – the bedchamber. There, he saw the worst. His friend lay on the truckle bed, fully dressed, and still. He thought at first that Corradino had taken his own life, that this had been the meaning of the farewell yestereve. But then, through new tears, he saw a telltale streak of black running from the corner of the open mouth to the coverlet. He turned over one of Corradino's cold hands – the fingertips were also black. Giacomo had seen such signals more times in his life than he wished to. Mercury. The plague of the glassblower had taken Corradino at last. Giacomo sat at the foot of the bed and wept.

He had known.

Corradino had known that he was dying, last night when he had visited. He *had* been saying goodbye. Giacomo stood at last and pulled the coverlet over the face that was so dear to him. As he did so he lamented, as fathers have always lamented as they beheld their dead sons: 'Lord, why did you not take me?'

That night, Giacomo returned at last to his house. It had been the most painful day of his long life, and he felt he would gladly go to sleep and never wake. He had reported Corradino's death to the mayor of Murano, and a *medico* had been sent to verify cause. The doctor had prodded Corradino with great care, snipping hair and letting blood, a thoroughness which Giacomo knew had been ordered by The Ten. In his dark robes and white mask with its long, beaked nose stuffed with herbs to prevent infection, the doctor looked for all the world like a vulture come to feed on the carrion of Corradino. But, if one of their great assets died, the Council always wished to make sure there was no misadventure. Only the knowledge of this prevented Giacomo from intervening to plead for his dead friend's dignity. He kept his peace. But when the *medico* at last released the body he seemed surprised that Giacomo requested permission to fulfill the proper rites for his friend. As the post-mortem was complete however, the doctor saw no reason not to grant this whim and Corradino was carried to Giacomo's house to be laid out.

Giacomo attended while the women he had paid made Corradino ready. They cleaned his face, arranged his hair and tied his feet together and his jaw closed. As candles burned around them they sewed the dead man into sack cloth, and Giacomo watched the face he loved disappear into darkness as the stitches closed the shroud. With his last glance of Corradino he thought how comely his son had been, that his curls shone in the candlelight, the cheeks held a faint flush and the lashes that lay across them were still lustrous. It was almost as if he slept. He chided himself; and, in a last act of leave-taking, Giacomo tenderly placed a golden ducat over each closed eye. He gave away a twelvemonth's wages without a thought. He had given the boy everything: his home, his skills with the glass, and all the love his old heart could hold. Corradino had been his heir in all things, so in place of an inheritance Giacomo paid the fare for Corradino's final journey. He turned away, his heart breaking.

At last two constables came to carry the body to the boat which would take it to Sant'Ariano, the burial island. Giacomo asked to come to the quay, but was prevented.

'*Signore*,' said the taller constable, his eyes shining with sympathy behind their mask, 'we have two cases of plague to carry too. We could not vouch for your safety.'

So Corradino had gone, the constables had gone and the women had gone, gratefully biting the coins that Giacomo had given them for their trouble.

He was once again alone, as he had been the night before, before all this sorry business had come to pass. He could cry now for the friend – the son – who had gone. But his tears had left him, and he felt nothing but a dry grief for his loss. Once again he took up his viol, exactly as he had done before his world changed. But all was not exactly as before – there was a piece of vellum twisted in the strings. Vellum that Giacomo would know anywhere – it was the fine Florentine vellum of Corradino's notebook. Giacomo remembered now, as his heart beat fast in his throat, how he had pulled Corradino to sit down right next to the instrument the night before. With shaking fingers Giacomo slipped the note out from under the strings. Corradino was not one for penmanship, as he had been untimely ripped from Monsieur Loisy's tutelage at the age of ten, but these letters were clear enough. He had carefully spelt out, in the middle of the page, the Latin tag:

NON OMNIS MORIAR

Corradino was no great reader – in fact the only volume he knew well was the Dante from his father. But Giacomo was a learned man, and had no need to search through the volumes in his chamber for the meaning of the phrase. It all fitted – the bloom on Corradino's cheeks, the shine of his hair, the loving leavetaking of the night before.

NON OMNIS MORIAR
I SHALL NOT ALTOGETHER DIE

Giacomo clasped the vellum to his heart before pressing it gently between the pages of his own copy of Dante. As he closed the book he smiled for the first time that day.

Corradino was still alive.

CHAPTER 19

The Fourth Estate

'Read this.'

The newspaper slapped down onto Adelino's desk in front of Leonora. She could smell the acrid printer's ink under her nose. Adelino turned his back and went to the window, struggling with some emotion she could not yet divine. Could it be anger? She supposed that the press had bungled the ads, or misspelled something. Warning bells only began to ring when she saw Vittoria Minotto's byline and photo on the folded page.

My interview? No, worse.

"Hapless *vetraio* Adelino della Vigna has spectacularly backed the wrong horse for his splashy advertising campaign. In an effort to flog the glass of his ailing Vetreria Della Vigna on Murano, he recently introduced the Manin range, an exclusive line of antique and modern glass. The range was to be sold on the back of famous *maestro* Corrado Manin, known as Corradino, and his decorative ancestor Leonora Manin, who lately became the first *maestra* on the island. Our readers will remember, just days ago, the glossy ads in these and other publications featuring the two Manins, and our eyes have been assailed by the posters adorning the walls of our fair city. But little did we know then what this paper has been able to discover, with the help of one of the master glassblowers of the *fornace,* Roberto del Piero."

Leonora went cold.

Roberto.

Shaking, her sweating fingertips blurring the print, she read on.

"'The whole thing is a joke,' says Signor del Piero. 'Corrado Manin was indeed a master glassblower, but he was a traitor to the Republic and his craft. He was solicited by French spies and went to Paris to sell our secrets to the French, who were then our greatest trade rivals. Corradino single-handedly smashed the Venetian glass monopoly. It would be laughable except for the fact that the affair holds a sinister history for my own family. My own ancestor Giacomo del Piero was Corradino's lifelong friend and mentor, and yet Corradino betrayed him and caused his death. He's a Murderer, not a Maestro.'"

This catchy piece of alliteration had obviously drawn

the editor's eye, as the words 'Murderer not Maestro' formed the subheading of the paragraph. Leonora swallowed and read below.

"Signor del Piero's grievances are modern as well as ancient. 'I approached the advertisers with my own story. Giacomo was Corradino's mentor – he taught him everything he knew. Moreover, there have been del Pieros working at the *fornace* ever since his day. I offered them the opportunity to introduce a line of glass in *my* family name, and they threw it back in my face. Clearly they preferred this bimbo who's only been in Venice a few months.' Signor del Piero is dismissive of Signorina Manin's talents. 'She can blow the glass a little, but really she's just an English girl with no talent and a yard of blonde hair.' Particularly hard, then, is the fact that after hundreds of years of service to the glassblowing industry, the family's run now seems to be over. 'I tried to alert Adelino to the truth, and his answer was to fire me. He'd rather keep his precious bimbo because he needs her for his ad campaign.'

"We should stress at this point that this paper is not in the habit of printing the vengeful vitriol of the wrongly dismissed. We have been shown documentary evidence of the treachery of Corrado Manin from what historians would term a 'Primary Source'.

"These revelations will be an undoubted embarrassment to Signor della Vigna, who has been touting for business with the aid of such copylines as 'The Glass that built the

Republic'. Such phrases must be ringing in his ears this morning, and may explain why he has so far refused to comment. Readers can expect to see the campaign withdrawn."

'Is this true? You're withdrawing the campaign?'

Adelino turned, his face bleak. 'What else can I do?' He took the paper from her hands and flipped over the folded page. The black headline bawled out at her. 'TREACHERY ON MURANO.' There flanking the type was the portrait of ten-year-old, innocent Corradino, and herself, in her vest and jeans by the furnace.

Then, all at once, of the sea of her thoughts one alone surfaced and consumed her body:

I'm going to be sick.

She rushed from the room and through the *fornace*, to the canalside where she vomited helplessly. How could she know that Corradino had done the same, four centuries before, the night before he became a traitor?

CHAPTER 20

The Eyes of the Old

Leonora stood outside the University of Ca' Foscari in Dorsoduro. She had come to meet Professore Padovani, the only link in the city to her family, to her past.

She had come home the previous night, from the scene at the *fornace*, distraught and upset, her nausea remaining with her as she left Murano. Even the welcoming sight of the night lights of San Marco did little to soothe her mood. She left the island boat at Ferrovia and waited, as she rarely did, for the number 82 *vaporetto* to take her up the Grand Canal to the Rialto. As the *vaporetto* roared to a stop, and the gateman expertly tied the boat, she thought of her father for the first time in weeks. His presence here, his very existence, seemed ephemeral when compared to the relationship she had with Corradino, dead for many centuries longer. She felt clearly now how much she had relied on Corradino, felt pride in him and even love for him. She could not have been more devastated by such accusations of treachery had they been directed at her own father. She felt her father to have been someone belonging to her mother alone – Leonora had never seen him and Bruno had never seen her. Their link was purely biological.

My connection to Corradino, paradoxically, seems much more real to me.

And yet Roberto del Piero had struck at the very roots of that cross-centuries bond. She felt vulnerable, exposed. Even the sight of the silver palaces roosting in the twilight along the canal did not give her the usual comfort. Autumn was here, and the friendly frontages of the buildings had assumed a shuttered look as the lifeblood of the tourist trade ebbed away from their faces like a fading blush. The decorative windows looked back, blank-eyed and uninviting now. She wondered if Corradino had betrayed all this, of what secret conferences he had had, what meetings he had held in these very buildings. As she disembarked at Rialto and ducked down the darkening *calli* to the Campo Manin her feelings of unease multiplied – she began to feel hunted, followed, to listen out for soft footfalls in the shadows. She felt tainted by the slur on Corradino.

If he has done this thing, the city remembers and condemns me too.

Leonora felt rejected by the stones that had lately welcomed her. Even when she walked at last into the Campo Manin she felt pursued. The beautiful shadows could hold ugliness too.

Don't Look Now . . .

She chided herself. For it wasn't a dwarfish red figure that she feared, but Roberto del Piero. She had ended his career at the *fornace*, and his family profession. He could, of course, work elsewhere, but it was she who had cuckooed him out of his nest.

She ran across the still-warm stones of the *campo* and fumbled for her keys. In a childish game she felt she was outrunning the unseen assassins.

If I can just reach my door . . .

As she fitted the key in her lock she expected a hand to pluck at her sleeve, or even clutch at her throat . . . struggling with the latch she wrenched the door open and fell inside. She backed the door closed and leaned in the dark, breathing hard. Seconds later she left her skin as the phone began to ring. Shaking, she moved into the kitchen and picked up the receiver. But it was not the rasping tones of a horror film cliché. It was him.

'Alessandro!'

She sank into a chair and switched on the lamp. As the

pool of light spread and she listened to the longed-for voice, the shades of her daymares fled.

He laughed at the fervour of her greeting.

'Detective Bardolino to you.'

'You passed!'

'Yes.' Pride in the voice. 'I have a week of orientation here and then I start at division, back in Venice.'

She could not dampen his enthusiasm with her own troubles. *Il Gazzettino* was a local paper, and news of her humiliation or Corradino's reputation would not yet have reached Vicenza. Plenty of time to talk of that face to face. She suddenly felt terribly tired, and besides, a small sense of shame lodged just below her heart would not let her tell this man of her tarnished ancestor. While Alessandro talked about his weeks away and the exam, Leonora felt the fear and panic abate. She felt confident in the circle of his conversation as if protected by his nativity. Of course Corradino was no traitor. It was not true. It was an ugly rumour perpetrated by his rival. And what did it matter anyway? Corradino was long dead, and his work lived on to testify for him.

But it does *matter. I want to know for myself, to find out for certain.*

Something Alessandro had said floated back from memory. 'When we first met, you told me that you might be able to help me find out more about my family ... my father. Well, I'd like to, if you can make any suggestions?'

Alessandro considered. 'When your mother and father were together in Venice, did they have any friends or colleagues that may still be here?'

'There was someone. A lecturer at Ca' Foscari. I met him when I was very little.'

'Can you remember his name?'

'It was Padovani. I remember because my mother explained to me that his name meant "comes from Padua". She taught me an old rhyme . . .'

'Ah yes, *Veneziani gran signori, Padovani gran dottori . . .*'

'*Vicentini mangia gatti, Veronesi tutti matti.*' Leonora finished. 'I always wondered why the Vicenzans ate cats in the rhyme. But I suppose it's better than being mad, like the Veronese.'

'Ah yes, but the best thing to be of all is a great lord, like the Venetians.' Alessandro interjected proudly.

'Anyway, Professore Padovani still sends Christmas cards to my mother. But I don't know if he's still at Ca' Foscari.'

She could hear him stretching on the other end of the line. He was clearly tired, but his voice was alert and she was encouraged that he was treating her enquiry in earnest. 'Then I think the thing to do is to talk to this man, if he is still there. He will certainly know something of your father, which seems a good place to start. Go tomorrow,' he said with his customary dispatch, 'because on Sunday I'm back for the day and we'll do something, if you're free.'

She clutched the receiver with joy, feeling like a teenager. But with a desperate effort for detachment, she stayed with her theme. 'D'you really think I can find out about him, after all these years?' And it was Corradino she meant.

'Sure. He only died in, what was it? 1972? And, you know, if you want to find something out, you should really have a Detective on your team.' She could hear him grinning down the phone as he signed off with promises to see her on Sunday.

Leonora felt a sudden resolve to unravel the mystery of Corradino, and felt that the *Professore* would be a good start. She couldn't wait for tomorrow. She couldn't explain to herself why she had not been entirely honest with Alessandro, had let him think that she wished to find out principally about her father.

She slept badly, and in the morning was sick again. Nerves, she thought.

But I know it isn't nerves.

Leonora entered the modest side gate leading into the University precincts from the Calle della Foscari. Once inside, Leonora was deafened by the antics going on around her. Though it was Saturday morning, a study day for most students, there seemed to be some sort of Rag taking place – Leonora recognized the same misrule, the same anarchic spirit, which had moved her to dress as a nurse and help push a hospital bed down the Charing Cross Road during Rag week at St Martin's.

Eggs and flour were flying everywhere, and she had to duck more than once as she crossed the desecrated lawn.

They must be graduating. I read somewhere that Italian students think that making cakes of themselves is a fitting way to mark their transition to Dottore. *Soon they'll all be gone, like the tourists.*

She perused the faculty lists on a noticeboard cloistered behind glass, with fading hope, but at last Leonora spotted; 'Professore Ermanno Padovani.'

He's head of the faculty for 'Storia del Rinascimento'. Renaissance History. I might just be in luck. 'Padovani gran dottori' *indeed.*

She mounted the ancient stairs and trawled the empty corridors reading the names on the history department doors. From here the screams and merriment from outside were muffled. It felt like there was no one in these upper floors at all, so when she reached the *Professore's* door at last, Leonora felt little hope of him being inside. But when she knocked and heard a faint '*Entrate*,' muffled by the oak, her insides fluttered with the knowledge that the man inside this room may have some of the answers that she sought. As Leonora entered the sight she beheld almost made her forget why she had come. Ahead was a wide, ornate window, made up of a quartet of the most perfect, intricate, Moorish frames of which Venice was so proud. And beyond – the most incredible vista of the San Marco bank of the Canal Grande, water shimmering at the foot of the splendid palaces, as if in supplication to their grandeur. Leonora was so lost in the view that the voice that addressed her was an audible shock.

'One of the privileges of having taught here for thirty years is that I get the best room in the faculty. One of the drawbacks is, sometimes I find it very hard to get any work done. You must have come in the back way, through the gate? A pity. It is not the best aspect of the place.'

Leonora turned to the old man, who had emerged from behind his book and desk with the aid of a stick. Kindly, white-bearded, beautifully dressed and with penetrating eyes, he looked faintly amused. She apologized. 'But it's so beautiful, for a . . .'

'You were going to say for a University? But it has not always been one. Ca' Foscari was formerly a palace built for the Bishops of Venice, and you know how prelates like their creature comforts. And surely, *Signorina*, you have beautiful seats of learning in your own country do you not? Oxford and Cambridge?'

Leonora started. She had flattered herself that her English accent was gone. But she was not chastened – it seemed that this was a man with a formidable intelligence, from whom nothing could be hidden. It seemed all the more likely that he could help her. She took a deep breath. '*Professore*, I apologize for disturbing you. I'd like to ask you a few ... historical questions, if you have a moment.'

The old man smiled, his bright eyes crinkling at the corners. 'Of course,' he said. 'I can spare more than that for the daughter of my old friend Elinor Manin. How are you, my dear Nora? Or,' the old eyes twinkled immoderately, 'is it *Leonora* now that you have become ... *assimilated*.'

Leonora marvelled at the quickness of the *Professore's* mind. Not only had he remembered her instantly, but he had divined, in a few short seconds, that she had changed her life and her name. She smiled.

'You're right. I am Leonora. And I'm amazed you remember me. I must have been ... what ... five years old?'

'Six,' countered Padovani. 'It was at a University drinks party in London. You proudly showed me your brand new shoes. They were nicer than the ones you have on today.' His eyes travelled to Leonora's battered converse trainers, which she shifted sheepishly on the wooden floor. 'And, you know, you mustn't give me too much credit for my perspicacity. You have become somewhat ... notorious ... since you arrived here, have you not?'

Il Gazzettino. Of course. The paper was taken by just about every household in Venice.

'But the rest of you has grown up so well, I suppose we must not be so exacting. The *Primavera*, yes? Botticelli is much more you than those Titian poses they put you in. But I suppose you have been told this many times, by younger men than me.'

Encouraged by his old-world charm, Leonora got to the point. 'I wanted to ask you some questions about my family . . . if you have a little time.'

The *Professore* smiled. 'Time is plentiful at my age.' He motioned to the window, where four easy chairs were placed for tutorials. 'Sit down then. I'm going to, so you might as well.'

They sat in front of the peerless view, the chairs comfortable, but not cosy enough to induce sleep in the drowsy scholar. Settling himself, the *Professore* began, 'At the risk of sounding like the villain of a bad movie – they always seem to be English, don't they, my dear? I wonder why – I've been expecting you. I take it Elinor doesn't know that you are here.'

Leonora shook her head. 'No. I mean, she knows that I'm in Venice, but she doesn't know that I've come to talk to you.'

The *Professore* nodded, and his gnarled hands tapped the head of his cane. 'I see. Then I must tell you, first of all, that I will not divulge anything which she has shared with me in confidence, but other than that, I will be as helpful as I can be.' The *Professore* looked frankly at Leonora, waiting. Her fingers were twisting the glass heart she wore on its ribbon – a sign, surely, of stress. He thought the trinket was a clue to which relative she would ask about first. And so it proved.

'What do you know of Corradino Manin?'

'Corrado Manin was the finest glassmaker of his time, and of any other. He escaped the murder of his family and hid on Murano, where he was taught the ways of the glass and became a *maestro*. He was particularly proficient at making mirrors, and became famous for it. It is said that the mercury of the mirrors finally killed him, as it killed many.'

'So he died on Murano?'

'I don't know for certain. But it seems likely.'

Leonora exhaled with relief, but persisted.

'Do you know anything about the story that he may have gone to France?'

For the first time in the interview, the Professor looked discomfited. 'Yes, I read that exposé. Your colleague seems to be harbouring quite a grievance. I'd like to know what the 'Primary Source' is that he thinks he has. I imagine that you would not feel comfortable approaching him yourself?'

'There's absolutely no way that Roberto would tell me anything, least of all help me to exonerate Corradino. He's so angry with me that I'm afraid of him. I keep expecting him to ambush me from the shadows.' She tried to laugh, but could see the *Professore* was not convinced. He did not probe further into her fears, but moved on.

'And the young lady at the paper? Might she be approached?'

Leonora shook her head. She had put in a call to *Il Gazzettino* as soon as she had read Roberto's revelations. She was eventually put through to a frosty sounding Vittoria, who had abandoned all pretence of friendliness. She was sorry, Signorina Manin, but the supporting documents of her sources were strictly confidential, particularly in this case as Signor Roberto del Piero had asked that they remain so. There was a chance that they'd be doing a follow-up story in which the source would be reproduced, and Signorina Manin could look forward to that.

'Hmm.' Padovani shrugged expressively 'Ah well. One of the wonderful things about the study of history is that there is never just *one* definitive source, but many. If facts are diamonds, then our sources are the facets, each set at a discrete angle to make up the whole gem. We can do some detective work of our own, and find those other facets.'

Leonora was encouraged by his use of the word 'we' while his reference to detection warmed her with the thought of Alessandro.

'It's possible that Corrado went abroad. But highly unlikely. It's true that French mirror-making took an enormous leap forward in the late seventeenth century, evidenced by the *Palais de Versailles*, which became the flagship for the enlightened century. Some say they had foreign intelligence, others say that they arrived at these methods through convergent evolution.'

'Convergent evolution?' queried Leonora.

The Professor explained. 'In Africa, from the primeval mulch of single-celled soup, there evolved an enormous mastodon with large ears which we now call the African elephant. In India, there evolved, by the same method, a creature the same in all respects save the size of its ears. Both creatures evolved independently, separated by seas and landmasses, by tectonics, to arrive at the same place. Neither 'copied' the other. They merely share a distant ancestor, as all glassware shares its mother; sand. They underwent convergent evolution.'

Leonora pressed the point. '*Professore*, why would you say that it was highly unlikely that Corradino went to France?'

'Because The Ten, the ruling body of the *Consiglio Maggiore*, took great exception to the defection of their artisans. They threatened their families with death if craftsmen took their secrets to foreign powers. Murano itself was something of a prison, although perhaps less so for a man like Corrado, who was possessed of a prodigious talent and was given dispensation to visit the city for his work.'

Leonora broke in with the question that seemed obvious to her. 'But *Professore*, why would The Ten hold any threat for Corradino, if all his family were dead?'

'Because, my dear young lady, not *all* his family were dead. I have but a rudimentary grasp of the Biological Sciences but I do know that, if they were all dead, there would be no descendants such as yourself, my dear. Corradino had a daughter.'

★ ★ ★

Leonora pressed her face into the towel, not caring how many grubby student hands had dried there before. She felt a fool – running out of the *Professore's* room like that, and skidding into the nearest bathroom to heave into the nearest toilet bowl. Why was this revelation such a shock to her? If she had even thought it through logically, there must have been someone else, some lineage, or else how was she here? How did she have the glass heart that Corradino passed down all the way to her? She held the heart for courage as she walked shakily back down the hall and timidly re-entered the *Professore's* room. Padovani courteously stood, with concern in his eyes. She sat again and apologized.

'Forgive me, I've been . . . unwell . . . for a couple of days now.'

The *Professore* nodded and took up his story. 'Corrado's daughter was also called Leonora. She was the product of an illegitimate union between Corrado and a noblewoman, Angelina dei Vescovi, who died in childbirth. Leonora was taken in to the Pietà orphanage and trained in music. She was given the name of Manin, but surnames were never used at the orphanage. The girls in the Pietà were always known by the instrument they played – '*cello*, *violino* – to maintain the anonymity of the bastard children of some very highly born families. She was always Leonora *della viola*, and was a very accomplished player. None would have known of her connection to Corradino, or even of her existence unless he himself told of it. Even The Ten had to respect the secrets of the Pietà, as the foundation had the weight of the church and its laws of sanctuary behind it. After Corradino's death Leonora was found by a distant cousin – a Milanese called Lorenzo Visconti-Manin – who was attempting to trace the disparate fragments of his family. The two fell in love and married, and she once again came into her rightful name. The Manins became a powerful force in Venice once again, and their descendant Lodovico Manin became a Doge, the last of Venice before the Republic fell.'

Leonora's head spun, but her nausea was gone in the hope that now consumed her. 'So Corradino would not have left, for fear of his daughter's safety.'

'No,' said the *Professore*. 'That is not what I meant. The Ten knew nothing of the child, for she was secreted in the Pietà by her grandfather and no one knew who had fathered her. Angelina never told the name of her seducer, and took the secret to her grave. I merely meant that I thought it unlikely that Corradino would have left Venice while Leonora lived. Visits to a secret daughter in the Pietà would be risky, but not impossible. And I imagine the temptation would be very hard to resist.'

Leonora was silent, digesting this.

So the treachery story could still be true, if unlikely. And what of this new character, the lost girl with my name that had no family but the Pietà and only music for her friend. At least she found love in the end.

She asked, 'how would we find out more? Can we ever know for sure if Corradino left Venice?'

'You could try the large library in San Marco – the Sansoviniana – they have guild records and also records of births and death, going back centuries. But I have told you all I know of Corradino's history, and this is the account that I gave Elinor.' The *Professore* stood to stretch his bad leg. 'My only other suggestion would be to try to find something out from the French end. I have some contacts at the Sorbonne who could help you.'

Leonora took his cue and stood. 'May I see you again? And will you contact me if you think of anything more?'

'Of course. And you may mention my name for a reference in the rare book collections of the Sansoviniana.'

I remember my first day here, when they would barely let me through the front door of the Sansoviniana. Now I am to be admitted to the inner sanctum.

The *Professore* moved to his desk to write down numbers and the names of various document collections that might be helpful. Leonora scribbled down her phone numbers and as the papers were exchanged Padovani wondered if Leonora was actually going to leave without asking of that other Manin, but at last she said: 'And my father? Did you know him?'

The *Professore* shook his head, with sympathy in his eyes. 'As is the manner of young women in love, Elinor saw little of her friends and kept Bruno to herself. I only heard of his death through the local news.'

At the mention of her father's name in this context, Leonora felt a wave of shame that she had not bothered to enquire after him before, so consumed was she with Corradino.

'Is there any family still in Venice?'

'I don't know. Elinor mentioned that Bruno's parents lived in Verona, but they died long since.'

Leonora knew of this but had not contemplated the loss before – of that immediate family that most take for granted; Grandparents. They had gone – without any of the usual meetings, knitted jumpers, chocolate bars, holiday outings. She collected herself – she knew that she must leave the *Professore*, and was anxious to begin her researches of the documents he had suggested, but felt she had a thousand more questions.

As she moved to the door, with murmurs of thanks and promises to return, the *Professore* embraced Leonora warmly. Holding her arms he said, 'one more thing. Tomorrow is the feast of All Souls, the *Festa dei Morte,* when the people of Venice honour their dead. If you would see your father, he is buried on San Michele. Perhaps you will visit him. He too should be mourned.'

Leonora felt reproach, but also affection.

I know I should go and see his grave. We should meet at last.

I'll ask Alessandro to come too.

She moved into the corridor and made to walk towards the stairs. The *Professore* called, 'Leonora!'

She turned. The old man looked directly at her, and said softly, 'There are some things an old man can see that a young man can't. Look after yourself.'

'I will,' she replied.

The oak door closed and she headed down the stairs.

I wonder how he knew?

CHAPTER 21

The Island of the Dead (part 1)

The number 41 *vaporetto* to the Isola San Michele resembled a flower garden. On this day, the festival of All Souls, Venetians all honoured their dead with floral tributes, and headed for the cemetery on the island of San Michele. Leonora was pressed close to Alessandro, but equally close on her other side was a sizeable matron carrying an immense bunch of chrysanthemums. Leonora stared at the huge ugly blooms, and breathed their pungent antiseptic scent. She had never liked the flower – not just for aesthetic sensibilities, but because she associated them with death. Looking around the boat, she could see that, as in France also, chrysanthemums were indeed the flower of choice for mourners.

Leonora and Alessandro had caught the boat from the Fondamenta Nuove. It was a short crossing – indeed the cemetery with its red walls and cloistered gates could be clearly seen from the city islands. Leonora was thankful for the brevity of the trip. With the crush of people and the smell of boat fuel, her nausea had returned. She moved closer to Alessandro and he dropped a reassuring kiss on her head – as he would to a child, she thought. She had told him that he needn't come with her, but he had protested that he wished to visit his grandmother's grave anyway. She knew this was only partly true – that he was there in support of her and her meeting with her father. She felt a warm thankfulness replace the sickness in her solar plexus. When he was with her she believed in him. She almost began to feel secure, that they had something like a relationship.

They disembarked with the crowds, and entered the iron gates of the cemetery. Alessandro steered Leonora to a booth where one could purchase a map of the gravesites.

'There are three cemeteries here,' said Alessandro 'all tended by Fransiscan monks as they always have been. Although as you'll see, a little more care is taken of the Catholic plots than those of the other two – the Protestants and the Greek orthodox,' he smiled wryly, 'so your father and my *nonna* are fortunate.'

Leonora registered his flippant ghoulishness and considered that it was his way of dealing with death. She was curious about this strange island where only the dead dwelt. She had the feeling that she would not like to live along the Fondamenta Nuove, where fancy would lead one to the window of an evening to watch for phosphorescent spirits rising over the sea. She gave herself a little shake and asked, 'When did this island become a cemetery?'

'In the days of Napoleon. Before that, the dead were taken to Sant'Ariano, which is just an ossuary now.'

'A what?'

'An island of bones.' Alessandro seemed to taste the words, as if contemplating the title for a sensational novel. 'When the time runs out for the bodies here, they get shifted away to make way for new ones.'

'What *can* you mean?'

Alessandro led her up the tended pathway to the Catholic quarter. 'I mean that Venetians are only allowed to be buried here for a certain length of time, after which they are dug up and moved.' He caught the look on Leonora's face. 'It has to be so. Because of room – it's limited.' He shrugged, callously.

'I didn't mean that . . .'

'Oh, I see. You mean you think he might not still be here? He will. You get forty years I think. And if your relatives pay, you can stay longer.'

Leonora suddenly felt angry as she followed Alessandro through the quiet courts. She felt that there was no permanence, no rest for these people. But as she watched the mourners walking quietly between the graves, like flowing water that would always find its way between and round its obstacles, she relented. This end, this rest that was not rest, was a fitting end for the shifting, itinerant seafaring people. Venetians lived their lives crossing from island to island, from Rialto to San Marco, Giudecca to Lido, Torcello to Murano. Why not continue after death, this relentless flux, with the sea as your steed? What could be better for those merchants and crusaders who had boarded the boats at Zattere and left them at Constantinople? And for her father too, who had jumped from shore to boat, from boat to shore, to earn his living all his adult life. Leonora realized that tears were sliding down her cheeks.

Idiot. You didn't even know him.

But when it came to it, as Alessandro led her through the ranks of almost military-style graves, and she was brought face to face with her father's name etched neatly in stone, she felt nothing but a dry emptiness. She felt no urge for tears. Alessandro murmured that he would find his grandmother, and melted away, but Leonora hardly noticed.

BRUNO GIOVANNI BATTISTA MANIN 1949-1972

He was only twenty-three when he died.

She didn't know what to do. She was visiting the bones of a twenty-three year old man – a man she had never met, a man who was still ten years younger than her living self.

And forever shall be . . .

The words – half remembered from school and Sunday church, rang their solemn refrain in her head. She was lost. At length, she lay down her tribute on the headstone – simple white daisies. Buy your favourite, don't try to guess his, Alessandro had said, and he had been right. Then she sat on the grass, looked at the stark letters and numerals again, and simply said: 'Hello, I'm Leonora.'

Alessandro found his grandmother in a matter of moments, and placed his roses at her headstone. He could scarcely remember her now, but though the complete memory eluded him, specifics remained. He remembered her black clothes, worn daily since the death of his grandfather. He remembered her *tagliatelle con burro e salvia*, which had never, in his opinion, been bettered by any trattoria. He remembered her wholly unexpected love for Vicenza Calcio, a love which had begun his own lifelong obsession with the team, and the game of football itself. He felt no grief, just fondness, as he crouched to flick dried twigs away from her plot and ran his thumbnail under a frill of lichen. He straightened up to look for Leonora, and quickly identified her bright head, bowed, her face hidden under her mass of hair. Discomfited, he thought she might be crying, then, as he saw her lips move, that she was praying. He crossed himself, but Leonora's eyes were open, and her demeanour more casual, more comfortable than one at prayer. He realized that, for the first time, she was having a conversation with her father.

She did not know how long she had been talking. She had begun at the beginning, and told her father all about her life: her childhood, her art, Stephen, the childlessness, the divorce, the move to Venice, Murano, the house in the Campo Manin, and Alessandro. She talked of Corradino, of her extraordinary fondness for her – for their – ancestor. She spoke of the stain of treachery of which she had just learned, of Roberto, Vittoria and *Professore* Padovani. She even spoke of Elinor, of their difficult relationship, and asked about the Elinor that Bruno knew – that different Elinor of long ago, the romantic and reckless Elinor, so different from the buttoned and bitter woman that Leonora knew. She talked herself to a standstill, and felt better. She looked up at last, stretched her aching legs, and beckoned to a hovering Alessandro that they could go. As he started towards her she turned for one private farewell. She laid her hand on the warm stone with affection. 'Goodbye. I'll come again.'

And I will.

Alessandro and she walked to the *vaporetto* stop and prepared to cross the Styx again – but this time the water would take them from the province of the dead back to the land of the living. She had found some peace here. She still needed to find the truth about Corradino but it had done her good to connect with her father – her immediate family – first. And he had been so easy to talk to. She had told him everything. Everything save one thing.

I didn't tell him I was pregnant.

CHAPTER 22

The Island of the Dead (part 2)

The feeling of grit in my mouth, grating between my teeth.

In his dream Corradino was on the Lido di Venezia, with his mother. The household were on a summer trip and the servants had roasted oysters on the beach while *piccolo* Corradino ran hither and thither in the surf, soaking his breeches with the whispering salt water. He was called to eat, and reclined on the blood-coloured velvet cushions with his mother's arm around him, her bosom smelling of vanilla. He tried an oyster for the first time, his eight-year-old palate first rejecting, then accepting the gelatinous creature as it slid down his throat. He tasted the oyster once it had left his mouth, and so began a lifelong partiality for this peasant food. The taste remained in the grittiness of the sand, left as a residue on his tongue, like sand washed up by a high tide; the *acqua alta*. In his dream he tasted the sand, the flesh of the oyster and the vanilla scent of his mother all at once, but when he woke at last, he knew he was far from the happiness of that day.

He felt the coarse sackcloth pressing on his face, planting a rough kiss on his lips like the greeting of his uncle Ugolino. Always bearded, it was ever a scratchy embrace – a traitor's kiss. Corradino struggled to breathe and turned his head slightly – it was better, but the stifling dark was hot and crushing and he was afraid. As his head turned he heard a metallic chink and felt two cold objects fall to the back of his head – the two ducat coins that Giacomo had pressed on his eyes after death, to pay the ferryman. He felt them move in his hair, cold metal for the dead sliding among the warm hair of the living. Perspiration soaked him in an instant as panic swelled in his throat and he fought the desperate urge to struggle and scream. They had not bound him, as they had promised not to, but they had no need – he could not feel his legs. A muffled scream escaped him once, then with a supreme effort he calmed himself. To keep the black panic at bay he began, for the next long moments, to remember with exactitude, with perfect detail, what the Frenchman had said.

'Corradino, have you heard of *Romeo e Giulietta*?'

Corradino was sitting in the confessional of his church, Santi Maria e Donato on the island of Murano. All the *maestri* worshipped here on Sundays. Religious observance was not required by the State, as the civic attitude was summed up in the phrase; '*Veneziani prima, poi cristiani*'

– 'Venetians first, then Christians'. But the glassblowers were more devout than most, as they appreciated the gifts which elevated them above the common man. Corradino, in the arrogance of a great artisan, often had the blasphemous notion that he and God shared the same satisfaction in the creation of beauty. In his humbler moods he felt himself a tool or instrument of the Creator. Sometimes he listened to the words of the mass, but on other days he spent long moments marvelling at the Byzantine splendour of the mosaic that adorned the nave floor. He felt a respect and a brotherhood for the long-dead-craftsmen who knew how to combine such abstract patterns with realistic beasts. In the universe of the mosaic nature was strange and sometimes inverted; here an eagle carried off a deer in his talons, there two roosters carried a helpless fox slung from a pole.

The mosaic is allegorickal – it describes my own existence to me. It is made of thousands of nuggets of glass just as my life is, and it depicts nature as it is and nature as it is not. Some of my daily life has remained the same, some is greatly changed.

Today he had come to confession as usual, but he did not confess to his usual priest. He realized as soon as the voice spoke in the warm dark that it was Duparcmieur.

They had never met in the same place twice, and no longer in Venice. The Frenchman had been a merchant on Burano where Corradino had gone to buy gold leaf,

Duparcmieur's costume flamboyant enough to make him disappear in the spectrum of the multicoloured fishing houses. He had been a boatman who murmured to Corradino in low tones as he rowed the ferry between Venice and Giudecca. And now, he was a Catholic priest.

He changes every time so completely, like the fabled lizards of the Indies who can dissemble as a leaf or a rock. I feel that I live in a dream, or a commedia *played out by actors in San Marco.*

But Duparcmieur was no comic muse – he dealt in Death. Today they were here to plan Corradino's demise, although the Frenchman's opening gambit seemed to belie the seriousness of their business.

'*Romeo e Giulietta*?' Corradino was bemused. But he had learned in their conversations that it were best to answer the Frenchman literally – apart from anything else, it saved time.

Although Corradino's formal education was halted at ten when Monsieur Loisy was wrested from him, Giacomo had done right by him and continued the boy's tutelage as best he could. So Corradino was able to reply with some confidence. 'It's an old tale, supposedly true, from Verona during the Italian wars, about two tragic lovers from opposing families. It was written up into a story, and embellished, by a monk; Matteo Bandello.'

'Very good.' Duparcmieur's voice passed clearly through

the grille, dry as sand, and low enough not to be overheard through the thick frontal drapes of the confessional.

'You may be interested to know that it was lately made into a play in England by one Master William Shakespeare. It was written in the time of *La Reine* Elizabeth, but I believe its popularity continues at court even now. It is the final act of the tragedy that concerns us; or, more specifically, you.'

Corradino waited. He had learned, too, that interruptions were fruitless.

'In the play, Giulietta takes a Mantuan poison in order to avoid an unwelcome marriage. The draught makes the body mimic death in every particular – the countenance grows paler, the pulses slow to an imperceptible rate, the fires of the humours are damped – but not extinguished. Pain is never felt – even attempts to bleed the victim yield no flow of blood, and give no pain. In the drama, Giulietta wakes, some days later, unharmed as if from a deep sleep. Of course by then, her beau has taken his own life and all is for nought. But this is not the burden of our tale.' Duparcmieur dismissed the fates of the long-dead lovers in a manner Corradino found chilling. 'The point is, my dear Corradino, that one thing your little city states make rather well – for it certainly isn't the food or wine,' he sniffed fastidiously, 'is poison.' He took a breath. 'I suppose that in all those years of internecine strife, your Guelfs and Ghibbelines, your Borgias and Medicis, the art became somewhat,' he searched for a phrase, 'more *developed* than in my own more civilized nation.'

This Corradino would not have. 'Perhaps you are forgetting the wonderful artistic heritage of our states, sponsored by those very warring families? Is art not civilization? Does France boast a Leonardo, or a Michelangelo? And perhaps you also forget that you have come to *me* to ask for *my* expertise to help *your* King?'

He heard the impossible man chuckling through the grille. 'You have fire in your belly, Corradino. That's good. But you must learn to love France, you know, it will be your country too soon enough, with the will of God. Now, to business.' The Frenchman's voice changed abruptly. 'When we leave this confessional, kneel and kiss my hand. In it I hold the draught I have procured for you. Not, it is true, from Mantua, but from somewhere in your own fair Republic. Take it tonight, and but three hours later you will fall into a deep state of sleep, and never wake in the morning. Instead you will sleep the day through. That night, you will wake one day exactly, almost to the moment, from the time you fell asleep.'

'And where will I be then?'

'Well, here you must inform me, Corradino. Who is it that will find your body?'

Corradino shivered at the term – Duparcmieur spoke as if he were already dead. He thought for a moment but needed no longer – he knew that if he did not appear at the *fornace* for the first time in ten years save for the time he had the water sickness, Giacomo would come to his house as he had that day too. The old man had brought him an eel from the market, and an orange, bright as a tiny sun, which was reputed to clear the sickness, and did.

'Giacomo – my . . . friend will find me.'

'Very well. And does he love you well enough to provide the proper rites for you? Or will you be put in the pauper's pit on Sant'Ariano? It matters not, we can plan for each eventuality.'

Corradino found that the only way to contemplate the plan was to adopt the impersonal tone of Duparcmieur. If he thought closely about the actuality he would drive himself distracted.

'He will pay for a burial.'

Corradino felt, rather than saw, Duparcmieur nod on the other side of the grille. 'Then he will send for the constables. But they will not be those of The Ten, they will be working for me. You will be taken to Sant'Ariano, and when you wake you will be buried under soil.'

Corradino choked, as if in anticipation of this fate. 'What?'

'My dear man,' said the Frenchman smoothly, 'consider that you may well be followed even after death by those that watch you now.' Duparcmieur, after some reflection, thought that he would not trouble Corradino with the possibility that The Ten may send their own *medico* to check that Corradino was truly dead, and that the doctor might, as had been known, plunge a surgical blade deep into the corpse's chest just to be sure. He merely continued; 'everything must appear true. My men will not bind you, and they will not bury you deep. You will easily be able to escape once your strength returns.'

'And when will that be?'

'Ah yes. Now listen well, Corradino. Your limbs will take some little time to regain their feeling. Your head and neck will wake first, as they reign supreme in the corporeal order. Then your heart and chestspoon and arms. Then as your humours heat in your stomach again your legs will gradually regain their feeling, with your feet waking last of all. Be not afraid as this process happens, for giving way to your fears will rob the vapours around you of their nourishing gases. Instead you must think of this conversation, remain calm, and wait to make your escape. Do you have a good knife?'

I will take no chances – I will make one myself. I will trust no other man's blade with an office such as this.

'Yes.'

'Then secrete it in your hose before you take the draught. You'll need it to cut the sacking and dig.' Again, the Frenchman thought that the possibility that The Ten's doctor would find and confiscate the knife was best kept from Corradino. The thought brought him to a more important concealment; 'and, Corradino, that book that you carry, which details your methods,' he met the glassblower's surprised gaze candidly, 'of course we know of it. You must hide that on your person too, and we must hope it is not discovered . . . ahem . . . *post mortem*. We are buying yourself *and* your secrets, Corradino, and if France is to steal a march on Venice in the matter of glassware, we cannot afford for your notebook to remain in the city. Unless, of course,' here the veiled eyes lifted, 'you wish to entrust the book to me now? No? I thought not.'

Corradino swallowed. His voice nearly failed as he asked, 'and if I get out, what next?'

'When, my dear fellow, when,' said Duparcmieur airily. 'Then you do exactly as I'm about to tell you.'

Corradino sat in his house on Murano as the sky darkened outside. He looked around the simple but homely room with affection, but soon his eyes were inexorably pulled back to the vial in his hands. He knew not how long he had been staring at the little bottle – roughly made green glass with a sedimentary liquid gleaming dully inside. It looked like canal water – had the Frenchman been duped? Or worse, had Corradino been given a deadly poison instead – had Duparcmieur realized that he had made a mistake in recruiting him but that Corradino now knew too much to live? Corradino chased such thoughts away by perusing the glasswork with a professional eye – unevenly made, but the ground glass stopper fit snugly, and there was quite a pleasing luminance to the bottle.

'Tis passing strange that my *destiny is now held inside a vial of glass.*

He thought suddenly of Giacomo, and felt sorry for what was to come. He felt like he was losing his father all over again, and experienced the crushing remorse that Giacomo was about to feel the pain of losing a son. He would visit him tonight, one last time.

Giacomo.

Could Corradino let him suffer, when he would still be alive, perhaps prospering in France with Leonora? Duparcmieur had warned him sternly to tell no one of the plan, or all would be discovered. But Giacomo? Surely it would be safe to tell him ... no ... to *hint* to him? Before he could change his mind, Corradino unstoppered the vial and drank back the draught. Fear almost made him vomit, but he swallowed back the bitter bile, for if he spat the poison all would be lost. His mouth tasted faintly of almonds, and he began to feel a strange sense of euphoria. Giddy, he reached for his quill and inkpot and sand, and scratched some words on a page of his book which he tore from its parent. As he sanded the words he fervently hoped they were true. Then he left the house for Giacomo's, tossing the bottle discreetly into the canal as he had been told, the poison already coursing through his veins.

★ ★ ★

If he reached down, his numb fingers crawling down his leg, a pale subterranean spider, he could feel the outline of the black *dente* inside his breeches. Wrapped beside it was the vellum book. His relief that his secrets had been buried with him was almost as great as finding that the knife had not been found. After three tries he pulled the blade from his stocking, ripping through the fabric. Slowly, so slowly, he fought the weight of the soil as he ponderously drew the knife up to his chest.

At least I have the means to end my life if I cannot free myself.

Once he was sure that his legs were awake, and that every toe could be moved in turn, Corradino began to cut the sacking over his trunk.

Night earth everywhere, dark and damp and heavy, in my eyes and in my mouth.

Corradino spat and coughed and heaved, his chest bursting as he dug ever upwards. *Giulietta* he thought, *Giulietta.* The name came incongruously to his mind in his panicked state, he repeated it in his head like an *Ave Maria*, then he said the *Ave Maria*, then he muddled the two in his head, the Blessed Virgin and the tragic heroine becoming one in his addled head, together with his mother Maria and *piccola* Leonora, whom all this was for. He dug and choked for what seemed hours, ever fearful that they had buried him too deep, that they had packed the earth down, that they never meant him to get out, that he was digging sideways and not upwards and would therefore dig forever until he drowned in soil. Then a coolness and a wetness on his fingertips. Blood? No – rain and a night breeze. He dug frantically, his lungs on fire, and gasped the night air in the most beautiful moment of his life. He staggered from his grave, weak, vomiting, and sat for a moment digging the earth out of his eyes. Rain pelted down and turned him to a man of mud. He thought he would never be afraid again.

But soon fear returned. He remembered the Frenchman's warning; 'Keep yourself low, and invisible. They may still be looking out for you. Get to the north side of the island, look for the lights of San Marco in the distance and follow them. Then look for me.'

Once again Corradino pressed into the ground. He crawled over the cemetery, face to face with numberless corpses, separated only by a stratus of earth. His hands clawed divots of soil and strange plants that bloomed on the flesh of the dead. He thought he heard ghastly whispers, and his memory did not spare him the details of Dante's *Inferno* and the dreadful inmates, mutilated sinners, traitors like his uncle, traitors like himself. He seemed to crawl for ever, every moment expecting to grasp a rotten limb or to feel the crunch of bones below. As his hands reached out to grasp the turf ahead of him, he felt a hundred spidery forms crawl over his arm. He stifled a scream and remembered that these were no insects of hell but the *mazzenette*, the soft-shell crabs that were fished in these islands. Tonight was full moon so the catch was larger, as the crabs responded eerily to the pull of the lunar tides. He shook the creatures from his sleeve and kept onward, but the creatures were on his face and in his hair. He kept his terror at bay by remembering that one of his favourite dishes as a child had been made from these very crabs. Graziella, their elderly cook at the Palazzo Manin, had taken him to the kitchens and shown him how she dropped the living creatures into her pancake mix to gorge themselves to death, whereupon the crabs were cooked, with an eggy softness both inside and outside the shell. Corradino crawled forever, crablike himself, his stomach turning with the thought that the crabs that he had enjoyed must have fed on the flesh of the dead. Never more would one pass his lips. Then at last he saw San Marco, the lights from a thousand windows shining like votive candles. His eyes made out a cloaked figure and a fishing bark in the quarterlight. Instantly his treacherous memory recalled the phantom at the *fornace* when he was ten. Had that angel of death come to claim him at last? Sweat mingled with the rain as he croaked out the agreed greeting: '*Vicentini mangia gatti.*'

The answer came back: '*Veronesi tutti matti.*'

Corradino had never thought he would be glad to see Gaston Duparcmieur. But he could have wept with joy as he went to board the boat, and grasped the proffered hand with real warmth.

As he hunched, chilled, in the bottom of the bark as it shot silently into the lagoon with no more than the faint plash of the oars, Corradino considered the truth of the passwords. The Veronese were mad indeed – Giulietta was a Veronese, and she must have been mad to put herself through what he had just experienced. But then he checked himself.

She was not mad, for she did what she did for love. And so did I.

CHAPTER 23

The Vessel

To have wanted something for so long, to have hoped against hope, until hope itself dies, and resignation sets in. To have almost forgotten what it was that you wanted so much. And then, at last, to be given the thing that you desired, and be filled with joy and terror in equal measure. Venice is a prism. Light enters white and leaves in a rainbow of colours. Everything is changed here. I am changed.

Leonora lay beside Alessandro with her hands on her bare stomach, holding the child within.

The cacophony of bells that rang through Venice always woke her, while the native Alessandro slept solidly through the city's song.

Be not afeared. The isle is full of noises,
Sounds, and sweet airs, that give delight and hurt not . . .

She never minded this waking – it was a delight to her to be pulled from her dreams by the bells, to lie in the gold morning light watching the curve of Alessandro's back, perhaps gently touching his warm hair, and to think idly of the day ahead. But today her thoughts were muddled as she attempted to absorb what had happened to her and the implications for her life. Her mind raced from the practical – what would she tell Adelino? What of her job? Did she still have one? – to the fantastical; she and Alessandro dandling a golden-headed child as their gondola swooped beneath the Bridge of Sighs. Her thoughts were ordered in one aspect – like a flock of gulls at a trawler they wheeled away singly but returned always to mass at the straining nets. All her thoughts came back to the child within her, and above all, how to tell Alessandro.

She had thought for so long that she was 'barren'. The old fashioned word stuck in her head. It seemed so expressive of everything in her life then – not just the childlessness but the sensation of being alone, left. 'Barren' described an empty, dark, Brontë moorland where nothing grew and no one ever trod. Her 'barrenness' had become a part of her, the label that she applied to herself. She carried it like a burden. So entrenched was her psyche that after the 'safe sex' of their first encounter, she had never used contraception with Alessandro. He, in the Italian way, had assumed that Leonora was 'taking care of it'. She said that she was.

I believed it myself.

So convinced was she that nothing could happen that even the classic sign that a schoolgirl would recognize with dread – morning nausea – had passed her by unnoticed. Even the absence of her periods she had attributed to the stress of the row at work and the press revelations, but in the end, she could ignore the signs no more that signalled that her barren body was actually bearing fruit. She did not understand the science of it – that what would not work with one man would work with another.

Perhaps fate or nature (for that goddess has many names) has a way of divining when one has found the right person. After all Stephen was the wrong person, and he had had no difficulty in getting Carol pregnant.

Stephen. She had not thought of him for weeks. He . . . they . . . must have had their child by now. What kind of father had he made? Leonora imagined he was somewhat of an absentee – there for school reports and hothousing but not for midnight feeds. He seemed a long way away. But Alessandro was here.

And he could be *the right man, I know it.*

But how would he take the news? Leonora had read enough literature and seen enough movies to know that the classic response of the foreign lothario was to disappear without trace at the first mention of a child. It was not lost on her that her situation uncannily reflected her mother's, and that Elinor and Bruno had had anything but a happy ending.

And yet, yesterday had been a day of almost perfect happiness. Though the wind was cold, the low orange November sun shone constantly, burnishing the city, making her friendly once more. When she was with Alessandro she felt the city loved her again. Only when she was alone did the palaces wear a different mask, and the shadows threaten her with figures and footfalls. After they returned from the cemetery Alessandro took her to the water-borne vegetable market at the Ponte dei Pugni, where the vendors sold their wares from *bragozzo* boats strung out under the bridge. As they wandered at the canalside, smelling the fragrant orange zucchini blossoms and the wizened porcini mushrooms, or handling the heavy bruise-black eggs that were the aubergines, Leonora felt a heady sensation of contentment. If only he were always here. If only they could bridge the distance that he had imposed between them, not the geographical distance necessitated by his training, but the psychological sense of removal that she felt at almost every moment they spent together.

There is something holding him back, I know it.

And now, she was aware that her news would change everything. It may cost her any semblance of togetherness they had. To stay the thought she pressed her belly harder.

At least I have you.

Her child. With her hands on her stomach, she imagined it growing, distending as it must over the next few months. She saw her stomach as a parison, growing to a perfect roundness as the breath of life filled it. She herself was now a vessel – the host for the child within. Venice had breathed a new life into her. She was an hourglass, swelling to mark the months before her burden would be delivered. The running sands, the baby, the glass, all seemed connected in an enormous, fateful plan. She felt as strong and as brittle as glass itself. All her old hopes sprang alive again – those long forgotten excitements that she remembered from back when she and Stephen were first trying. Names, nursery colours, imagining the face of the child by mentally combining her features with his. And now, even if Alessandro left, she had his child. Her features would be combined with his now. 'Our child,' she said aloud to her belly.

Alessandro rolled over sleepily. 'What did you say?'

The moment had come.

She turned to him so they faced each other. Her swollen breasts fell sideways on the coverlet and a skein of gold hair fell across her face. As he brushed it away Alessandro thought she had never looked more beautiful, as if lit from within. He reached for her but she stopped him with the words. She had never liked the bald clinical statement "I'm pregnant," so instead she said, 'I'm going to have your child.'

Shock registered on his face, and after a dazed moment his hands searched for her belly and rested there with hers. Then he lowered his head and she felt his soft curls as he laid his rough cheek on her stomach. She felt a wetness, and when he raised his face it was running with tears. From that moment she knew that it would be alright.

It was alright. Alessandro was delighted and called everyone he knew with the news that he was going to have a son. 'How do you know?' laughed Leonora as he refused to consider the alternative. 'I just do,' he said. She teased him with being a 'typical Italian', but he did not rise, saying, 'No, no, *cara*, if we had a girl I would love her just as much. But I *know* this is a boy.' And he refused to be moved.

For the rest of the morning he treated her like the glass of her metaphor, bringing water, getting her chairs, and lifting even the lightest burdens for her. She teased him, but her teasing came of sheer relief and gladness.

And yet . . .

All too soon, he was gone. Today was a public holiday, the day after All Souls Sunday, but tomorrow his course began again. He must return this afternoon, to complete his reading before tomorrow morning. As he left the house he kissed her with extra tenderness, but in all the sweetness Leonora thought of the week ahead without him. And after that, when he took up his post in Venice, what then?

I dare not ask.

Leonora fidgeted around the house, fruitlessly beginning tasks she could not finish, and then decided to go to the Sansoviniana Library and do some digging about Corradino. For tomorrow she must go back to the *fornace*, to face Adelino's wrath over the shattered ad campaign and now this news.

And then what?

She had to be honest with herself. In all his excitement Alessandro had never once mentioned future plans. All talk had been of the child, and while Leonora did not expect a Victorian proposal of marriage, she now thought it strange that he had never once mentioned the possibility of moving in.

As she walked across the *campo*, Leonora felt the city begin to retreat from her again. She felt her lover and her profession slipping away and the cold, empty Venice of winter closing in. She thought of the tourists and trippers, the pleasure-seekers and lotus-eaters who had now gone.

They never saw the city like this. This was the facet of the place that was for residents only. The dark days, the old stones, and the emptiness. She held her head high and thought only of her child.

I must find out about Corradino before the baby is born. I must reconcile my past before I turn to the future. For Corradino is the baby's past too.

CHAPTER 24

Banished

'I'm sorry, Leonora.'

To be fair, he did look sorry. Adelino also looked old and ill.

'I've had to cancel the campaign. They're calling in my debts. I can't possibly keep you on just now.' He walked to the window of his office, as he always did, searching for comfort in the peerless view.

Leonora felt a lurch in her stomach.

Was that the baby? Or the realization that I've just lost the job that I came here for?

She put a hand down there and he turned in time to catch the gesture. He waved at her stomach.

'And now with your ... wonderful news, there are not just financial considerations but implications for your health. All the chemicals and pigments that we use here, to say nothing of the heat. You'd have to leave soon anyway. When are you due? February?'

She nodded.

'Well.' He sat heavily at his desk. 'Let's just call this maternity leave. I'll have to see how things go here. I must re-trench.'

Leonora found her voice, 'And afterwards?'

Adelino shook his head. 'I really don't know. It depends on business. We always have a slump in between Christmas and *Carnevale*. It could be the end of me.' He took off his glasses and rubbed his eyes. 'To be honest Leonora, I can't afford to pay you anything, apart from your money to the end of the month. You could sue me, I suppose, for maternity pay, or whatever you call it. It would certainly be a first on this island. But there's nothing to give you.'

'I never asked.' She felt absurdly like crying – as if she had done this to him. Although she never wanted a part of the ad campaign, and although it was *his* greed that had sunk his ships, she felt responsible.

'I'd love to say that you could come back. But the truth is, I just don't know. And certainly for the moment, in the light of all the press your presence here is somewhat . . .'

She finished for him, 'Embarrassing?'

Adelino's eyes, small and unfamiliar without his glasses, dropped to the desk.

There was one more thing she must know. 'And Roberto? Will you reinstate him?'

'Leonora, you're not listening. I can't employ *anyone* else at present, however accomplished. Even if . . .'

'Even if what? You've tried, haven't you?'

Adelino let out a long sigh. 'I went to see him, yes. But his neighbours said he'd gone away.'

'Gone? Where?'

'They don't know. They think abroad.'

Leonora looked at him. She wanted to feel anger but felt instead only pity. Her sadness at the inevitable course of the interview was only tempered by relief that Roberto had gone from the city.

She got up. She walked down the stairs, through the hot door, and onto the factory floor. The men stopped to stare, but without Roberto's malign presence she felt animosity but no sense of danger. She felt the heat of the furnaces, so well-loved, so final. The *maestri* swung their blowpipe *canne* in cooling arcs like so many pendulums. Tick, tock. Time is up. She looked at the pieces of glass, a rainbow of colours, ranged around the workshop in various states of evolution. She smelled the silica and sulphur and turned for the door before the flames blurred in her tears. It felt so odd, this muddle of emotions. In one sense, she was happier than she had ever been. She was going to have a child, a child that grew inside her every day. She held the heart at her throat. The baby was *this* size now – the size of the heart she wore. But at the same time, she had lost what she came here for. Her creative outlet, her livelihood. Outside she took her leave of the street sign.

The Fondamenta Manin. If I could just find out that Corradino was innocent, if he could become a hero again, could he save this place that I have helped to ruin?

CHAPTER 25

The King

Corradino felt sick. He didn't know whether the stench was worse inside or outside of the carriage – outside the bewildering sounds and rotten smells of Paris, and inside the overpowering perfume of the powdered and pomaded Duparcmieur, all dressed up for their audience with the King. Corradino, too, was richly dressed in fine brocade; his transition from the mud-covered-risen-dead to aristocrat-amongst-craftsmen had been accomplished on the voyage. He felt even sicker now than he had then, when he was shuttled from bark to boat, from boat to ship, from ship to carriage.

I could vomit on my fine new breeches.

Paris seemed to him a bewildering and hellish place. Against all sense it was the *space* that oppressed him – the tight canals and *calli* of Venice and Murano had made him feel secure, but here the streets were wide and he felt vulnerable.

And the stench.

The smell of human ordure was everywhere – no wonder Duparcmieur constantly held a small perfumed kerchief to his nose. At least in Venice there was an efficient and healthy disposal of wastes; with a canal on every doorstep, you could merely throw your filth into the water, or shit directly into the canal. Here it seemed that the sluggish brown Seine was a central artery of human waste that infected the whole city with its stench and miasma of pests.

And the noise! In Venice there was barely a sound to be heard beyond the gentle splashing waters as gondolas cleaved through the canal's surface. The only cacophonies were the pleasing sounds of *Carnevale* merriment or play-making. Here Corradino's head rang to the sound of horses' hooves, and the rumble of carriage wheels. Before today the greatest number of horses that Corradino had seen together were the four bronze statues standing silent sentinel over Venice from the top of the Basilica di San Marco. Here there were thousands of the creatures – big, ugly and unpredictable. The foul sweet aroma of their leavings was everywhere in the streets, steaming piles which the well dressed citizens stepped delicately over.

The buildings, while tall and grand, had none of the delicate traceries of the Venetian palaces on the Canal

Grande. But they were certainly imposing. One great white church reached high into the sky, with twin towers and spires of jagged teeth.

'Observe,' said Duparcmieur, 'the magnificent gargoyles watching over us.'

A comical word. What can the fellow mean?

As Corradino craned out of the carriage he saw, high up, malevolent demons crouched in the masonry, gazing down on him with ill intent. He drew back in, suddenly afraid, and as the carriage drew up at a particularly impressive edifice Corradino felt a wholly unwanted pang for the city he had left behind.

'We're here,' said Duparcmieur, as a powdered and liveried footman sprang to open the carriage door.

The King's presence chamber was gilded and grand, but, to Corradino's mind, not a patch on the Palazzo Ducale where he had been with his father for an audience with the Doge.

And the *King* himself – wholly unexpected.

Slumped in a beautifully carved chair elevated on a dais, the monarch's face was all but obscured by the curls of his wig as he leaned to the floor where a small dog played around his ringed hand. The dog slavered for a treat concealed in the King's chubby palm. Ever a student of detail,

Corradino noted the richness of the rings on the plump fingers, and the white powder clogged in the creases between the royal digits. Although they had been announced, the King spoke as if to himself.

'A gift from the English King. *Epagneul de Roi Charles.* A "King Charles spaniel".' A strange fit seemed to come over him as he began to snuffle like a truffling pig.

Corradino waited for the Royal aides to step forward with a draught of medicine, or to burn a feather under the King's nose to bring him out of his malady, when he realized the King was *laughing*.

'The English King is a dog! The English King is a dog! And a little one too!' Louis enjoyed his own wit for some further moments, before returning to the game. 'I shall call you Minou. A good French name. *Yes* I will. *Yes* I will.'

The spaniel circled the hand, impatient now, and was rewarded for her persistence as the King relinquished the comfit. The dog gobbled the bon-bon, and then squatted, shivering and straining, to shit on the rug. There was silence as the court regarded the perfect turd glistening on the priceless Persian weave. Corradino looked to the King, anticipating anger, but the fit had overtaken him again – the King threw back his head in mirth and Corradino at last saw his face. Contorted like the gargoyle he had seen earlier, eyes closed and streaming, with a slick of mucus from nose to mouth. Corradino felt nothing but contempt for this man who was said to be the greatest monarch in Christendom. He glanced to Duparcmieur, who bowed low and made as if to leave, clearly acknowledging that the planned audience would not take place today. Corradino followed suit and they had all but reached the door when a voice stayed them.

'Duparcmieur!'

Both men turned to meet the sight of a different man sitting on the throne. The face was composed, the wig arranged, the eyes flint.

'So you have brought me the Venetian to complete my vision, yes?'

Duparcmieur's smooth mask slipped for an instant in the face of such a startling transition, but soon the practised urbanity was back.

'Yes, Majesty. Allow me to present Signor Corrado Manin of the fair city of Venice. I believe and trust that you will not be disappointed in his artistry.'

'Hmmmm.' The King tapped his teeth with a nail, both teeth and nail yellow against the powdered white cheeks. And then, abruptly, 'Have you seen the Sainte Chapelle?'

Corradino realized he was being addressed. He bowed low. 'No, Your Majesty.'

'You should. It is really quite beautiful. It is considered a marvellous example of stained glasswork.' For a moment the King's face seemed to shine with pride at his city's finest jewel. 'But of course, it is in fact, no more beautiful to me than Minou's little tribute there.' To underline his startling *volte face*, he indicated the dog's waste, still sitting on the rug. 'Little nuggets of glass, multicoloured fancies, tiny bon-bons, minute panes all muddled together. Good enough for a child. Good enough for God.' He rose from his chair. 'But I am King. I want glorious, clean glass, huge pieces, mirrors of white and gold to reflect my Majesty. Can you do that for me, *Signore*?'

Corradino was afraid, but he knew his capabilities. 'Yes,' he said in ringing tones. 'I can.'

The King smiled pleasantly. 'Good.' He came close – Duparcmieur lowered his head but Corradino met the royal eyes. 'If you please me, we will reward you greatly. Fail me, and you will find me no more merciful than your own Venetian overlords, with their embarrassingly *thorough* methods of justice.' The King turned and walked back to his throne, deliberately stepping in the dog turd on the way. As the great doors closed on Duparcmieur and himself, Corradino could see the underside of the King's satin slipper, smeared with shit.

Duparcmieur was surprisingly cheerful in the carriage. 'Good. You've met the King, and he seems pleased with you. I thought that went terribly well.'

Corradino was amazed and silent.

'Do you not think he is indeed the most glorious of monarchs?'

'My experience of monarchs is limited to that one audience, Duparcmieur, but I'll admit he had an . . . interesting . . . manner.'

In truth your King is a disgusting child, but to speak my thought would show little diplomacy, and may even be dangerous.

'You find him charming? I do. He seemed in a very good mood today.'

I hope that I am never witness to his bad mood.

Duparcmieur leaned forward in a businesslike fashion.'Now, we'll take you to your lodgings in Trianon – quite well appointed, I think you'll find. We have provided work clothes for you there. When you are properly attired for work I'll take you to the site of the palace at Versailles. I think you will be impressed by the building work – it looks marvellous already. Although, you have seen many marvels today, to be sure.'

Corradino grimly agreed. He had seen a King who was not a King. Thinking of the monarch's double nature he voiced a concern which had grown in his chestspoon over the last hours. 'Duparcmieur. How can I know that I can trust you and your – the King? How do I know that you will bring Leonora to me as you promised, and that you will not kill me when I have told my secrets?'

Duparcmieur met his troubled eyes with a candid gaze. Either the eyes of a man telling the truth or the eyes of a practised liar.

'My dear fellow, you have my word. I don't know how you run things in Venice, but in France a man's word is his bond.'

'Oh in Venice too. Even The Ten keep their word once given, for good or ill.'

'Then you understand me. I propose that you teach our foreman your ways with the mirror for one month, to show good faith. Then we bring Leonora to you. Then you remain for the next eleven months to oversee the work in the palace. At the end of the year you are free, to live with your daughter, and you can work with the glass or not, just as you choose.'

It sounds too wonderful to be true.

'Your foreman of the glassworks, what kind of man is he?'

'His name is Guillaume Seve. He is very experienced, a man of mature years, a good craftsman.'

Corradino shook his head. 'No good. I need a young man, someone with natural aptitude, a willingness to learn, but who has not already learned all the wrong methods. Someone who will learn from me, a *servente*, not someone older than me.'

'Very well.' Duparcmieur thought for a moment. 'Then that would probably be Jacques Chauvire, just an apprentice, but talented. He is but one and twenty.'

Corradino nodded. 'Perfect. It will take time, and dedication. Such things cannot be taught in a short span.'

Duparcmieur sat back. 'All will be well,' he said airily.

'You'll have everything you need – time, materials, men. The palace will be magnificent, you'll see.'

★ ★ ★

The palace already was. Sitting in new work clothes, the leather of his apron and wrist bands smelling sweetly, Corradino sat with his back to the half built palace facing the gardens. His back rested on newly-hewn masonry warmed by the setting sun, he watched the gardeners shaping the gorgeous green lawns for as far as the eye could see, while waterworkers diverted natural sources into the huge ornamental lakes which began to fill before his eyes – great mirrors themselves. Despite the distant chink of the mason's hammer and the banging of carpentry Corradino felt at peace for the first time since he arrived in France. A shadow cut his sun and he looked up – a gangly youth with tousled hair and dark eyes held a hand to him.

'I'm Jacques Chauvire.'

Corradino took the hand and pulled himself to his feet. The boy, expecting a handshake, smiled at the unexpectedness of the action. Corradino's eyes were level with his. The boy had good eyes, dark and true. He had no need to search for their meaning like he did with Duparcmieur. Nor was it lost on him that the name Jacques was the French version of Giacomo, the family he had left behind.

'Let's get to work, Jacques,' said Corradino. He threw a friendly arm around the boy's shoulders, turned his back on the vista and they walked together to the foundry.

The boy will do.

CHAPTER 26

Purgatorio

When I entered the fornace at Versailles I was at home at last.

As Jacques opened the secret chamber to which only he and his new master had the key, Corradino saw that all that he had asked for had been given to him. There were the water vats, the silvering tanks. There was the furnace, with the coals stoked and ready, and a glowing red gather of *cristallo* glass at its heart. There were his *pontelli*, his blowpipes, his paddles. There were his *scagno* saddles and *borselle* pliers. There were his pigments; lapis blue, scarab red and leaf gold among them. There were his bottles and flasks of nitrates and sulfates and mercuries. Here then, at home, he could work once again.

His printless fingers itched to touch the rods and pigments, to make something again after his long month at sea and on road. The presence of Jacques at his shoulder felt incongruous, so used was he to working alone. But today was the day he must at last share his methods, and he felt a sick reluctance in his chestspoon. Not because he thought the boy's skills would ever exceed his, but because he alone had made mirrors in this way for ten years now, and he felt he was giving away a precious possession; a part of himself, a skill which had defined him for so long.

A skill which has saved my life, for 'twas for this that The Ten spared me. Once this has gone from my grasp what do I have to protect me from the King?

Would Louis decide, once Corradino had told his secret, that he would be better out of the way? And yet what choice did he have? He was in Purgatory, waiting for Leonora to be brought to him, and the sharing of his methods had been part of the bargain which would bring her to these shores. He was in Limbo. A wholly unwanted memory of Dante's couplets chimed in his head. He recalled that, in *Il Purgatorio*, his namesake had been killed by a French King. Corradino, the doomed Prince of Sicily, was executed by Charles of Anjou following an unsuccessful coup. *That* Corradino's father, King Manfred, had been murdered too.

But as he turned and met Jacques' warm brown eyes – eager and shining, reflecting Corradino's own love of his trade – he felt comforted and set aside such gloomy thoughts. He had no son to pass his skills to, and perhaps never would, so this was his chance to share in his knowledge and enjoy teaching if he might.

There is Leonora of course, but no woman has ever been a glassblower, nor ever will.

All he hoped for his daughter was that she would be happy, marry well, and enjoy the family life that had been wrested from him.

'So,' he said to Jacques, with a firmness that belied his doubts, 'we begin.'

He took up the largest blowpipe, and reached into the fire for the molten *cristallo.* As he felt the heat blast his face he thought again of the words of Dante, but this time his favourite couplet: '*Even so rained down the everlasting heat, And, as steel kindles tinder, kindled the sands.*' Corradino was kindling the sands now, coaxing crystalline beauty from a quintessence of dust. He took such a large amount of gather on the end of his pipe that he had to constantly turn the rod as he blew the parison.

Jacques looked confused, and tentatively questioned his master. '*Maître*, I thought we were to make a mirror, not to blow glass?'

Corradino slid his eyes sideways as he blew. There was merriment there.

When the parison was blown Corradino spun the bubble on the end of the pipe and transferred it to his *pontello*. He then took the parison to the water tank and let it rest there, floating like a buoy. As it cooled he took a sharp blade and cut swiftly down the length of the bubble so the sides of the cylinder relaxed flat onto the surface of the water tank, and the amber glass cooled on the surface to a flat clear pane.

'So . . .' breathed Jacques into a reverent silence, '. . . that is how it is done.'

Corradino squatted and squinted with a practised eye down the surface of the tank. He nodded. 'Yes. That is how. 'Twas but an accident when I discovered it, but it is the only way to make a pane of such a size, with the same thickness throughout.'

'And the water?'

'Water, when stilled, is completely flat, wherever it lies on the earth. It is the original mirror – nature's mirror. Even if its tank or vessel is tilted, it will always find its true level. I just hope that the French waters of your pestilent river will make as fine a glass as the sweet *acqua* of Venice's lagoon. Now, we must dress the new-born.' He lifted the cooled pane tenderly and laid it on the surface of the neighbouring vat, which housed a molten silver compound so bright it resembled a mirror itself. 'This is mercury and silver sulfate,' said Corradino, 'but only on the surface. Here too there is water underneath.'

'Why, *Maître?*'

'Because these silvering compounds are very costly. Even for your King it would be too lavish to fill a whole tank with them. But there is sufficient on the surface to cover the glass with the correct thin skin to produce a reflection. You must always take care that you cover the entire surface of the tank, lest there are empty patches which will leave the glass clear. And take care of the mercury – it is an evil compound, and one that enters the skin of a man with ease. Many of our trade have died from its arts – I know of one such very close to me.' He smiled at his black jest as he recalled how he had imitated a mercury poisoning – blackening his own tongue with charcoal and letting the spittle run from his mouth on his 'deathbed'. But when he recalled how the sight of him must have greeted Giacomo he ceased to smile.

He turned back to Jacques. 'Just take care to let as little of the mixture touch you as you can. Here;' he demonstrated, using two small wads of leather to lift out the huge silvered pane. 'The silvering dries very quickly – see? It has almost parched in the heat of the furnace.'

Jacques looked on in awe as the compounds dried, and as they did, his blurred image resolved into a pin-sharp, bright perfection.

'Now, you see that the edges are rough, where I cut the parison? We score down the edges using the same knife and a metal rule,' Corradino suited the action to the words. 'It's only necessary to break the very surface of the silvering, because, as you see, the glass will snap off cleanly along the line you have made. Here there are many metal rules provided for us, for as you know, the crowning panes of our mirrors in the *palazzo* are to be curved, and for those you will need one of these.' Corradino held up a flexible length of metal, which he curved into shape. As Jacques nodded he turned back to the mirrored pane where it lay on the cutting saddle. 'At the last, we take a chamois leather,' he did so, 'dip it in alum, and polish the surface to both protect and brighten the pane. See?'

Jacques had thought the mirror could not be any brighter, but now the glass seemed to sing. His wonder and admiration showed in his face, and Corradino could see that his apprentice was full of questions. '*Maître*, how are mirrors made by others?'

'There have always been mirrors. The Arab infidels used to polish their shields in order to see their images. But in other nations they attempt to roll out the glass thinly from one piece, as if making a pie. The results are passable but it is impossible to make a very large pane this way – the glass cools and hardens, and is lumpy and uneven. But with breath you can make a parison as large as your winds will allow, and when you treat the glass as a cylinder its dimensions open out to more than double the shape you have made. 'Tis simple mathematicks.' He shrugged to deflect the admiration he saw in Jacques' eyes. But he saw something else too – he saw the boy's hands twitch towards the fire just as his own had done.

I know I have babbled aplenty – that I speak more words when talking of my work than at any other time. Those that know me may think me as dumb as an oyster. Let them but speak to me of the glass, they will hear what a prattling parrot I am become. Enough.

He uttered the words he thought he would never say. 'Now you try.'

CHAPTER 27

A Champion

Signor Aldo Savini, curator of rare books at the Libreria Sansoviniana in San Marco, was slightly surprised when asked by a blonde beauty to help her lift down the guild records of the glass and mirror makers of the seventeenth century. But she must be a registered reader. He checked her newly laminated card – she was clearly a Venetian from her name. He shrugged, and handed her a pair of thin cotton gloves from a dispenser. 'You must wear these, *Signorina.* These volumes are very old and fragile. Also you must use the bookstand provided, to minimize damage to the spine, and only turn the pages by the laminated marker. Don't touch the paper itself.'

La Signorina nodded seriously throughout his instruction. Her eyes were green but had silver shards in the centre, the colour of the olive leaves on the farm where Aldo Savini grew up. The librarian suddenly felt his heart quicken and pushed his glasses up his nose, as he always did when flustered. Aldo Savini was not yet forty, and beneath his sweater-vest and tie beat a romantic heart. As he helped the *Signorina* lift down the ancient volumes for the relevant date, her gold hair brushed his arm and he could smell her coconut shampoo mingled with the old leather and vellum of the books. As she smiled and thanked him, Aldo Savini thought he would kill dragons for Signorina Manin.

Aldo Savini saw '*la Principessa*' as he had secretly dubbed her, many times over the next few months. Always she had some peculiar request, which stimulated him as a librarian almost as much as her appearance stimulated him as a man. Guild records, inventories, wills, records of birth and death, letters, bills of works, he had found all these for her. Her questions, posed in perfect Veneziano, intrigued him too. They always revolved around the same man, Corrado Manin. Even Aldo Savini, in his cloistered life, had heard of the man. *La Principessa* hounded him with questions as she had soon found out that Aldo had trained in Paleography at the University of Bologna, and could read the cramped ancient writing where her reading failed her. Do these documents mention Corrado Manin? This mirror that the *Contessa* Dandolo left to the Frari church, was it a Manin? This bill of works for the Palazzo Bruni, does it mention the Manin candlebra? What year was the *palazzo* built? This ship's register, does the entry say Manin, or Marin? These records of death that cite poisoning, does this symbol mean mercury, or some other compound? Aldo Savini became fascinated by the quest, as he was fascinated by her. Apparently she had some help from Ca' Foscari, as she used to shuttle back and forth from the library to the university for advice, and arrive back with a crop of new leads. He divined soon that her helper was Ermanno Padovani, an eminent scholar who had many volumes in this very library. Some Sundays the *Principessa* did not come at all, and Aldo knew that she continued her search elsewhere, the *Professore* having given her, it seemed, fairly comprehensive access to the deepest and most precious sequestered archives of the city.

In his romantic mind, Aldo Savini became a knight championing the cause of the blonde *Principessa*. He saw himself facing the black knight, Ermanno Padovani, in the lists of bibliographical knowledge. He was determined to provide her with some sort of breakthrough, before the *Professore*, so he would be her hero.

Over the coming months of deepest winter, Aldo Savini's chivalric fantasy took a fresh turn. Because it soon became clear that the *Principessa* was pregnant. He saw her belly swell, her angel face take on a rounded, cherubic aspect. Once he saw her, lost in a ship's register, with her hair swept to one side of her swan's neck, writing in a notebook that was balanced on her belly. His heart nearly failed. He, Aldo Savini, would protect her from her foul seducer, whomever he might be. He would help her finish her quest. He must think hard for that breakthrough. And then one day, the breakthrough came.

For many weeks now, Aldo had realized that certain French elements were creeping into the search. Questions about shipping, about the Palace of Versailles, about glass trade to Paris, about the court of Louis XIV the Sun King. Then it struck him – if the *Principessa* was interested in any of the courts of Europe in the seventeenth century, there was one ubiquitous character who would always be able to help her, a personage who hailed from this very city.

The Venetian Ambassador.

La Principessa had been very excited when he showed her the document. After reading it three times, she dragged the volume of letters over to his desk with a speed that made him fear for her condition, which was now very advanced. She badgered him about making a copy, till at last he took the letter in question to the private inner sanctum where the specialized scanners and printers lay dormant. Squat and expensive, these machines could copy even the most delicate parchment with the use of infra-red laser technology. Not for these documents the exposure to the harsh bands of light of the office photocopier, thought Aldo Savini tenderly. He took the pages back to the *Principessa*, who waited at his desk. She grasped the pages to her belly, face-up as if she did not want the child to read the contents from within her. She looked agitated, but not particularly happy. Still, ever good mannered, she gave him one of her peerless smiles.

'Thank you, Signor Savini,' she said.

He pushed his glasses up his nose, gathering courage, but she had already turned before he had uttered the name 'Aldo.'

She had not heard him – she was walking away through the bookstacks, her mind already elsewhere. And in the grand chivalric tradition to which Aldo Savini was so attached, he never saw her again.

CHAPTER 28

The Ambassador

When Jules Hardouin-Mansart, chief architect of the Palace of Versailles, showed Corradino the plans for what he called the '*Salon des Glaces*' even Corradino had a moment of thinking that it could not be done. There were to be twenty-one huge mirrors, each with twenty-one panes. Each pane was to be exquisite, flat, true and with a crystal-clear reflection. There was to be no bevel at the edge, so that the glass would appear as one piece, with no interruptions to the reflected image. Moreover, each glass was to reflect exactly the window opposite it, so exterior light and interior light were partnered, to create, as Hardouin-Mansart said, the lightest room in the world. There was also to be fantastic series of frescoes on the ceiling, depicting the King's life and the glories of France. These were to be painted by Royal Painter Charles Le Brun and his apprentices.

Le Brun himself was a constant presence at the site,

relentlessly questioning Corradino about the direction of light, the angle of reflection, and the implications for his painting. Slowly, Le Brun's wondrous panels came to life – high above, gesso doves fluttered in the stratosphere, and bare-breasted beauties reclined on fat clouds while they watched the golden triumphal chariots of the King. Corradino recognized a kindred talent, but felt the weight of the task presented to him. His glass must reflect these glories.

Even the designer of the great gardens, André Le Nôtre, visited the hall to inspect how his artistry would be reflected in the mirrored wall.

Despite his reservations, however, Corradino found that all help was there at his disposal – conferences with carpenters and masons, the assistance of the latest measuring equipment, mathematicians from Paris. The *fornace* – purpose built in the kitchen gardens of the palace – was well equipped, and Jacques Chauvire worked hard and progressed well. As Corradino taught Jacques his secret method the boy blossomed, and together master and apprentice began to make larger and larger panes. Corradino gradually had to remelt less of Jacques' work, and by the end of Corradino's first month in Paris Jacques had made his first passable square mirror pane.

At night Corradino went back to his well furnished house in the nearby village of Trianon. With six chambers, a maid and a small vegetable garden, it afforded greater luxury than he had known since leaving the Palazzo Manin.

He began to relax – to feel, for the first time in years, that he was not being watched. Sometimes, in the dying sunlight when he stood at the end of his garden watching the enormous palace grow, with a goblet of fine French wine in his hand, thinking of Leonora, he was almost happy.

This new sense of ease was destined to be short-lived.

On the momentous day that the first silvered panes were set in place in the Hall of Mirrors, Corradino stood, arms akimbo, supervising the work as the last glass was set in place. Quite a gaggle had formed to watch the work, including Hardouin-Mansart and Le Nôtre. Privileged company indeed, and at length they were rewarded as the mirror was complete and the crowd stood back in awe. A hush descended as the men surveyed their handiwork – the mirror arched above them, high and clear, gilded struts crossing the panes like light caged with gold. As well as their own reflections, the assembly saw the half-completed gardens, and the half-filled lakes stretching out into the distance, as far as the eye could see, in an optical miracle of design. The thing was truly a marvel, and all assembled could see what wonders they could expect when the hall was complete. No one moved, unable to tear their eyes away. Talk, once hushed, died into silence. But not just through admiration, or respect for the craftsmanship they all witnessed. They were silent for the presence of royalty. The King had entered the room.

Louis strode toward the mirror, and those gathered bowed to the floor instantly. Corradino bent low, his heart thudding.

Will this capricious King approve of my work?

Soon he had greater anxiety to reckon with – his lowered eyes raked the royal slippers, then moved to the pair of shoes next to them – *Bauta* slippers with red laces, sold only on the Rialto.

Venetian shoes.

Corradino's hair crisped on his scalp. He dared not raise his eyes, but as the crowd around him straightened up he contrived to shuffle to the back of the throng, as Hardouin-Mansart and Le Nôtre moved forward to be presented. The King was speaking. Blood thrummed in Corradino's ears so loudly that he could not, at once, hear what was said.

'So Ambassador, *pas mal, hein*? Perhaps even you will be forced to admit that my little *château*, when complete, will rival your crumbling *palazzi*?'

The Ambassador bowed politely, but Corradino could see that his eyes were hooded, and their gaze cool and guarded. He thought he knew the man slightly, a member of the Venetian Guilini family, attaché to the *Arsenale* years ago when Corradino's father was trading with the Baltic.

A taciturn, but highly intelligent youth he had been then. He must have risen through the influence of his family to this exalted state, but looked as if his intellect merited the position. Dressed in the finest Venetian velvets and satins with hair and beard trimmed and oiled, the Ambassador looked not like a dandy but a self possessed, confident, and highly dangerous man.

The King spotted Hardouin-Mansart and Le Nôtre at the front of the throng. He beckoned with a fat beringed hand and the pair bowed low as the King began desultory introductions. 'This is Hardouin-Mansart, my palace architect. And that's Le Nôtre who's doing the gardens. It goes well?' He waved away their answers. 'Yes, yes, but this mirror is better than both your efforts, no? I imagine you two are jealous? Going to get one of your masons to drop a brick on it, Jules?' The King laughed at his own sally as the court joined in. Then, as Corradino began to relax, Louis uttered a question which froze his blood. 'Where's my *Maître des Glaces*? Can't have you two taking all the bouquets . . .' His eyes raked the crowd, found Corradino's. Corradino's heart thumped so he thought he would expire. A smile flitted over the King's features like a summer cloud. 'There's the fellow.'

I am undone – my life is ended.

But the fat hand beckoned Jacques Chauvire. Guillaume Seve, passed over for the job, gave Jacques an officious little shove, and the boy stumbled forward awkwardly, twisting his leather cap in his hand.

Baldasar Guilini regarded Jacques balefully from under an arched eyebrow. He made a circuit of the boy on his Venetian heels, looking him up and down. Then he walked to the mirror, freeing his hand, finger by finger, from his chamois glove. He reached out his index finger and touched the cool, flat glass, leaving a smoky print. Corradino, despite himself, winced as if a seducer had laid a finger on his daughter.

Baldasar turned back to Jacques.

'Something wrong, Ambassador?' asked Louis, who seemed to be suppressing the mirth of a private jest.

The Ambassador visibly recollected himself. 'Forgive me, Majesty, I was thinking that this man – Chauvire, is it – is very young to create such mastery.'

Jacques shifted his weight, as Louis replied, 'Perhaps it is hard to accept that France has at last attained the quality of glasswork that the Venetians have enjoyed these past many years.'

Baldasar looked from the mirror to Jacques and back again. 'How many panes in this mirror, *Maître*?' he gave the title a gentle, ironic stress.

Jacques, properly, looked to the King, who nodded that he may answer. 'Twenty-one, *Gracieux Monsieur*.'

'And how many years have you been on this earth?'

'Twenty-one, *Gracieux Monsieur*.'

'How fitting. There is a pleasing symmetry about that,

don't you find? Indeed, it is a work of passing beauty for one of such *tender* years. It has clarity, lucidity; one might almost say a *Venetian* quality about it.' His eyes raked the crowd and Corradino shifted, dropping his eyes, obscured behind one of the burlier masons.

'I congratulate you, Majesty.' The Ambassador bowed once again, but his eyes were thoughtful behind his diplomatic visage.

'Well, well.' The King waved away the compliment modestly as if he had crafted the mirror himself. He moved off down the hall, with Ambassador and coterie in tow. Then, briefly, the Royal head turned. Quick as a flash, Louis' eyes found Corradino. One eye closed for an instant. Then the King turned back and continued on, the whole incredible incident taking no more than an instant, and the court not even faltering in its progress. Corradino, as he allowed himself to breathe again, tried to comprehend what he had just seen.

The King had *winked* at him.

It is a game to him. A piece of amusement. The fact that my life is forfeit if I am discovered, that whole pantomime with Jacques, it is all a game; a piece of Royal folly to pass the hours.

Sweating, glass-limbed, he put a hand to his thudding heart, as if to keep that organ from leaping from his chest. Guilini had not seen him, would not even know him if he had, as Corradino had been but eight years old when he met the adolescent Guilini at the *Arsenale* on business with his father. But was Louis capricious enough to reveal the true identity of his *Maître des Glaces* over brandy after the Ambassadorial dinner? No, reasoned Corradino, the King's national pride, already fully displayed, would dictate that the credit for the Hall of Mirrors would be attributed to French craftsmen, now and for all time in the future. Then, how long would an Ambassador stay? Not more than a week, two weeks? Best to lie low till he heard Guilini had gone. Shaken, Corradino returned to the *fornace*, waving away Jacques' agonized apologies that he had been given credit for Corradino's work. I must talk to Duparcmieur, thought Corradino. I must bring Leonora to me.

But Corradino had forgotten one thing in his reasoning. The mirror itself had betrayed him. In the moment when Louis had looked back, Baldasar Guilini, quick as a cat, had seen the exchange in the mirrored panes. Corradino had been right, Guilini had not recognized him yet. But he knew him for an Italian, and it was but a short step from thence to know him for a Venetian.

That night, after the Ambassadorial dinner in his honour, and the brandy over which Louis told him nothing, Baldasar Guilini returned to his quarters in the *Palais Royal*. He refused the attentions of the courtesan he had brought from Venice, and instead, sat down at his ornate gilded writing desk.

Alone, with the heavy drapes closed, in the warm perfumed closeness of his elaborate chambers, he took up his quill and began to write a letter. At length he sanded the parchment, folded it twice, and heated a stick of red wax at his candle. He pressed the molten wax to the paper, where it lay like a gout of blood. He turned his signet ring and with the ease of long practice impressed the wax clearly with its design – the winged lion of San Marco. He turned the parchment and wrote the direction on the face for Louis' messenger, who waited outside his door.

It was to His Excellency the Doge of Venice.

CHAPTER 29

Before Dawn

Leonora walked all the way home from San Marco. The photocopy of the Ambassador's letter was in her bag, and she felt its presence burning through the canvas. It was early evening, and the streets were deserted. She knew why – it was the eve of *Carnevale*, and all the citizens of Venice were getting ready – putting the finishing touches to their costumes, grabbing much needed sleep before the nights of revelry to come. Tomorrow the tourists would be back in full force and the city would wake from her winter sleep. The shuttered and cold city known only to her residents, would resume her bloom – the princess, once kissed, would slough off her hundred years sleep and blossom for her suitors once more.

And yet the darkest hour comes just before dawn. Leonora's walk home was beset by dreaded shadows once more – not just the spirit of Roberto this time (had he left Venice? Or was he still here?) but also the malign presence of the Ambassador whose words she had just read. Words that condemned Corradino. These twin presences stalked her home. The night froze with the water underfoot and in the air, her breath smoked. She tried to hurry, but the burden of her baby sat hard upon her hips and her pelvis ached. Eight months of growth and icy pavings did not allow a speedy progress. The palaces and houses shunned her with their blank frontages. All was green and grey where once it had been gold and amber. She remembered something that Alessandro had said; that in Venice the moonlight was green because the light reflected from the canal. It was so tonight, but the greenish tint was ghostly, ghastly: it turned living flesh to the hue of the dead. The canal itself was a trough of cold green glass. The city had cooled and hardened. There is no sanctuary here, the houses said. You are no longer one of our own. Even the statue of Daniele Manin, turned by twilight to a greenish ghoul, accused her from his plinth. His copper embodiment proof of his own loyalty; he questioned hers. Her bright windows were a lighthouse beacon to guide her to safe mooring.

Lighted? Someone is there? Alessandro?

Her heart beat hard and painfully as she fitted her key in the lock – but it was not he but his cousin. Marta was seated at the table, *Il Gazzettino* spread in front of her. She looked up and smiled as Leonora entered, pink-cheeked with cold and expectation.

'Fa freddo, vero?'

Leonora nodded, shedding gloves and scarves. 'Freezing.'

Rent day. I had forgotten. Thank God I got the rest of my month's wages from Adelino. Christ knows what will happen next month though. I couldn't bear to lose this place too.

As she crossed the kitchen to get the money from inside her Moroccan tagine dish (a hiding place which would be immediately obvious to even the most amateur burglar) she heard Marta tactfully fold the offending paper away. She paid over her month in advance and offered Marta a glass of wine. Her landlady seemed to hesitate.

'I'm not sure . . . I . . . actually, yes, please.'

Leonora opened a bottle of Valpolicella and ran the tap for herself. As the water rushed over her hand, running to bone-chilling coldness, she considered her friend from the corner of her eye. The cousin of the man she loved. They really shared nothing in the physiognomy of the face – there were no resemblances to catch at her heart. And yet today she divined something of him in Marta – The familiar hesitation, distance, discomfort. She filled her glass with water and brought the two drinks to the table.

What is she hiding?

Leonora sat and the silence persisted. Then, as if making

up her mind, Marta spoke at last. 'Is Alessandro coming here tonight?'

Leonora looked up from her glass, surprise registering. Throughout her pregnancy, she had not seen as much of him as she would have liked, but they had had enough shared time to foster the notion that they were a couple. When they were together he was the model boyfriend and expectant father – talking to the growing bump, imagining the future child and helping her make the inevitable and exciting changes to the flat. But the notion of cohabitation had become a bone of contention – for some reason he studiously avoided the issue. The flat evolved slowly to accommodate the baby, but in all the plans he never mentioned making a space for himself. Major festivals were spent together, and Alessandro had suggested that he come tonight and that they go to the *Carnevale* together. So Leonora answered his cousin, 'He's coming here after work.'

Marta nodded. She hesitated, took a deep breath, and twitched the paper towards her again. 'I didn't realize that he still saw Vittoria. I just saw them in the Do Mori on my way here.'

Leonora registered her tone before she realized what Marta was saying. She had heard that studied nonchalance once before in her life. She realized when and where and was suddenly as cold as she had been outside.

Jane. In Hampstead. The friend who told me about Stephen.

In her cold horror she grasped at the name Marta had spoken. 'Vittoria?'

Marta sighed. 'Vittoria Minotto. She and Sandro used to live together, then she got promoted away from Venice. But now she's back. But you know that of course. You . . . met her.'

Yes; she took away my livelihood. And now Sandro too?

Marta looked bewildered. 'You mean he didn't tell you?'

'No. Yes. I mean – he told me about a journalist he had been seeing, but I never thought . . . I never put the two together.'

Stupid, stupid.

Marta frowned. 'But surely, after the article?'

Leonora shook her head. 'He was away when it all happened. Doing his detective's course. I'm not sure how much he knows about it.' Her head was spinning. That woman, that sexy, vicious female, had been *his*? And with *her* he had consented to live, when *she*, the mother of his child, was to cope alone? Involuntarily she put a hand on her bump in what had become an accustomed gesture.

Marta took it for distress. 'Are you going to be alright?'

Leonora forced a smile. She suddenly wanted Marta to go. She needed to think. She knew what it must have cost

Marta to warn her – the Venetians were, like most Italians, extremely loyal to their families. Leonora chatted with forced cheerfulness for what seemed an eternity but must only have been moments. At last Marta got up for her coat. She turned as she reached the door.

'It's nothing,' she said haltingly. 'It's very civilized to be on good terms with your ex. Sandro never did like bad blood or ill will. He likes things to be easy.'

Easy.

So now, at last, she knew the source of the distance. He had lived with Vittoria and been hurt. She had left him. And now she was back, what?

Where do I fit in?

She stayed for long moments at the table, nursing her glass of water, looking at the door through which Marta had left, through which Alessandro was shortly to come. She considered, as the shock drained away and anger replaced it, how she would confront him.

No. That's not the way. Not again.

With Stephen she had faced him out with what she knew, and he had left. This time she would learn the lessons of history. She had to assume Alessandro's innocence as the alternative was too horrible to contemplate – to be alone in a city which now felt alien to her, with a child and no job.

No. I will wait, and hope, and give him the benefit of the doubt.

She knew she was a coward. When he came in from the winter night she embraced him warmly. They ate dinner and talked animatedly of the child and the *Carnevale* to come. He seemed excited about something, hyper. Her heart chilled as she thought that Vittoria was the reason. In denial she took him to her bed and pleased him as much as she could. Only afterwards did she ask him one question, hating herself.

'Marta was here tonight. You just missed her. I thought you were going to be here by seven. What happened?'

His voice was thick with sleep. 'I had to work late. That art theft at the Ca' D'Oro. It's dragging on for ever.'

You've been caught in a lie. Proof.

She turned uncomfortably, her bump ungainly, and shoved at the pillows. She did not want him to see the tears that ran into the linen. The child kicked her, reacting to her movement, and she cupped its form, crying for them both. She felt a touch to her back.

Alessandro murmured 'I love you.'

He has never once said that before. And now it's too late.

CHAPTER 30

Carnevale

Carnevale. The Doge's Palace, that great confection, is *en fête*. The delicate, blanched façade hides the dark and ermetic chambers within. The edifice itself wears a mask. Costumed characters, garish and bright, tangle round the pillars of the white loggia like a gaudy ribbon. Above their heads, like a grey tooth in a peerless smile, sit the two discoloured pillars that stand out from their fellows. Legend has it that these two columns are permanently stained with the blood of the criminals that were hung and quartered there. The revellers do not think of this. They laugh and squawk like parrots at a bagpiper. Venice *La Serenissima* is, today, far from serene. Here a moon capers with a princess, there a *Pierrot* converses with an elephant. Today, a cat can look at a King.

By the bridge of the Riva degli Schiavoni, a man and a woman hail a gondola. The man is dressed as Sandro Botticelli, with a close cap on his curling hair, and

Renaissance robes. The woman seems as if she has stepped from his work, so closely does she resemble *La Primavera*. Her gilded hair is twisted about her cherub's face, and gold filaments snatch at the sun. Her hooded green eyes are the colour of a wine bottle, the pupils distended with promise. Her sprigged white dress catches in the wind and her escort hands her into the rocking boat with care – for she is heavily pregnant.

Leonora settled back in the cushions. She had decided that *La Primavera* was the obvious choice for her *Carnevale* costume; as Spring herself was pregnant with the coming Summer, Leonora could find comfort in the flowing robes. The dress was loose and airy, the cushions soft under her back. Her glass heart sat in the notch of her throat; its cool round weight a constant reassurance that she needed more than she knew. Her child squirmed beneath the ceinture of her dress, and its father's hand clasped hers. She looked replete; the oft-used term 'blooming' could have been coined for her. Outwardly, she was as serene as the glassy lagoon under the winter sun. But beneath her surface there was darkness and turmoil in the depths. Two evils, from the past and present, were the tides that tugged at her innards. She doubted the fidelity of the man whose hand she held. And between her filling breasts lay the scratchy secret of the Ambassador's letter. She recalled her dream of the sunlit day when the three of them rode the gondola. Well, here they were – the child unborn but inside her belly. For the baby's sake she wanted resolution – of her quest and her relationship too. The past, as was fitting, should be dealt with first. She began to talk. She told Alessandro everything. Of Corradino. Of Roberto. Of the revelations in *Il Gazzettino*. She watched him carefully when she mentioned Vittoria, but he showed no surprise, no shifty glances or shamefaced blushes. He merely frowned.

Vittoria can wait. For now I want his opinion as a professional.

She went on to speak of Padovani, of her researches in the Sansoviniana. Leonora freed the much-read letter, and handed it to Alessandro. The shadow of the Bridge of Sighs dipped them in darkness and with a quizzical arch of the brow, he began to read, waiting only for the shadow of the bridge to pass.

CHAPTER 31

The Piombi

Giacomo walked over the Bridge of Sighs with the shuffling steps of terror. Through the fine lattice of the windows he looked what may be his last on the Riva degli Schiavoni, where *Carnevale* was in full swing. The passage was small and airless after the massive rooms in which he had been questioned with their magnificence of frescoed gilt. He knew that this was no mere accident but design. The condemned man leaving light and space and warmth to enter the crushing damp darkness of that most dreaded place – the Piombi prison. Named for the leads that slated the roofs, he knew as well as every citizen of Venice that no one left the fabled prison alive.

The perspiration of fear sat between the old man's shoulder blades. His terror had begun last night when they had taken him, and washed over him in waves all day as he had been questioned, relentlessly, by the same dark, masked figure. He looked through the last window with something akin to love for his lost city. But he did not sigh. Instead, a thin stream of urine trickled down his leg to the stone floor. The guard behind him cursed, and dropped a rag which he scuffed along with his boot, erasing the trail. The old ones always lost control at this point – they knew their days were numbered. Even a young man could quickly get lung fever from the damp of the Piombi, or be driven mad by the dark. For the old, it was assured. He gave Giacomo a vicious shove through the yawning mouth of the prison portal, and as he entered the dark a trick of memory recalled to Giacomo, word for word, the letter that they had read to him, the letter that had brought him here.

Most esteemed and excellent Doge, Duke of the Republic of Venice, Seneschal of the Three Islands and Emperor of Constantinople,

Lately summering, at your Excellency's pleasure, at the court of His Majesty Louis XIV of France, I have today made an unsettling discovery which may pertain to the security of one of our trading monopolies. This discovery touches on the mirror work which His Majesty has commissioned for the decoration of his new palace here at Versailles, where I am newly quartered.

I will tax your Excellency's patience no longer but say, in brief, that it is my belief that a citizen of our own fair Republic is assisting the French with their labours. Excellency, I must write that I believe the traitor to be one of our own Murano glassmakers (so fine is the work) who is even now unburdening the secrets of our Guilds to the foreign craftsmen.

I have had sight of the man whom I believe to be a Venetian. He is of his middle years, dark, well-favoured, and of youthful appearance. I will endeavour to discover his name, but casual enquiry reveals he may be under some kind of Royal protection, as well a craftsman of his status may be.

Excellency, if your humble servant may be so bold, I urge you to make such necessary enquiries of the Murano community, of any absence among their number – even a death.

For my own part I will take further steps to bring the identity of this man into the light.

Make haste, Excellency, I beg of you, else our monopoly is lost.

Your servant,

Baldasar Guilini, Venetian Ambassador to the Court of France.

CHAPTER 32

The Lost Heart

The letter fluttered in Alessandro's fingers. The breeze stirred their costumes as they stood, on the Riva bridge, facing the Bridge of Sighs, their gondola ride over. The sun was hot at their backs, and Leonora turned to warm the baby. She was silent – she did not want to say it. Alessandro spoke first. 'It's him.'

It was still a shock to hear it like that.

'It has to be – the age, description, everything. And the date – it's written just a few months after Corradino's "death".'

Leonora nodded. 'I know.'

She turned back to lean on the parapet with him.

'I have to go to France.'

'Yes.'

'I have to find out for sure. *Professore* Padovani has some contacts at the Sorbonne. They'll have more records there.'

Alessandro nodded. 'Next year, when the baby can travel, we'll all go. I can take leave, and ...'

'I have to go *now*.'

Alessandro shut his eyes. When he opened them his voice was level.

'Leonora, you are eight months pregnant. You cannot possibly travel now. You can't fly, for one thing.'

'I can go by train – or by boat like Corradino.'

'*Fuck* Corradino!' The explosion shocked them both. The silence that followed seemed to still the very revelers themselves. Alessandro tempered his voice. 'Any journey at this stage will put you under enormous stress. And what if you go into labour on the train? Or in France? Our baby should be born here, in Venice, as *I* was and as *you* were. Not in some hospital in Paris. I won't allow it.'

'You won't *allow* it?' Leonora was stung – she knew he spoke the truth, that she was losing the battle, but she perversely resented Alessandro's propriatorial tone.

'You're carrying *my* child.'

'Then act like it!' Leonora clutched at the glass heart and lost her head. All her resolutions, to be measured and dispassionate, faded away as her rage boiled. 'Why don't you commit to me? Why can't you be in my life all the time, instead of coming and going like the tide? Is it because of Vittoria?'

'*What*?'

'Yes, you think I don't know, but your own cousin told

me what you wouldn't. You're still seeing her aren't you? Last night, in fact, when you were "working late"?'

Her voice had risen, and passers by were looking on with curiosity at this piece of street theatre. Alessandro drew her below the loggia and forced her to sit on one of the cool marble benches.

'Sit down. You're getting far too agitated for someone of your condition.'

'I like your sudden concern.'

His voice was measured. 'Leonora, whether you know it or not, you and this child are the most important people in my life.'

'And Vittoria?' she spat. The woman that tied me in knots, and rubbished me in public for all to read? Why are you still seeing her if you are so loyal?'

'*Listen.*' He sighed. 'It's true I asked to see her. *Wait,*' as Leonora cried out. 'I knew all about Corradino, and the article. *You* didn't tell me, couldn't share your inner life with me. You let me think that you were looking for your father, but I knew of the real object of your interest. I went to see Roberto after Vittoria's article, to see if I could find out the truth with my new "official" status.' He sketched inverted commas in the air. 'But it seems he has emigrated, to France of all places, taking his secrets with him. That only left Vittoria.' He turned to look at Leonora full in the face. 'Last night was the one and only time that I've seen her. I asked her to show me Roberto's "Primary Source" – the proof that Corradino was a traitor. For old time's sake, she agreed.'

Leonora's mouth was dry. 'What was it?'

'A letter. The last letter written by his ancestor Giacomo del Piero, as he was dying in the *Piombi*.'

They both turned as one to look through the loggia arches at the dark barred windows of the watery prison. Alessandro went on. 'I didn't tell you any of this because the letter is pretty conclusive. He denounces Corradino as a traitor.'

Leonora tried to order her thoughts. 'Then why did Roberto not simply have the contents of the letter published?'

'Because the end of the letter shows Giacomo in a pretty bad light. He reveals the existence of Corradino's daughter, and her whereabouts.'

'The *Pietà*.'

'Yes. I imagine Roberto was as precious about his ancestor's reputation as you are about yours. Denouncing an apprentice who has betrayed you is one thing, but condemning an innocent orphan girl to death is quite another.'

'But she didn't die. She survived, and married, and lived happily ever after.'

'Well, Roberto must not have known that. And anyway, it's the denunciation itself which makes Giacomo look so bad.'

Leonora nodded. 'Why didn't you tell me you were looking into all this for me? Why have you been so distant?'

'How could I be intimate with you when you weren't honest with me? You held Corradino to yourself, even when the ad campaigns and the article made him so public. You thought that because I was away from Venice I wouldn't know. You thought that somehow I would like you less if you were the descendant of a traitor rather than the *maestro* you had boasted of. How could I tell you that someone that mattered so much to you mattered nothing to me? It's *you* I love and you have to find yourself first, before I can find you.' He turned back to the canal. 'And now, you are putting your obsession with a distant ancestor above the wellbeing of your own child. You're crazy. You should be thinking of *him*.'

'I'm *doing* this for him! I have to know before he is born! That's why I have to go to France. Don't you see? If Giacomo revealed Leonora's existence to The Ten *and yet she lived* then Corradino must have saved her somehow. I have to *know*.' Leonora clutched her glass heart for reassurance.

Alessandro caught the gesture and turned on her. 'Why? So you can boast about him at dinner parties? Is your own life not enough? Do you need Corradino to define you? Why can you not simply say, I'm Leonora, I am a glass-blower?'

'But I'm not! I'm not any more! That's why I have to clear his name. My job depends on his reputation. If he is redeemed then the Manin line will sell again and my family's profession is mine again.'

'Why must you rely on Corradino, and that stupid talisman you wear? Why can't you rely on *me*?'

Before Leonora could stop him he snatched the heart from her throat and threw it into the canal. It flew as far as the Bridge of Sighs, winking once as it disappeared into the arching shadow. They only heard, but did not see, the brief splash as the heart disappeared.

They both froze in shock at what had happened. At how much they could hurt one another. The glass heart, gone, meant they had reached a place from which there was no return. In this new insane universe where the centuries had telescoped, Alessandro faced the truth.

Corradino had become his rival.

Eyes shining with tears, Alessandro left her, pushing through the crowd and stumbling towards the Arsenale.

Leonora tried to call out, to tell him that he was right, as she knew he was. That she would not go to France. But she could make no sound. She tried to move but her feet were lead. Only when his black curls had completely disappeared from sight did she realize what was happening, as a band of pain wound tight around her belly, strong enough to make her gasp and clasp the balustrade. Concerned hands fluttered at her back, bystanders stopped to ask if she was alright. But she was not alright.

I am in labour.

CHAPTER 33

The Phantom

Giacomo didn't know how long he had been in the cell. From the length of his whiskers he knew it was many days, perhaps weeks. Weeks of silence. He heard only the rasp of his own breath and the hacking of his new cough. He could not see the walls that held him, but by the touch of their cool slime he knew he was in one of the cells that lay below the water level of the canal. His fear was as cold as the stone.

The silence was complete – so quiet he fancied he was alone in the prison. But he knew this was not the case, that only the thickness of the walls kept the cries of others from him. He thought he would have preferred to hear them. Anything but this solitary dark.

The smell of his own waste was everywhere. For the first days he had confined his excretions to the corners of the cell, finding the conjunction of two walls with his searching hands. Soon he had ceased to bother, and the stench was such that he prayed for his breath to stop.

For the first hours of his incarceration he felt the tingle of horrid expectation bump his flesh. Every moment he expected the door to open and the terrible dark phantom to enter, to ask more questions. They had read him the Ambassador's letter. They thought someone from Murano was helping the French King with his palace. The questions were relentless. Did anyone regularly send letters from the *fornace*? Had anyone been absent from the *fornace*? Ill? Dead? He had cried when he had told them of Corradino's death, as he missed the boy terribly – whether alive or dead, he was no longer with Giacomo day by day. Separation was death too.

They paid his grief no heed. What had Corradino died of? When was this? Then hours in an ante-room while they questioned someone else. From the snatches that Giacomo heard he divined that it was a doctor. The questioning was hard to hear through the oaken doors. But the screams were easy to hear. At the end of the interview the *medico* was taken away, pleading and broken. For the first time that day, Giacomo began to fear for his life as he was led back in to the vast chamber to face the spectre in the black mask. In his fancy he thought it was the same man that had come, years ago, for Corradino at the *fornace*. When he had saved the boy's life. But he knew it could not be. The figure stalked his fitful sleep – as potent as Death itself. But as the time wore on and he waited he knew what they were doing. Dread was their weapon. They wanted to drive him mad.

He fought it. God knows he did. But his fanciful mind in his ailing flesh peopled his cell with figures from his past. The whore he had tumbled in Cannaregio as a young man. She had brought his babe to him – called him Roberto after Giacomo's father, in an attempt to appeal to his instincts. But Giacomo had gone back to the glass, and Roberto and she had gone to Vicenza. Now she sat, with accusing eyes, holding the babe up to him. He looked inside the swaddle and saw the gaping maw of a child's skull, crawling with maggots. Giacomo's screams were muffled by the damp.

Sometimes Corradino himself visited, and mocked the old man with a secret that he would not tell. Giacomo rolled himself into a ball, hugging his own wasted flesh, forehead pressed to the slick wall, so he would not see the shades that loomed from the dark. But in his lucid moments, when his mind was well, he knew his body was sick. His coughs had become agonizing paroxysms that burned his chest, and in the last few fits he had tasted the metallic tang of blood in his mouth. He wished for a glass dagger – one of Corradino's would be best – to end his life.

Days later, he knew not when, a freezing voice spoke to him.

'You suffer greatly.' It was a statement, not a question.

Giacomo turned from the wall that had become his friend. The cell was lit by a single, blessed candle. But Giacomo's relief at the light was short lived. For in the corner, deep in shadow, he saw the spectre of his nightmares. By now, he was used to the ghosts. Even this one would go if he hugged his wall.

He made as if to turn back.

'Heed me, for I am real. I am not one of your imaginings. I can be merciful. I can bring you food, water; even set you free if you tell me what I want to know.'

Giacomo could not speak for some moments, his voice weak from the coughs and screams.

The figure took his hesitation for defiance. Had he but known it, Giacomo would have told him anything, everything, if only he could.

'Do you know why no man ever escapes from here?'

Giacomo knew very well. He desperately tried to say yes, for he did not want to hear it again, not here.

'Because if a guard ever lets a prisoner escape, that guard must finish the prisoner's sentence.'

At last Giacomo could croak. 'I know.'

The faceless figure inclined its cowled head. 'Then you see, I am your only hope.'

Hope. Hope from the Devil.

'We went to Sant'Ariano. To your friend's grave. Do you know what we found?'

Silence.

'We found loose earth and torn sackcloth. Your friend has gone.'

The clouds parted for Giacomo, as realization dawned. *Non omnis moriar.* Corradino did *not* altogether die. He felt like singing. His secret hope since he had read the Latin words had come to pass. His son *was* alive. The note which he had kept *was* an assurance, an instruction that he should not grieve. Praise God. Giacomo felt warm for the first time in months. But the voice went on:

'That night a ship was chartered from Mestre to Marseilles. Two men boarded from a fishing bark which was found with earth in the bottom. Your friend Corrado Manin has gone to France. He is the one we seek.'

A fast as joy and relief came, they left again. Giacomo felt the bile rise as he knew what had been done to him, to Murano, to the art of glass and mirror-making to which he had devoted his life. His dry eyes sprang fresh tears in the dark, but they were not the cold tears of grief but the hot tears of anger. *I shall not altogether die*. No, but you have killed me, and our trade too. Corradino, my son, how could you? You have given our secrets away. *Non omnis moriar.*

The words were echoed in the hideous voice. '*Non omnis moriar.*'

Giacomo's blood froze. They had been to his house. Of course they had. They had the note.

'I see these words have some significance. We found his letter to you.'

Giacomo cursed himself. Sentiment had made him keep

the note – the last thing that Corradino wrote, or so he thought. This note, which meant his own death, was a keepsake from a man who had betrayed him. If Giacomo had known what was planned, he would have killed Corradino himself. The irony was exquisite.

'You helped him.' Again, a statement.

'No!'

'You knew what he planned. He wrote you the note.'

'No, I swear it.' A scream at the last.

'You will die here.'

They left him then. The light, the phantom and the guard outside. As the footsteps receded, Giacomo began to scream. The pain in his chest and throat were nothing. The betrayal hurt the most.

Wordless, nameless hours later. His hours were filled with Corradino, laughing at him, taking his expertise and charity, and yes, love, for years and now making the best glass of his life for the French. The palaces in Giacomo's head were made of walls of crystal. The chairs, tables and food were glass. Corradino sat at the table which groaned with glass food. He ate his fill of the glass delicacies till the blood ran from his mouth, laughing all the time with a glass King. He must be stopped.

Giacomo felt death approach him. And Death came. Again with a guard and a candle.

The door was opened and the phantom entered. 'Well? Are you ready?'

Giacomo's voice was weak, but just audible.

'If I tell you, will you give me materials to write to my son Roberto?'

It was like bargaining with the Devil and it took the last of Giacomo's courage. The terrible shade inclined its cowled head. 'I will send you a scribe if you tell me what I need. And I will send you all comforts for your last hours. Now, hurry. Your life is ebbing away.'

'My son . . . he is in Vicenza. He bears the del Piero name. I wish him . . . I want him to know, and his sons to know, that Corradino finished me, and that he, not I, was the traitor.'

'It shall be accomplished. Now, what do you have to tell me?'

'Corradino, he . . . has a daughter.'

CHAPTER 34

The Mask Falls

The *Salon de Thé* in Petit Trianon reminded Corradino very much of the Cantina Do Mori and as he entered the café for his assignation he missed Venice like a blow to the belly. As he sought the privacy of the backroom as instructed in Duparcmieur's note he passed the patrons who had borrowed the latest eastern fashions for their dress – the Byzantine look was the latest in style, and the gaudy velvets made these genteel Parisians resemble Venetians. The enclosed and exclusive rear area of the café was highly decorated with frescoes and mirrors.

The French, it seems, steal all of their ideas from Venice. Even me they stole.

As he sat and waited he began to wonder anew why Duparcmieur had chosen to meet here, in a mirror image of their first interview. Duparcmieur had been in the habit of coming to Corradino's house, or talking to him in the Palace itself. It was no secret to his colleagues that Duparcmieur was his protector, and that through him, Corradino had a loftier patron; the King himself.

Perhaps there were some delicate negotiations to conduct which demanded a convivial atmosphere. After all it was close on a year since Corradino had come to France, and they were nearing the appointed time for Leonora to come to him. Corradino set his jaw. He would not budge in the matter of Leonora. Every day he thought of her and how it would be when they were together at last – holding her sweet face in his hands, playing in the palace gardens as he worked, or touching their fingers together in their special way – this time without the grille of the Pietà in between. Unconsciously, Corradino spread out his hand in a star of longing – he could almost feel her little pads pressed to his hard, printless fingertips.

I hope she has not forgotten. I cannot wait.

He felt a back settle against his – the bones of a spine behind the nap of fine velvet.

Duparcmieur.

'Why here?' asked Corradino.

'Why not?'

The voice was not French. Not Duparcmieur. But the

perfect, aristocratic patois of the Veneto. As he had done a year before at the Cantina Do Mori, Corradino glanced into the mirror at his side. His guts shrivelled within him.

'I apologize for this unconventional meeting,' said Ambassador Baldasar Guilini smoothly. 'However, as we have met before, I thought such *convivial* surroundings would not offend you. Do you recall our meeting?'

Corradino swallowed. His thoughts flapped like moths in a bottle. He must not give himself away.

'At the Palace, Excellency?'

'Yes, then. But before, a long time before. At the *Arsenale*. You came with your father – he was ratifying a trading treaty with the Dardanelles. Saffron, was it? Or Salt? Forgive me, I forget the particulars of the case. But I remember your father – a noble fellow, Corrado Manin. You resemble him physically, which is your good fortune.' The Ambassador shifted. 'Your ill fortune, of course, is that you resemble him also in your propensity for treachery to the Republic.'

Corradino's frozen heart plummeted. He knew that it was over.

I am unmasked. I am dead. Should I run?

Corradino cast swift glances left and right at the laughing patrons. Any one of them could be assassins, agents of The Ten. It was no good.

As if echoing his resignation, the Ambassador continued. 'It's too late for you, of course. But if you make certain amends, you may be able to save your daughter.'

Fear clutched Corradino's throat with a strangling grip.

How could they know? Dear God, please, not *Leonora.*

'What do you mean?' he choked, in a last desperate parry. 'What daughter?'

'Signor Manin, please. The one in the Pietà of course. Leonora. The issue of your little *amour* with her mother Angelina dei Vescovi. We knew of the affair, of course. But not of the child. I expect old Prince Nunzio was ashamed of the matter, as well he might be. No, we are obliged to your mentor Giacomo del Piero for that information. It's too late for him as well, of course.' Baldasar Guilini sniffed fastidiously, as if he smelled rotten carrion.

Corradino felt his blood turn to water. Giacomo dead! And turned traitor on him, in a reflection of his own sin! He glimpsed down the pit of horrors that must have forced Giacomo to such a pass, and fought to restrain his terror. He must save Leonora, at any cost. 'What must I do?' It was a whisper.

'There is but one thing you can do to secure her safety. If you do this, she will be unharmed and may live out her days in peace in the Pietà or in marriage.'

'What? Dear God, what, anything.'

'We are aware, of course, that you have passed on

somewhat of your *specialist* knowledge to an apprentice. He, of course, will be taken care of.'

Jesu, not Jacques too. He was young; at least Giacomo had been old. A sorry pair of men, at either end of life's journey, who shared a name, a way with the glass, and a friendship for me – the man who has murdered them both.

'What must I do?' Now, almost a scream. Corradino looked savagely in the mirror, tired of the charade.

The Ambassador steepled his hands before his face and blinked his hooded eyes. 'You must go back.'

CHAPTER 35

Pity

Alessandro had no clear plan. He walked down the Riva degli Schiavoni in a daze, through the colourful crowds. He did not know if he was angry or sad or sorry or all these things. He didn't know whether to go back to Leonora or just see her back at her flat later. He didn't know whether to go back at all.

He needed peace to soothe his aching head. As he stumbled along in the direction of the Arsenale a dark door welcomed him. He fell through it.

Dark, peace and cool respite from the sun. A church. He was alone at last save for a single sacristan lighting candles for mass in the Lady chapel. A smell of incense that recalled the childhood masses at which he served as an altar boy. Alessandro had not been one for church since. But as he sank into the cool wooden pew he realized he had been to *this* church before. For over his head, looming from the dark, was an exquisite chandelier. A veritable cathedral of spider-spun silk, which he remembered from times past.

The Pietà.

Alessandro smiled at the irony. He had come here to escape Corradino, and yet his work was all around. And yet, Alessandro too had history here – for it was here that he had first seen Leonora. In that moment he knew he would go back, knew he couldn't be without her. She was stubborn and wrongheaded, but he loved her. Baby or no baby, he would go back.

A baby. Corradino had had a child too. Another Leonora. With a jolt, Alessandro recalled what his Leonora had said: 'But she didn't die . . . she lived happily ever after.' The fairytale phrase revolved in his head, to be joined by another.

Once upon a time Corradino's daughter had lived *here*.

All at once, like a revelation, Alessandro saw how it had been. He saw in his mind the literal, pictorial definition of the Pietà, seen a thousand times repeated as a favoured motif of the Renaissance artists. The embodiment of pity; the Virgin Mary cradling the dead, crucified Jesus. But what Alessandro saw now in his mind's eye was the inversion of this trope. He and his unborn baby, and Corradino holding his daughter in his arms. *His* baby. Alessandro rose like one who had witnessed a miracle. Corradino could not leave his child behind for ever any more than Alessandro could. Leonora was right – he *must* have saved her. He would cross oceans, weather storms, fight dragons for the flesh of his flesh, blood of his blood. Corradino may have been an artist and a genius but he was still a man, and they shared this common bond. Just men after all. Alessandro moved through the pews on respectful feet and approached the sacristan who was lighting the flames, and as he asked what he had to ask he felt the first flicker of humanity, the first warmth of fellowship, for Corradino Manin.

CHAPTER 36

Mercury

Jacques waited for Corradino in the secret furnace room at Versailles. He was not concerned by his master's lateness, although it was, 'tis true, the first time he had been there before Corradino. Jacques knew his master had the most exalted of protectors – perhaps some business with the King kept him?

As he waited he raddled the coals, and polished some of the tools, idly twitching things into their proper places, anxious to begin the work of the day. At the last he crossed to the silvering vat, which he half filled with water from a pail. Then he reached for the flask of liquid mercury and poured the compound gingerly onto the surface where it spread like oil. Jacques was careful not to pour too quickly, for then the element could break into globules which spoiled the perfect sheet of silver. As he set the flask back down on the bench a perfectly round drop of the liquid jumped onto his index finger. From habit borne of spills when cooking his meagre supper he almost carried the finger to his mouth, then he remembered Corradino's warning that the mere taste of mercury could mean death. He wiped the digit carefully on his jerkin till all traces were gone. Then he was drawn, inexorably, back to the tank as the liquid settled and stilled into a mirrored sheet. He was so busy watching his undulating reflection that he did not turn to heed the key in the lock. He knew, in any case, that it was his master that entered as none but the two of them had the key.

Jacques was still watching his own image so closely that he did not see the gloved hand which caught the back of his neck and pushed his face into the silver poison.

CHAPTER 37

The Labours of Spring

It was not the first time that the Ospedale Civili Riuniti di Venezia had admitted a woman in labour who was wearing *Carnevale* costume. This was Venice, after all. How could it be otherwise? And yet a significant crowd formed and even the most hardened obstetricians were moved by the sight of *La Primavera* herself twisting in the agony of her burden. The sprigged dress was soaked with birthing waters and clung to her legs.

In the delivery room decisions were made quickly. It had taken a long while for the *Signorina* to get here, as she was unaccompanied, and despite the fact that this was her first baby the birth was well advanced. It was already too late for an epidural, and moreover, the baby was breech. The nuns attempted to offer comfort and relief, but, despite the pain of her labour, Leonora was sensible of the fact that she was alone, here in the very hospital where she herself was born, and the baby was coming. Every couple of minutes a toothsome steel trap closed on her belly and back, and she cried out for Alessandro. She was haunted by Professore Padovani's story of another Leonora's mother.

Angelina dei Vescovi, who died in childbirth . . . died in childbirth.

She felt the same pains as that long-dead beauty. The pain made them sisters over the span of centuries. At last she lost consciousness, albeit briefly, and the nuns thanked Jesus for the brief respite in what would surely be a long night. The obstetrician, a man of many years of experience whose ideas weren't working, noticed that even in her unconscious state *La Primavera* clutched at her throat, as if searching for a trinket that wasn't there.

CHAPTER 38

The Watcher in the Shadows

As Corradino Manin looked on the lights of San Marco for the last time, Venice from the lagoon seemed to him a golden constellation in the dark blue velvet dusk. How many of those windowpanes, that adorned his city like costly gems, had he made with his own hands? Now they were stars lit to guide him at the end of the journey of his life. Guide him home at last.

As the boat drew into San Zaccaria he thought not – for once – of how he would interpret the vista in glass with a *pulegoso* of leaf gold and hot lapis, but instead that he would never see this beloved sight again. He stood in the prow of the boat, a brine-flecked figurehead, and looked left to Santa Maria della Salute, straining to see the white-domed bulk looming in its newness from the dark. The foundations of the great church had been laid in 1631, the year of Corradino's birth, to thank the Virgin for delivering the city from the Plague. His childhood and adulthood had kept pace with the growing edifice. Now it was complete, in 1681, the year of his death. He had never seen its full splendour in daylight, and now never would. He heard a *traghetto* man mournfully calling for passenger trade as he traversed the Canal Grande. His black boat recalled a funeral gondola. Corradino shivered.

He considered whether he should remove his white *bauta* mask as soon as his feet touched the shore; a poetic moment – a grand gesture on his return to the *Serenissima*.

No, there is one more thing I must do before they find me.

He closed his black cloak over his shoulders against the darkling mists and made his way across the Piazzetta under cover of his tricorn and *bauta*. The traditional *tabarro* costume, black from head to foot save the white mask, should make him anonymous enough to buy the time he needed. The *bauta* itself, a spectral slab of a mask shaped like a gravedigger's shovel, had the short nose and long chin which would eerily alter his voice if he should speak. Little wonder, he thought, that the mask borrowed its name from the '*baubau*', the 'bad beast' which parents invoked to terrify their errant children.

From habit borne of superstition Corradino moved swiftly through the two columns of San Marco and the San Teodoro that rose, white and symmetrical, into the dark. The Saint and the chimera that topped their pediments were lost in the blackness. It was bad luck to linger there, as criminals were executed between the pillars – hung from above or buried alive below. Corradino made the sign of the cross, caught himself, and smiled. What more bad luck could befall him? And yet his step still quickened.

There is one misfortune that could yet undo me: to be prevented from completing my final task.

As he entered the Piazza San Marco he noted that all that was familiar and beloved had taken on an evil and threatening cast. In the bright moon the shadow of the Campanile was a dark knife slashing across the square. Roosting pigeons flew like malevolent phantoms in his face. Regiments of dark arches had the square surrounded – who lurked in their shadows? The great doors of the Basilica were open; Corradino saw the gleam of candles from the golden belly of the church. He was briefly cheered – an island of brightness in this threatening landscape.

Perhaps it is not too late to enter this house of God, throw myself on the mercy of the priests and seek sanctuary?

But those who sought him also paid for this jewelled shrine that housed the bones of Venice's shrivelled Saint, and tiled the walls with the priceless glittering mosaics that now sent the candlelight out into the night. There could be no sanctuary within for Corradino. No mercy.

Past the Basilica then and under the arch of the Torre dell'Orologio he hurried, allowing himself one more glance at the face of the huge clock, where tonight it seemed the fantastical beasts of the zodiac revolved in a more solemn measure. A dance of death. Thereafter Corradino tortured himself no more with final glances, but fixed his eyes on the paving underfoot. Even this gave him no respite, for all he could think of was the beautiful *tessere* glasswork he used to make; fusing hot nuggets of irregular glass together, all shapes and hues, before blowing the whole into a wondrous vessel delicate and colourful as a butterfly's wing.

I know I will never touch the glass again.

As he entered the Merceria dell'Orologio the market traders were packing away their pitches for the night. Corradino passed a glass-seller, with his wares ranked jewel-like on his stall. In his mind's eye the goblets and trinkets began to glow rosily and their shapes began to shift – he could almost feel the heat of the furnace again, and smell the sulphur and silica. Since childhood such sights and smells had always reassured him. Now the memory seemed a premonition of hellfires. For was hell not where traitors were placed? The Florentine, Dante, was clear on the subject. Would Corradino – like Brutus and Cassius and Judas – be devoured by Lucifer, the Devil's tears mingling with his blood as he was ripped asunder? Or perhaps, like the traitors that had betrayed their families, he would be encased for all eternity in '. . . *un lago che per gelo avea di vetro e non d'acqua sembiante* . . . a lake that, frozen fast, had lost the look of water and seemed glass.' Corradino recalled the words of the poet and almost smiled. Yes, a fitting punishment – glass had been his life, why not his death also?

Not if I do this last thing. Not if I am granted absolution.

With a new urgency he doubled back as he had planned and took the narrow bridges and winding alleys or *calles* that led back to the Riva degli Schiavoni. Here and there shrines were set into the corners of the houses – well-tended flames burned and illumined the face of the Virgin.

I dare not look in her eyes, not yet.

At last the lights of the Orphanage at the Ospedale della Pietà drew near and as he saw the candlelight warmth he heard too the music of the viols.

Perhaps it is she that plays – I wish it were so – but I will never know.

He passed the grille without a glance inside and banged on the door. As the maid approached with a candle he did not wait for her inquisition before hissing: 'Padre Tommaso – *subito*!' He knew the maid – a surly, taciturn wench who delighted in being obstructive, but tonight his voice carried such urgency that even she turned at once and soon the priest came.

'*Signore*?'

Corradino opened his cloak and found the leather gourd of French gold. Into the bag he tucked the vellum notebook, so she would know how it had been and one day, perhaps, forgive him. He took a swift glance around the dim alley – no, no-one could have drawn close enough to see him.

They must not know she has the book.

In a voice too low for any but the priest to hear he said: '*Padre*, I give you this money for the care of the orphans of the Pietà.' The mask changed Corradino's voice as he had intended. The priest made as if to take the bag with the usual formula of thanks, but Corradino held it back until the father was forced to meet his eyes. Father Tommaso alone must know him for who he was. 'For the orphans,' said Corradino again, with emphasis.

Recognition reached the priest at last. He turned over the hand that held the bag and looked closely at the fingertips – smooth with no prints. He began to speak but the eyes in the mask flashed a warning. Changing his mind the father said, 'I will make sure they receive it,' and then, as if he knew; 'may God bless you.' A warm hand and a cold one clasped for an instant and the door was closed.

Corradino continued on, he knew not where, until he

was well away from the Orphanage.

Then, finally, he removed his mask.

Shall I walk on till they find me? How will it be done?

At once, he knew where he should go. The night darkened as he passed through the streets, the canals whispering goodbye as they splashed the *calli*, and now at last Corradino could hear footsteps behind keeping pace. At last he reached the Calle della Morta – the street of death – and stopped. The footsteps stopped too. Corradino faced the water and, without turning, said, 'Will Leonora be safe?'

The pause seemed interminable – splash, splash – then a voice as dry as dust replied.

'Yes. You have the word of The Ten.'

Corradino breathed relief and waited for the final act.

As the knife entered his back he felt the pain a moment after the recognition had already made him smile. The subtlety, the clarity with which the blade insinuated itself between his ribs could only mean one thing. He started to laugh. Here was the poetry, the irony he had searched for on the dock. What an idiot, romanticizing himself, supposing himself a hero in the drama and pathos of his final sacrifice. All the time it was *they* who had planned the final act with such a sense of theatre, of what was fitting, an amusing *Carnevale* exit. A Venetian exit. They had used a glass dagger – Murano glass.

Most likely one of my own making.

He laughed harder with the last of his breath. He felt the assassin's final twist of the blade to snap handle from haft, felt his skin close behind the blade to leave no more than an innocent graze at the point of entry. Corradino pitched forward into the water and just before he broke the surface he met his own eyes in his reflection for the first and last time in his life. He saw a fool laughing at his own death. As he submerged in the freezing depths, the water closed behind his body to leave no more than an innocent graze at the point of entry.

From the shadows of the Calle della Morte, Salvatore Navarro – the new foreman of the *fornace* on Murano – watched, terrified. He had been given this time and place by an agent of The Ten and been told to attend on pain of death. Coming so lately upon the death in the Piombi of his predecessor Giacomo del Piero, he had dared not refuse. As he watched the demise of the great Corradino Manin, a man he had looked up to since his days as a *garzon*, he knew he was here as a witness. That he was expected to go back to Murano and tell all that he had seen.

And that he, and all other glassblowers through him, were being given a warning.

CHAPTER 39

The Notebook

Alessandro followed the sacristan as they wound upward in a small spiral staircase leading from the vestry of the Pietà.

'It's not a library as such, mostly old music books and some records,' the sacristan continued, his words punctuated by the whispering of his flowing robes. 'Once, of course, we had a very significant collection of Vivaldi's handwritten scores. After his popularity revived in the nineteen-thirties we had our book collection properly stored at the correct temperature and insured. That collection is in a museum in Vienna where he died. Are you a student of Vivaldi?' The sacristan did not seem to need an answer but launched into his well rehearsed guidebook version of the red priest's life. Alessandro climbed higher and fought to remain polite. At other times he would have been deeply interested in the history, today he was fired with a quite indecent urge to push past the kind old man and rush ahead into the library. Each turn of the stair seemed the thread of a screw that wound Alessandro's impatience ever tighter. At last they reached an ancient door and Alessandro fidgeted whilst the sacristan went through what seemed like dozens of keys. At last the right one fitted. Turned.

The small room was barely lit by one arched window. Golden motes of dust danced in its light. The draught of the opening door caused the dead-leaf rustle of pages which whispered that no one had read these volumes for years. From floor to ceiling they were piled, not shelved; the dusty bookstacks of Prospero. Alessandro forgot the cant of his guide as he looked around. It would not take long to find what he sought, if it was here, if it existed. He turned decisively.

'*Padre*. I am most grateful for your guidance. Could I beg you to excuse me while I take a little look around here? I'm sure you have other things to do. I'll be most careful, I promise.'

The sacristan set back a little, but then his eyes crinkled. They held the exquisite trust of a man of God, one that believes the world holds no ill. He patted Alessandro's arm. 'A private matter. I see. I'll be downstairs.'

Alessandro flashed his most charming of smiles as the robe whispered from the room.

Then he turned to his task.

There were perhaps a thousand volumes here. Not many.

But if what he sought was here, it would betray itself by its size. He anticipated his search would take a few hours. But after perusing only two floor-to-ceiling stack's worth of books, finding only leather bound music scores and hymnbooks, he saw it. Wedged between the horizontal stacks was a small vellum volume, bound in fine calfskin, the best Venetian workmanship. As he had guessed, the size told the secret.

A book of days. A notebook. A diary.

Alessandro sank to the floor and the velvet of his costume rose around him. He could have been a man from another age as he sat in the pool of cloth, in this ancient chamber, the light from the window turning him back to a painting. His hands shook as he realized this was it – the notebook whose existence he had assumed but not been certain. Surely this was the grail at the end of Leonora's quest? But as he turned the fine pages, wondering at the crabbed script, the detailed drawings, the scrawled measurements and mathematics, a new notion held him. What if this book confirmed her fears?

And so it was. Alessandro's fingertips were suddenly soaked, and the thin vellum began to bubble beneath their wetness till he hurriedly wiped his hands on his robe. For here it was, proof – irrevocable and incontrovertible. The last pages were measurements and drawings that pertained to the Hall of Mirrors at Versailles. Alessandro sat back as the enormity engulfed him. In a legacy of treachery, that room had once housed Vittorio Orlando, Prime Minister of Italy. Had Orlando and the other signatories – Woodrow Wilson, Lloyd George, Georges Clemenceau – looked into Corradino's glass as they had cut the heart and soul out of Germany in that 'Treaty' of 1919, and set in train the inevitable grinding machine which led to the Second World War? Ill deeds bred ill deeds, never more so than here. Alessandro could have wept. He had solved the mystery, but brought the answer Leonora dreaded.

Leonora.

His eye caught her name on the page – the last pair of pages in the book. Here the writing was different – scrawled, passionate, not exact and mathematical, and here and there was a splash of brine or tears. So Alessandro sat and read the letter Corradino had written to his daughter, which could have been written to Leonora, *his* Leonora, herself.

CHAPTER 40

The Ruby

Someone was screaming and crying. Twisting in blood and mess on the sheets. It sounded like Leonora's own voice.

How many hours have I been this way?

Concerned nuns and a doctor in blue scrubs collected at her stirupped feet. Monitoring belts bound her heaving belly. A machine chattered at her side with a needle spiking over reams of graph paper in improbable peaks. The pain darkened her eyes and she called again for Alessandro, as she had done at every labouring of her body. At last, miraculously, he answered. Not as an ephemeral pain-filled daydream – for she had relived their time together to get her through this – but as a strong presence, here by her bed, his firm dry hand holding her damp one tight. She clasped his fingers, hard enough to bruise bone. The fog cleared and she saw him clearly then, raining kisses on her hand

and forehead. He held something in his hand – a book. He whispered something in her ear – through the thrum of blood in her head as she pushed again, she heard:

'He came back! Corradino came back!'

The pain abated. She knew its dark ways now – there was time enough for her to say what she had to before it came again.

'I don't care. Don't leave me.'

She heard him say, 'never again,' before the pain made her insensible. She was not aware that, as she laboured, he slipped onto her third finger a ring with a ruby red as the banked fires of a furnace. He had been carrying the little box around with him all day – he had meant to propose at the Carnevale, and that had been the reason for his excitement of last night. This was not as he had planned it. This way she knew nothing of the question that had been asked of her. He could have waited for tomorrow, for hearts and flowers, and the bending of one knee. But he wanted her to have the ring now.

In case tomorrow was too late.

CHAPTER 41

The Letter (part 1)

Leonora was still. Alessandro, his eyes still wet, still held her hand. The hand that wore his ring. Her suffering was over.

And the prize? He slept too, in a clear plastic box next to the bed. A small, perfect bundle with a face crumpled from his ordeal, but to Alessandro the most beautiful thing in the world beside Leonora. He would battle tigers for him. His son. He should be in a casket of gold, not this incongruous tupperware.

Alessandro had been there just in time for the birth. The events of last night were as a dream to him – returning in triumph to an empty house, fearing that Leonora had gone away, then spying the winking red light of the answer phone. The message from the hospital. The mad dash to get here, fearing he knew not what.

She stirred. Her eyes opened and the bloom returned to her cheeks, Spring no more, but full blown Summer, rich, abundant and with a healthy son. He thanked God for the first time since he was a child.

He kissed her gently as she smiled, and the baby, as if sensing his mother's wakefulness, woke too. They smiled at each other as the boy opened his eyes, their dynamic for ever changed from two to three. A triangle now. Alessandro tenderly picked up his son and held him to his chest. Tiny, heavy and real. He moved to the door.

'Where are you going?' A new mother's anxiety.

'My son and I are going for a walk,' his heart thrilled at the words. 'You should rest. But before you do, read that.' He nodded to the vellum notebook where it lay on the coverlet.

'On the final page is a letter for you.'

'For *me*?' But Alessandro had left the room with their son. Their son. She barely had the patience to read, so cocooned was she in her new happiness. But her name on the parchment caught her eye.

Leonora mia,

I will not see you again. Mid-way through the journey of my life, I took the wrong path, the right way being lost. I have sinned against the State, and now I must be punished. Moreover, two fine men, Giacomo del Piero and Jacques Chauvire, died because of what I did. But I want you to think kindly of me if you can. Do you remember when I came to see you last, and we said farewell, and I gave you your heart of glass? I went to France and gave away the secrets of that glass. But now I will make amends. Now I am coming back home, to Venice, so you will be safe and the glass will be safe. And you will *be safe, I have been promised. I will walk back through Venice once more, and leave this book for you. By the time I reach the other side of the city, I know they will find me and finish me. Keep your glass heart close, and think of me. I want you to think of the way we touched our hands together that last day, do you remember? Our special way? Every finger and the thumb? If you should read this, remember that Leonora, remember me that way, on that day. And Leonora, my own Leonora, remember how much your father loved you, loves you still.*

Tears dropped on the coverlet and soaked the hospital gown they had given her, when they had taken Spring's raiment away. She cried at last for Corradino, but also for Giacomo, for her mother, for her father and for Stephen. They were her past. But by the time her future came back into the room, she was smiling and ready to hold her son. The notebook was tucked away, tidied carefully onto the night stand, ready to return home to the Pietà and the kindly sacristan who had understood why Alessandro needed to take it away.

CHAPTER 42

The Letter (part 2)

Padre Tommaso climbed the stair to the girls tiring chamber, expecting to find the bride-to-be surrounded by her contemporaries, all twittering over her dress and hair. Instead, his heart failed him as he beheld the girl that had become as a daughter to him, the girl that had been like his own since the defection of her father, the girl that had been the delight of his old age. She was alone, kneeling in the sun of the dorter window, her bright head bent.

She was at prayer.

He knew as he watched that the trinket she held at her throat as she prayed was no cross but the heart of glass that her father had given her the day before he had disappeared for ever. Then Corradino was in her thoughts today. It was natural, he supposed, that an orphan should think of her dead parents on her wedding day. It made it easier to tell her what he had to. He waited with his head bowed while she finished her intercessions and chose his words.

She smiled up at him. '*Padre*? Are they ready for me?'

'Yes, child. But before we go, may I speak with you a little?'

A slight frown crossed her perfect features and then cleared. 'Of course.'

The *Padre* lowered himself slowly onto a faldstool, as his bones were no longer young. He gazed at this peerless beauty and tried to remember her as Corradino would have seen her last – without the silver brocade gown, the ringleted hair set with moonstones, and all the trappings of a woman who was shortly to marry into one of the most powerful families in Northern Italy. 'Leonora, are you happy in this match? Is Signor Visconti-Manin truly the choice of your heart? Your head is not turned by his riches? I know his gold must be tempting to one orphaned such as yourself . . .'

'No, *Padre*,' Leonora interrupted with a rush, 'I truly love him. His riches mean nothing to me. Do not forget that when he first came to Venice he was merely a younger son, and he came as a student of history, anxious to find the Venetian branch of his family. Only now after the death of his brother and father, has he assumed the riches that were never his before. I love him – I loved him long before his inheritance. He is kind and good and loving. He wishes to settle here in Venice and bring up his children in the Manin name. I hope . . . you will still be my confessor.'

'*Cara mia*, of course I will. These old eyes would miss you too much, else.' The priest sighed and smiled, his mind at rest. Corradino would be glad that his daughter was to be happily matched. Now he must come to the burden of his visit. 'Leonora, do you remember your father?'

'Of course I remember him. Very fondly, for all that he left me never to return.' She clasped the glass heart. 'He gave me this, and I have worn it always as he said. Why do you speak of him now? No man ever heard from him again.'

Padre Tommaso clasped his hands. 'That is not entirely true. He returned here, just once, and gave me something for you.'

The girl stood, straight as a willow wand, her green eyes wide. 'He came back? When? Is he still alive?'

'Leonora. No. This was many years ago, you were still a child. Only now that you are a woman, might you be able to understand.'

'Understand what? What did he leave for me?'

'He left enough gold for your education, and a handsome dowry. And . . . this.' The gnarled old hand proffered the vellum notebook. 'Your father was a genius. But he was not without sin. Great sin. Read this, and form your own mind. But do not neglect to read the final pages. I will leave you for a moment.'

Padre Tommaso retired into the next chamber, and once there he prayed too. Leonora took so long that he was afraid for the patience of the congregation downstairs in the church. He was also afraid he had taken the wrong course in showing her the book. But at last the door opened and she came out. Tears had turned her eyes to glass.

'My child!' The *Padre* was distraught. 'I was wrong to have shown you.'

Leonora fell into his arms and clasped his frail body tightly. 'Oh, no, Father, no. You were right. Don't you see? Now I can forgive him.'

As Padre Tommaso led Leonora Manin down the aisle of Santa Maria della Pietà, the place that had been her home for one and twenty years, the orphaned girls sang with especial beauty. It seemed to the priest that today they attained divinity in their music, but perhaps it was the more earthly longing – that they too might one day make a match like this – that gave wings to their song. Lorenzo Visconti-Manin stood at the altar in magnificent cloth of gold, and Padre Tommaso felt a misgiving at the man's grandeur until the groom turned to see his bride and his eyes were also wet with tears. As the priest surrendered Leonora to her husband, the couple did not join hands as was customary. With a shared smile and in a practised ritual that Padre Tommaso did not understand, they reached out their right hands and, starlike, placed fingertip to fingertip, thumb to thumb.

CHAPTER 43

At the Do Mori

When Salvatore Navarro went to the Cantina Do Mori to receive a commission, and the voice of the one that greeted him was French and not Venetian, he was not surprised. Only very, very frightened. He was not surprised because They had warned him that this may come to pass. All he could think of was Corradino Manin's body, falling forward into the chilled waters of the canal, a glass blade in his back and his robes darkening as they accepted the water and dragged him down to Hell. Salvatore left at once, without even listening to the Frenchman's proposals. He knocked over a table in his haste to be away, as if every instant he spent in the man's company implicated him further as a traitor.

Salvatore gulped the twilight air and raced down the Calle dei Mori to the canalside. He waited, dreading following footsteps until with relief he heard the familiar mournful cry; '*gondola gondola gondola,*' and hailed the gondolier. It was not until he had settled back into the velvet cushions, and directed the boatman to the Doge's palace, that he began to shake.

Still inside the Do Mori, Duparcmieur shrugged and took another leisurely sip of his wine. Salvatore could not be persuaded, and Duparcmieur had lost Corradino in a spectacular fashion, but someone soon would be persuaded by the King's gold. He glanced at his goblet and calculated – yes – he had time to finish his wine and still be safely away before Salvatore denounced him to The Ten, and they came looking. He drank deeply. Really, the wine was excellent here.

CHAPTER 44

Leonora's Heart

The birth had been difficult, so the hospital kept Leonora for another day. Never an easy patient, she was anxious to go home and was delighted to be discharged. The three of them took a boat from the hospital as she was still feeling weak, and she looked at the palaces and bridges and gloried in the city. With an open heart she loved Venice again and the city loved her back. She belonged. She had done something as fundamental as giving birth here. She had given *La Serenissima* another son. And as for Corradino – he was forgiven by her and the city too. Carnevale was here, winter was gone. She longed to see her flat again. Better still was the clutter that greeted her as she opened the door – all of Alessandro's things were stacked in the hall. He had moved in overnight. She caught sight of the ruby on her hand as she opened the door and thought of the moment of quiet in the hospital yesterday when he had asked her properly and she had said yes. Alessandro followed her up the stairs with their precious cargo in a carry-cradle which he placed tenderly beside her bed. Their bed. The Madonna of the Sacred Heart smiled benignly down on the three of them from her frame. The heart she held glowed in her hands and Leonora understood her at last. The heart was the Virgin's Son.

In the crazy first weeks of constant feeding and broken sleep Alessandro was home on paternity leave, so he was there when they received an unexpected visitor. Adelino crept quietly into the flat behind a barrage of flowers, kissed mother and father on both cheeks and waggled his fingers at the son. The baby was lying on a sheepskin in the living room, captivated as his mother and grandmother had been by the reflected crystal filigree of the water shimmering on the ceiling. He captured one of Adelino's gnarled digits and seemed happy to hold on.

'He is very strong,' Adelino pronounced, 'very good for his future profession.' Adelino ballooned his cheeks as if blowing a parison, and popped them to amuse the child. He sat on the proffered chair which Alessandro politely vacated to perch on the bed. 'Now; I bring two gifts,' said the old man, 'one for the mother and one for the son. The father I have brought nothing for, but it seems he has everything he wants already. Now, ladies first.' He produced a folded newspaper from his pocket and handed it to Leonora. She received it with the shock of memory which reminded her of darker times.

Il Gazzettino.

She looked at Alessandro in time to see a smile of complicity pass between the two men. 'Go on,' said her fiancé. 'Read it.'

She opened the folds to read the headline. 'MAESTRO AND MARTYR. Corrado Manin returned to certain death for the love of his secret daughter. Read the astonishing true story of self-sacrifice of one of our city's greatest sons.' Her eyes moved down to the byline. 'An exclusive by Vittoria Minotto.'

Leonora raised a brow. 'Vittoria?'

Alessandro smiled. 'I sent her Corradino's notebook. With the sacristan's permission of course. It's safe back in the Pietà now. I wanted it to be a surprise for you.'

'It certainly is. She changed her tune!'

Alessandro sat down beside his son and tickled the baby's belly. 'Not really. If you'd had the misfortune to know her as long as I have you'd realize that the only thing that matters to Vittoria is an exclusive. She's not a bad person, but she will shift sides with ease to get the best story. That's why we would never have worked. Her job was always much more important than people.'

Adelino had the grace to look sheepish at the mention of work. 'Speaking of jobs, we'd ... *I'd* like you back, as soon as your family can spare you.'

Leonora looked down for a moment, remembering her ignominious departure.

'We *need* you back. *All* of us; the *maestri* too. We're going to be pretty busy. That edition only came out this morning and we've already had hundreds of enquiries about the Manin line. The public is a funny beast – they think Corradino is a hero. We're thinking of going national with the ad campaign. Chiara and Semi are very excited.'

Leonora started to laugh. 'I bet they are.' But she began to remember other things, the smell of the *forno*, the hot glass growing beneath her breath, taking shape in her hands. She had loved it, but she did not want to give in at once. 'How do I know you want me back to be a glassblower, and not just to be some figurehead for your world domination?'

'Ah, you must let me come to my second gift,' said Adelino, patting all his pockets in a mock pantomime which elicited a reluctant smile from Leonora. Then, from the last pocket, he pulled, in the manner of a magician revealing a string of handkerchiefs, a length of familiar blue ribbon. Transfixed, Leonora's jaw dropped as the glass heart popped out of Adelino's pocket. Perfect as ever, imprisoning light in its core. Leonora looked at Alessandro, who shook his head, equally amazed.

'But how did you . . . when did you . . .'

'How did you fish it out of the canal?' They spoke together in a rush.

Adelino drew his white brows together. 'What do you mean?'

Alessandro told the tale, by now ashamed of his part in

it. 'So you see, the heart is ... was ... somewhere under the Bridge of Sighs. I'm just surprised that it was found.'

Adelino smiled. 'No, no. This is not Corradino's heart. That one has found its rest, and just as well. Leave it for the city and the sea to claim.'

As it claimed Corradino. Yes, it was a fitting end.

'This,' Adelino waved the heart, which winked in the sun, 'is one of the ones *you* made at the *fornace*, Leonora. *This* is why I want you back. You must be a better glassblower than you think to mistake your workmanship for your ancestor's.' He smiled expansively, including them all in this new word.

Leonora examined the heart and could not see the flaws she had imagined before. 'Very well,' she said. 'I'll be back. But not yet. I have my son to take care of at the moment. Give me a few months. You can use all the ad material in the meantime.' She smiled. 'But I'm sure you would anyway.' Adelino's grin, the grin of a merchant, a pirate, a buccaneer, had returned.

She looked down at the heart where it shone in her hand. 'I'll keep it close as you asked,' she said quietly, a whisper to a long-dead man who had loved his child too. She made as if to tie the heart round her neck, in its old place, but Adelino stopped her.

'Hey, hey, what are you doing? It's not for you!' The familiar twinkle was back.

'It's not?'

'No, it's for Corradino,' said Adelino, pointing to the baby.

Leonora and Alessandro exchanged a look. Started to smile.

'Here, Corradino,' Leonora dangled the heart over the sheepskin rug, 'how do you like your birthright?'

One tiny hand reached up for the bright glass, closed over it, and didn't let go.

THE END

Acknowledgements

Writing a book is a solitary experience, but I was lucky enough to have someone along for the journey. So most of all I'd like to thank my husband Sacha Bennett for being my editor, muse, psychiatrist, nanny, chef and printer; in short, my everything.

Once the book was finished I had lots of help from some fantastic people: thanks to my brilliant agent Teresa Chris for her constant faith in me, and to Simon Petherick, Tamsin Griffiths and the team at Beautiful Books for getting behind the novel in such a big way. Thanks to friend and writer Helene Wiggin for her encouragement and advice, and to Nigel Bliss for going to the right wedding! Thanks also to my Dad Adelin Fiorato for knowing his way round Dante, and to my Mum Barbara Fiorato for correcting my French.

If this book has a message I guess it is that family are everything. So thank you to Conrad and Ruby for letting mummy write, and for teaching me that when you have a child it's like letting your heart walk around outside of your body.

Last but not least, thank you to the Glassblowers of Murano, who work miracles every day.

Reading
Group
Gold

THE GLASSBLOWER OF MURANO

by Marina Fiorato

About the Author

• A Conversation with Marina Fiorato

Behind the Novel

• "The History of Murano"
An Original Essay by the Author

Keep on Reading

• Recommended Reading
• Reading Group Questions

A Reading Group Gold Selection

For more reading group suggestions
visit www.readinggroupgold.com.

ST. MARTIN'S GRIFFIN

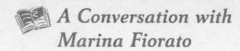

A Conversation with Marina Fiorato

Could you tell us a little bit about your personal and professional background, and when it was you decided to lead a literary life?

I was born and educated in the north of England and at university I studied history. I then rebelled against my parents' academic background by going to art school and entering the film and music business! I began by generating onscreen graphics and I was lucky enough to work on films like *Tomb Raider* with Angelina Jolie and *Proof of Life* with Russell Crowe. I shifted into rock music and worked with U2 and the Rolling Stones and Aerosmith, but when I became pregnant with my first child I took maternity leave. It was then that my old life found me again, and it was after I had my son that I had the idea for the story for *Glassblower.* I wrote the book while I was on leave and never returned to my job. I think I had been trying to be something I was not, and then, when I had a child of my own, ideas of heritage and my Venetian origins became enormously important. My old interests had found me with a vengeance—it was like being tapped on the shoulder by my past.

"My old interests had found me with a vengeance—it was like being tapped on the shoulder by my past."

Is there a book or author that inspired you to become a writer?

I grew up reading Pamela Kaufman's books about Alix of Wanthwaite and her wonderful earthy writing and sense of period really inspired me—she invokes the sounds, sights, and even smells of the past so well! In more recent writing I love the prose of Thomas Harris. In the Florentine section of *Hannibal* I think he really manages to evoke the beauty but also the brutality of Italy at the same time. It's a modern tale but so Renaissance in spirit.

You studied history at Oxford University and the University of Venice, where you specialized in the study of Shakespeare's plays as an historical source. How has your education influenced your writing?

I studied a lot of Shakespeare in school and was inspired by both the language and the sheer drama of his storytelling. I'm like a magpie when I write; I steal shiny bits of the work of my betters and weave them into my own prose! There is so much Shakespeare in *The Glassblower of Murano,* from pieces of plot to direct quotes. I was particularly inspired in this case by *The Merchant of Venice,* which is one of the plays I studied in detail for my master's degree, but I also lifted a plotline from *Romeo and Juliet.* There's even a quote from *The Tempest* in there somewhere. At least I steal from the best!

Do you scrupulously adhere to historical facts in your novels, or do you take liberties if the story can benefit from the change?

I do try, as far as possible, to be reasonably accurate—I think because of my training in historical research that any blatant inaccuracies would really jar. If push came to shove, though, I would sacrifice total accuracy for the cause of the story. It's not my job as a novelist to create a piece of historical documentation. What I'd like to think is that my books might serve to interest people in a certain period or character, and serve as a jumping-off point for them to then go away and research their interests from proper historical sources. My historical hero, Corradino Manin, is fictional so I wasn't bound by the constraints of writing about a real person; that gave me a certain amount of freedom. The context, though, the world in which he lives, does have to be accurate. There are real historical figures in the book, like Louis XIV, but as they tend to be marginal there is not the obligation to feverishly research them.

Are there any parallels between you and Leonora? Can you tell us a bit about your own travels in Venice and experiences with glassblowing?

There are a number of parallels between myself and Leonora, mostly to do with our heritage. Like her, I have a Venetian family. I was actually lucky enough to study at the University of Venice for six months and I lived on the Lido, taking the *vaporetto* into Ca' Foscari every day, which was wonderful. While there I remember taking a tourist trip to Murano, where I saw a glassblower make a tiny, perfect crystal horse in about sixty seconds. I remember that it seemed like a miracle, and the episode stayed with me; in fact it's included in the book when Giacomo makes a glass horse for the young Corradino. I returned to Venice years later to get married, in a little church on the Grand Canal. The whole wedding party was in eighteenth-century dress, which was fabulous, and we took boats out to the islands for the reception. It was unforgettable.

"I love the way glass is such a shifting entity. In many ways it has as many faces as Venice itself."

You've mentioned that one of your favorite blown-glass windows in Venice is at Ca' Foscari, a palace on the waterfront of the Grand Canal. What do you see when you look at that window, in particular, and all blown glass, in general? What is it about Venice, blown glass, and the process of glassblowing that you hoped to reveal to your readers?

There are hundreds of beautiful windows on the Grand Canal, but Ca' Foscari has a special resonance for me because of studying there. Originally a palace, Ca' Foscari is now used as a university and stands in a particularly beautiful bend of the canal; what fascinates me is that the window itself is as beautiful as what you can see through it. I like the way that these windows also tell the story of Venice's history—they are a wonderful hybrid of western and eastern design and exemplify Venice's identity, a republic standing astride two empires.

Blown glass fascinates me because, like most great crafts, it's incredibly difficult to achieve a good result. I used the word *miraculous* in the book and I think it's deserved. I love the way glass is such a shifting entity. In many ways it has as many faces as Venice itself, and I think that nature of changeability, of having many faces, is what I wanted to reveal about the city. Glass begins life as a powder which becomes liquid, then solid; there's only a very short window to work with glass before it hardens, and it takes a true artist to do it. Incredible, too, that such beauty comes from humble sand—true artistry from a quintessence of dust.

Venice is so unchanging; it's essentially the same place architecturally as it was in the seventeenth century. There are few places in the world about which one can say this, because most cities have changed to accommodate roads and sprawling suburbs. But because Venice as a "character" was the same then as now, I thought it would be really interesting to take a look at ideas of heritage and continuity of a particular Venetian family, with a peculiar creative genius. I was interested in whether or not a skill like glassblowing is passed down in the same way that, say, facial characteristics are. Is glassblowing in the Venetian DNA? Are these skills built into the Venetian genome, and how much does the city itself create artists by a kind of osmosis which has nothing to do with the century they are in? These are the kinds of questions which interested me.

Geoff Budd

Marina's wedding kiss

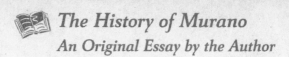

The History of Murano

An Original Essay by the Author

When writing the historical strand of *The Glassblower of Murano* it was important to me to get some sense of the significance of glass in Venice at the end of the seventeenth century. And when you visit, the evidence is before your eyes; the city seems to be almost made of glass. As well as boasting the most beautiful windows in the world, exquisite chandeliers hang from the frescoed ceilings of every palazzo, the basilica is clothed in jewel-like mosaics comprised of nuggets of glass covered in lapis and gold; and at the other end of the scale the streets in the Merceria dell'Orologio behind San Marco are crowded with bijoux little shops crammed with glass fancies, beads, and bonbons.

"Murano is the glass heart of Venice."

But it is Murano, one of the trio of islands set far into the Venetian lagoon, which is and was the glass heart of Venice. In 1291, an edict of the Great Council, Venice's ruling body, decreed that all glass furnaces should be moved to the island after a series of serious fires which threatened the city. In the Renaissance period, glass was a priceless monopoly for the Republic of Venice, and at the heart of their mystery was the closely guarded secret of how to make mirrors. The manufacture of mirrors of reasonable size and reflectivity was deeply problematic until the glassblowers of Murano stumbled across the optimum method through an accident of glassblowing. Thereafter they began to make mirrors brighter, clearer, and larger than any in the world. Venetian mirrors quickly became the Republic's most valuable commodity, more precious than saffron; more costly than gold.

The Council of Ten, the vicious ruling junta of Venice's Great Council, quickly realized the value of the glass-blowers of Murano, and threatened them with death if they ever divulged their methods. Often, the glassblowers' entire families were kept as hostages by the state. Venetian law was very clear on the matter:

If any worker or artist should transport his talents to

another country, and if he does not obey the order to return, all of his closest relatives will be put in prison.

Incredibly, despite such threats, some of the glassblowers of Murano did betray their secrets and their city. In the 1680s, Louis XIV, the Sun King, was in the throes of his Grand Design: the Palace of Versailles, for which he planned to construct a great chamber made entirely out of mirrors, and needed assistance from the best of the best. Thus, many of Murano's glassblowers were secretly transported to Paris. Recruited by Pierre de Bonzi, the French Ambassador to Venice, they were tempted by tales of foreign lands, exotic women, and great riches. By the autumn of 1665, twenty Murano fugitives had been spirited away to Paris where they began work upon the task of making the dream of a king a reality.

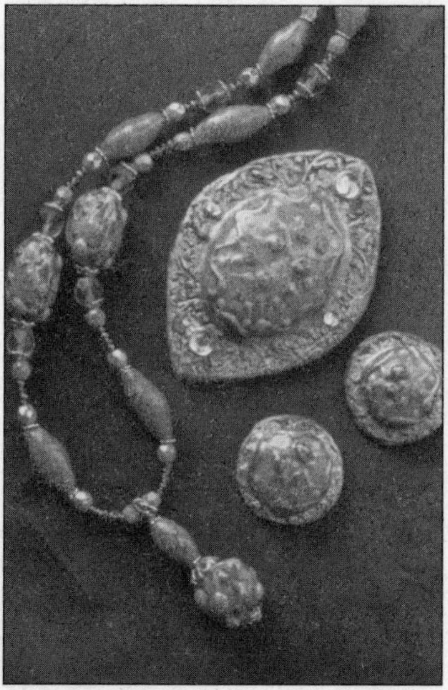

Ai Buangsuwon

Fiorato beads. Image courtesy of Ann Mitchell and Karen Mitchell of AnKara Designs, www.ankaradesigns.com.

"It's great to be, in some small way, part of such a wonderful tradition."

As we now know, the Hall of Mirrors in Versailles was built and remains for all to see—a cathedral of glass that is undeniably one of the modern wonders of the architectural world. Not only does the work mitigate the treachery of those brave souls from Murano, it is also a tribute to the craftsmen of France, who would someday become the forerunners for the genius of Baccarat and Lalique.

On a more personal note, I made a discovery of my own while researching the history of glassmaking in Murano: I was delighted to discover that *Fiorato,* my Venetian family name (which means "floral"), is also the name for a type of Murano glass. Fiorato glass features tiny glass flowers enameled and fused into beads. Fiorato beads are tiny, but they are beautiful. It felt great to be, in some small way, part of such a wonderful tradition.

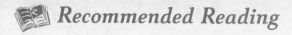

Recommended Reading

The Count of Monte Cristo
by Alexandre Dumas

A wonderful epic tale of a man who comes back from the "dead." A direct influence on my historical plotline.

The Comfort of Strangers
by Ian McEwan

An extremely dark take of Venice, in contrast to the way in which the city is usually portrayed in literature. McEwan creates a wonderful sense of unease throughout. Here, the city is dangerous; it can kill, and it does.

Brideshead Revisited
by Evelyn Waugh

One of my favorite novels. Tucked in the central section is one of the most golden, languid portraits of Venice ever written. Entirely seductive, the city here is the polar opposite of the one in *The Comfort of Strangers*.

Hannibal
by Thomas Harris

Another one of my favorites. Not a Venetian setting but half of the novel is set in Florence and it's a wonderful portrait of a city which has never left the beautiful, brutal Renaissance. Everything is here; the art, the corruption of those in power, and, of course, the bloodletting.

Through a Glass, Darkly
by Donna Leon

Donna Leon knows Venice so well that every detail places you in the city. I'm a big fan of her Guido Brunetti detective novels, but this is my favorite; a great tale of murder set in the glass factories of Murano.

Death in Venice
by Thomas Mann

Another wonderful portrait of Venice, this time seen from the Lido (where I used to live). In this novella the city is sick; death stalks Venice in the shape of a mysterious disease, in a marked contrast to the youthful perfection of the Adonis of the Hotel des Bains.

The Merchant of Venice
by William Shakespeare

Not a novel, I know, but a wonderful play and a direct influence on my book. *The Merchant of Venice,* as the name suggests, is proof positive that trade was the lifeblood of the city in Shakespeare's day. Interesting too, that *every* section of society engaged in trade, even the nobility; in other Renaissance kingdoms, nobles thought trade was a dirty word.

Reading Group Questions

1. Glass and Venice are both metaphors for change in the novel. How do they mirror the changing reflections of the characters? In particular, discuss this facet of the novel in relation to the roles of Leonora and Corradino.

2. Marina Fiorato uses imagery of glass: its beauty yet changeability; its strength yet fragility, throughout her novel. How does this portray an unfamiliar, dark, and sinister side to the most romantic European city?

3. Do you think Corradino Manin did the right thing by his "betrayal"?

4. Discuss the narrative structure of *The Glassblower of Murano*. In what ways do the two intertwined strands of the novel, the story set in the Renaissance and Leonora's modern-day narrative, shape the story?

5. Marina Fiorato says in her acknowledgments that having a child is like letting your heart walk around outside your body. Discuss the various relationships between parent and child in the story. How do they vary, and in what ways are they similar? What do you think is signified by Leonora's gift of the glass heart pendant to her child?

6. How important was it for Leonora to leave everything behind and move to Venice, and what do her discoveries teach her about family?

7. Think about the male-dominated *fornace* on Murano. Leonora has an uncertain relationship with the *maestros* in the factory because she is a woman in what remains a man's world. How do you think this relationship affects her view of her own femininity?

8. Is it acceptable—because of the importance of glassblowing to Venetian heritage—for Leonora to be treated as an outsider by the *maestros*?

9. The story of *The Glassblower of Murano* is centered around Corradino's secret and Leonora's search for the truth. Discuss the various elements of mystery in these pages. What types of narrative devices does Marina Fiorato use to keep the reader guessing?

10. Few places are as romanticized, celebrated, and praised as Venice. Have you traveled to Venice? If so, do you agree with the portrayal of Venice in the story? If not, how did reading this book confirm or deny your preconceived notions of one of the world's most famous places?